BROKEN JOURNEY

BROKEN JOURNEY

Janet Woods

This first world edition published in Great Britain 2007 by
SEVERN HOUSE PUBLISHERS LTD of
9–15 High Street, Sutton, Surrey SM1 1DF.
This first world edition published in the USA 2007 by
SEVERN HOUSE PUBLISHERS INC of
595 Madison Avenue, New York, N.Y. 10022.

British Library Cataloguing in Publication Data

Woods, Janet, 1939-
    Broken journey
    1.   Friendship - Fiction
    I.   Title
    823.9'14 [F]

    ISBN-13: 978-0-7278-6495-6

All Severn House titles are printed on acid-free paper.

Typeset by Palimpsest Book Production Ltd.,
Grangemouth, Stirlingshire, Scotland.
Printed and bound in Great Britain by
MPG Books Ltd., Bodmin, Cornwall.

To my son, Andy Tutt
with love.

One

Postmark
20th September 1984

Dear Jillian,
My name is Neil James, and I believe I'm the son
you gave up for adoption. I've sat down many times
to write to you, but found it difficult to start. It's
impossible to analyze why I felt a burning desire to
track you down, and I'm not quite sure how I should
address you – or whether you will even welcome
contact.

Perhaps I should start by telling you I had a happy
and enjoyable childhood . . .

Jilly's smile had several layers of incredulity to it. Heart
thumping, she crossed to the window and held the letter
against her heart, gazing out of the window into a golden
afternoon. Her husband was raking the carpet of autumn
leaves into a pile.

'Dear God,' she whispered, tears blurring her eyes, 'after
all these years!'

Her finger traced around the outside edge of the airmail
envelope. To think he lived in Australia, of all places. What
a coincidence.

She laughed with the sheer relief of knowing. After all
the denials, the shame she'd been forced to experience, the
silent grieving and the tears she'd never been allowed to
shed, she now tasted freedom. She wanted to hug the happiness inside her. At the same time she wanted to shout it to
the world. But she must take small steps.

Her mind was fraught with the difficulties. What if he

didn't like her? Or she him? It would make no difference. He was alive and safe.

Her emotions were in turmoil. Inside, she could feel herself unravelling. Mirroring the circus she was painting on the nursery wall, there was a circus going on inside her, clowns doing somersaults and a brass band playing *oompah-pah!* The audience stood, clapping their hands and cheering.

She did a little quickstep around the room, her heels rapping on the bare boards, the love she'd kept suppressed all the years they'd been apart almost bursting out of her. But there was another emotion too, overriding the euphoria of the moment: caution. So, where to start?

They had something in common, Jilly thought as she went downstairs, her elation overcoming her need to cry all the tears she'd held back in one big flood. She'd had a happy childhood, too – at least, until her father had come home from the war.

1 June 1944

Not a gleam of light could be seen in the village of Blackbriar Caundle. The moon was a luminous crescent in a dark sky peppered with stars.

Inside Rose Cottage, Sylvia Turner had just finished serving dinner to the children.

Of the three, only five-year-old Jilly was hers. Twice her age, twins Audrey and Peter were the children born to the first Mrs Turner, after whom the cottage was named.

Rose Turner's children had the blue eyes of their father and light brown hair as straight as a yard of pump water. Sylvia's own daughter had a mop of dark unruly curls. Jilly's eyes were brown, exactly like Sylvia's own.

Tonight for dinner there was a tin of Spam, provided by her American friend, Gary Carstairs. With it, some leftover cabbage and mashed potato was fried together in dripping to become bubble and squeak.

Sylvia gazed at her daughter. 'Clear your plate, Jilly love.'

'I'm not hungry.'

'I'll have it,' Peter said.

'No you won't. Jilly is too thin as it is. Eat it, love, else you won't get any pudding. We can't afford to waste food when we have to eke out every scrap we get.'

Jilly looked at her half-siblings and screwed up her face. 'I don't want any. I don't like tapioca.'

'Tapioca is made of frogspawn, and it hatches into frogs that wriggle around inside you,' Peter said, making a face at her.

Jilly held her stomach and went into a fit of giggles, nearly falling off the chair as she rolled around on it.

'Stop it, Peter. Jilly, you sit up straight and eat. Tapioca is good for you, and there's some blackberry jam to go on it. Count yourself lucky we've got it. Hurry up now, the lot of you. Clear the table when you've finished. I've got to get ready to go out. Lieutenant Carstairs is picking me up.'

When she came downstairs Sylvia was wearing the dress she kept for going out in, the blue one with the little bolero jacket. A scarf was tied carefully over her hair. She turned her head to gaze over her shoulder, raising first one leg, then the other, asking, 'Are my seams straight, Audrey?'

'Yes. You look really pretty in that dress, too, but you've got some lipstick on your teeth.'

'Damn!' Sylvia rubbed at it with her finger and grimaced at herself in the bevelled, butterfly shaped mirror hanging over the fireplace. 'Now, make sure you look after Jilly, you two. She's to be in bed by eight, and the pair of you as soon as it gets dark, to save electricity. Make sure you leave the night light burning. And don't touch the blackout curtains, unless you want Jerry to drop a bomb on you.'

With that warning, Sylvia kissed them all as she heard the sound of a jeep outside. She picked up her jacket and slipped her gas mask over her shoulder. 'Here's the lieutenant. He might have some cocoa for you.'

There was more than cocoa: a tin of corned beef, real coffee, more jam, a packet of biscuits, a tin of butter, two pairs of nylons, a carton of cigarettes and a bottle of bourbon came out of the pack he carried. And he had a special treat. Four bars of chocolate.

Sylvia broke a small piece of chocolate for each of them. 'Jilly, I'm giving yours to Audrey. You can have it when you've finished your tapioca.' She smiled when Jilly picked up her spoon and began to attack the slimy pudding.

Sylvia knew she'd have to pay for the goods, but it was a fair exchange. Besides, it was comforting, having a man to cuddle up to from time to time, especially when the kids were at school.

Jilly was too young to be aware of what her mother and Gary got up to behind locked doors. Rose Cottage was a good distance from her neighbours, so Sylvia escaped observation from the locals, too. Not that they bothered with her much. They treated Sylvia as a usurper, even though she hadn't met John until four years after his wife had died. Rose Turner had been a paragon of middle-class values by all accounts – the type of woman who'd found her way on to every committee. In contrast, the villagers seemed to regard Sylvia as the wicked stepmother. What was worse, they treated Jilly with the same disdain.

As for Gary, he was always careful. In civilian life he'd been a businessman. He had a wife and two kids back home, and didn't want any complications. Neither did she, come to that. Except for Jilly, Sylvia had no family. She was illegitimate, and had been brought up by her grandfather, who'd been a farm labourer. She'd married John Turner for a home he could provide. Need had brought them together.

Sylvia had heard a rumour that landing craft were being loaded in the harbour at Poole, and the American divisions were about to move out. She knew better than to ask Gary. He didn't like talking about the war. He enjoyed himself when he was off base, as if the war didn't exist. He'd taught her to dance the jitterbug at the American Red Cross Club in Bridport, and the energetic dance had left them both breathless and laughing.

Sylvia was back home just after midnight, both of them a bit the worse for wear. Gary pressed against her as she fitted the key into the lock, breathing against her ear, 'Aren't you going to ask me in for a drink, babe?'

'We'll have to be quiet; I don't want the kids woken up. Shush,' she said when he stumbled against her in the dark, for the kids had forgotten to light the night light.

She set a match to the wick, then poured him a drink,

which he downed in one go. He gave a slight shudder, said in a slurred voice, 'Let's go upstairs.'

'Not upstairs, Gary. The kids.'

'Here then.' He began to undo her bodice and placed his hands over her breasts, fondling her as his mouth covered hers. She hoped he wouldn't take as long as he had in the field earlier, as they settled themselves on the floor, half under the table. She wasn't really interested tonight because her monthly curse was due, but she faked arousal because she could feel the urgency in him. The sooner she got it over with the sooner she could go to bed.

Jilly had nearly dropped off to sleep again when there came the sound of grunting.

She shook Audrey awake, whispering, 'D'you suppose the Jerries are under our window? They might shoot us!'

Desperate for a wee, Jilly daren't get out of bed. Peter had told her the floor was covered in spiders at night and they'd run up under her nightgown if she set a foot on the floor.

Audrey cuddled her close in the double bed they shared. 'It sounds more like the butcher's sow has got out of her sty. She's looking for her piglets, I expect.'

'Peter said the butcher cut their throats and sold them on the black market. He said he watched him do it and they squealed really loud. The butcher told Peter that he'd be doing exactly the same to the Jerry if he was younger, or if they set foot in Blackbriar Caundle.'

'I expect he would. Mr Hadly is a fierce old man. I don't like him.'

'What's the black market?'

'I'm not sure. A market with blackout curtains, I expect.'

'Peter's going to make me watch Mr Hadly kill my bunny rabbit.' Tears welled in Jilly's eyes and she began to snivel with the misery brought by the thought. 'He said we're going to eat him. Why does he have to be killed?'

'Peter's teasing you. But Mum told you not to get attached to that rabbit. One of these days he might escape from his cage and go back to the wild, like the last one. Things will be different when our dad comes home from the war, I expect.'

'What's he like, our dad?'

'I don't know, I can't really remember him. There's a picture of him in the photograph album.' Audrey turned over. 'Now be quiet. I want to sleep.'

Jilly turned towards the wall. She waited until she was bursting, then said, 'I want a wee, Audrey.'

'Hold it until morning,' Audrey said sleepily.

But although Jilly tried, she couldn't. And she couldn't sleep. There were noises in the house she wasn't used to.

Lying on the wet patch, thinking of the spiders on the floor and hoping they didn't think to climb on the bed, Jilly was just beginning to fall asleep when she heard a faint throbbing sound.

Scrambling from under the covers she knelt on the bed and drew the curtain to one side as the throbbing grew louder and louder. She pressed her face against the cool glass of the windowpane. She could make out the shapes of the bombers as they came back over the coast; one trailed a plume of smoke from one of its engines.

The sky was filled with them. Dense black crosses blotted out the stars like gigantic, noisy bats, so the air around Jilly beat and throbbed, the bed under her vibrated and the smiley moon appeared and disappeared behind them, as if it were playing hide-and-seek. The noise made the windowpanes rattle and her ears ache.

They were English planes, full of brave pilots and gunners, Peter had told her. When he grew up he was going to be a pilot and fly one too and drop bombs on the Jerry.

Jilly loved the menacing noise they made, as if they were live, growling creatures venturing into the gloaming to do battle. They returned before dawn and she always woke, feeling comforted by them.

Audrey always slept through the noise, the blanket pulled over her head so only the end of her nose poked out to suck in air.

When the bombers throbbed away into the distance Jilly got back under the covers. The warm patch was now cold, so she pulled her pillow down over it and sprawled over the top. Presently, her eyes grew heavy and drooped shut.

As she dozed, she heard a plane by itself, not a bomber

though. Its engine kept surging and missing a beat. It was some way off.

The noise stopped, then came a dull thump. Then there was silence.

Jilly's eyes flicked open again. Perhaps it was a German plane. It might have dropped a bomb. If so, she hoped it was on the church so she wouldn't have to go to Sunday school.

Distracted, Sylvia said, 'I think one of the planes came down.'

'Could be.' Gary drew on his jacket, then took a wad of paper money from his pocket and dropped it on the table.

'What's that for?'

He was awkward, shuffling from one foot to the other, as if there was something unpleasant on his mind he was eager to avoid. 'I don't really need it where I'm going. I thought it might come in handy. Buy something for the kids with it, wouldya?'

'You're going tomorrow, aren't you?'

'I shouldn't be at all surprised.' He shrugged and cracked a faint smile. 'The war can't last for ever. Tell you what, I'll send you a postcard when it's over.'

'I'd like that, Gary, however long it takes . . . just to know you're safe.'

He gave her a hug and placed a kiss against her hair. 'So long . . .'

Sylvia silently sang the words to the tune they'd danced to earlier in the night: *It's been good to know ya . . .*

He reached out, gently touching her face with his fingertip. 'You're OK for a Limey. Thanks for the dance. Did I ever tell you that you have a great pair of pins? I'll miss you, babe. You're my kind of gal.'

'Take care, Gary.'

His reply was quietly confident before he closed the door behind him. 'You know me, Sylvia, I'm the original Lieutenant Cautious.'

Tears pricked her eyes as she heard the noise of the jeep disappear into the distance. She'd grown to like the generous Gary Carstairs more than she should.

*   *   *

The stairs creaked as her mother crept up them, waking Jilly. The door quietly opened and her mother set the candle on the dresser. First, she kissed the blanket over Audrey's head, then she leaned over her to kiss Jilly's cheek. Her mouth nuzzled warmly where Jilly's jawbone met her ear. She giggled, then slid her arms around her mother's neck and hugged her tight.

'What are you doing awake?'

'The planes woke me. Where do they go every night?'

'Across the Channel, but you mustn't worry about it. I love you, Jilly girl. You're the sunshine in my heart.'

'Your only sunshine?' But she already knew the answer to that.

'That's right. You make me happy when skies are grey.' Her mother's voice was slurred, her breath smelt funny and there were tears glittering on her cheeks.

'Why are you crying, Mum?'

'Because sometimes things get me down a bit. People you love go away, and you don't know if you'll ever see them again.'

'Like my dad did?'

She sighed. 'Yes, my love, like your dad did. I hope you never have to be parted from someone you care deeply about. Go to sleep now, I don't want you to fall asleep in Sunday school like you did last week.'

'I thought I heard a plane fall out of the sky.'

'I expect you were dreaming.'

'Peter told me there were spiders on the floor. Be careful they don't run up your legs.'

Her mother chuckled. 'Peter was teasing you. But if I go running off down the road flapping my skirt in the air and showing off my knickers and suspenders, with spiders dangling from my petticoat, you'll know they climbed up the ladders in my stockings.'

Reassured, Jilly giggled and allowed her eyes to drift shut.

'Don't forget your gas mask.'

'Do I have to go to Sunday school?'

'Yes. You want to grow up to be good, don't you? Besides, I want you all out of the way so I can give the cottage a good clean through.'

Audrey and Peter didn't add their complaints to Jilly's. They were being picked up by their uncle Derek in his motor car and taken to spend the day with him and Auntie Blanche in their posh house in Branksome Woods.

'It's not fair. Why can't I go in Uncle Derek's car too?'

'Because they're not your relatives,' Peter said loftily.

'Why not?'

Her mother sighed. 'Because they're not.'

Audrey said rather smugly, 'I expect we'll be taken to the cinema. And we'll have jelly and cake for tea. Uncle Derek is a doctor. Auntie Blanche is really pretty, and has lovely jewellery. They said our mother married beneath her, since Dad was just a farm worker.'

'Oh, la-di-da. Perhaps your mother was desperate. After all, she wasn't much to look at. And without farm workers there wouldn't be any cake for the likes of your auntie Blanche to eat. Besides, she sold tickets in a theatre box office before she married, so she's got nothing to blow trumpets about.'

Consumed with envy, Jilly said to Audrey, 'Why don't you go and live with them if they're so rich?'

'They have important work to do. Auntie Blanche is on committees, and our uncle works in a hospital. We might go to live with them when we're eleven and start at grammar school. Uncle Derek said he owes it to our own dear, departed mother to see that we get a good education.'

Peter pushed her. 'You're not supposed to tell anyone.'

Tartly, Jilly's mother said, 'And first you have to pass the exam.'

'Oh, we will,' Peter told her. 'Uncle Derek's on the examination board. He's very important. He gets extra petrol rations and everything, because he's a doctor.'

'I don't want to stay with them, anyway. I hate them,' Jilly poked into the conversation.

Audrey said loftily, 'They wouldn't have you, since you've got dirty habits. You still wet the bed. Auntie Blanche said you'll turn out to be common.'

'You wet the bed at her age, too, you little madam,' Sylvia said, clipping Audrey round the ear. 'You needn't parade your airs and graces and your fancy relatives around here.

It's not as if they're gentry. Pay no mind to her, Jilly love. Go on, off with you.'

Wishing she had posh relatives too, Jilly picked up her gas mask box. Pulling her head and arm though the strap she let the box rest on her hip. She hated wearing the mask. It fitted tightly around her face and smelled strongly of rubber. She could hardly see through the two round metal eyes. Sometimes, she panicked when she put it on, and felt sick.

'You'll just have to get used to it. It's better than being gassed,' her mother had told her firmly. 'And if you're sick in it, it will go all over your face, so you'd better be careful.'

As soon as she was on her own, Jilly had turned on the gas cooker's taps and had stuck her nose where the jets were. The gas had smelled like rotten eggs, and her head had gone all dizzy, so she had to rush outside straight away and breathe in some proper air before she died. Her mother had been right. But she'd forgotten to turn the taps off and she'd got into awful trouble when her mother came in from the garden and scolded her.

'What a waste of gas. Now I've got none to cook dinner on. It was just as well I forgot to put money in the meter, and a good job I didn't light a fag as soon as I came in. We'd have been blown to kingdom come with the house full of gas! Next time you touch the gas taps you're going over my knee, Jilly Turner. Here, put a bit of extra chocolate in your pocket. That pair can eat their cake instead.'

Sunday school was boring. Mrs Green, the vicar's mother, wore round glasses. She had a nose like a chicken's beak and it seemed to stab as she spoke, as though she was pecking crumbs out of the air. There were white hairs sticking out of her chin and she was very stern.

Jilly was colouring in a picture of Jesus. There was a garland of flowers around him and a halo of light. His eyes rolled upwards. He carried a lamb under his arm, and children were gathered at his feet, their hands together in prayer. She concentrated hard not to go over the lines, then turned to Alec Frampton, who was one of the evacuee children. He lived at the Crutchlys' farm and was three years older than her.

'What do the words say?'

'Can't you read yet?' he said loftily. 'It says, "Suffer little children to come unto me."'

'What does that mean?'

'That Jesus wants little children to suffer and die, then go and live with him in heaven.'

Jilly stared at him. 'I don't want to die and go to heaven.' Taking the crayon she scribbled all over the drawing, screwed it up and threw it on the floor.

'You pick that up, Jilly Turner,' said Mrs Green.

'I will not! Jesus is mean, and I'm not ever going to heaven.'

Mrs Green looked shocked. 'That wouldn't surprise anyone around here. Very well, you can place your hands on your head until you decide to apologize for your blasphemous behaviour.'

Jilly's arms began to ache after five minutes. She gazed at the other children. Amy Waterhouse caught her eye and winked. She looked over at Mrs Green, who was reading the bible, silently mouthing the words, her face red from the affront. Amy poked a tongue out at the old lady, then grinned at Jilly.

Jilly tried not to giggle. She was tired of standing still and began to fidget, first lifting one leg, then lowering it and raising the other.

'I know where there's a crashed plane,' Alec whispered from the corner of his mouth when Mrs Green suddenly stood up and left the room.

'Where?'

'I'll show you after Sunday school.'

'Won't you get in trouble with Farmer Crutchly?'

'All he wants is free labour. He can beat me if he wants. I don't care.'

Jilly admired Alec. He was scared of nothing. He was good at school, too, better than everyone – even Peter. The Crutchlys were mean to him and called him Smart Alec. But Alec knew everything that happened in the district. His mother was dead from the bombing and his dad was away at the war. His dad's uncle, a man called Reginald Fry, couldn't look after him, Peter had told her. He did important war work. 'I think he's a spy,' Alec had whispered to her in the school playground.

'Fry the spy,' she'd said and giggled.

Jilly was beginning to get pins and needles. She took the opportunity to hop in a circle, flapping her arms. The elastic in her knicker leg was loose and it slid down her thigh. She stopped to pull it up.

Somewhere in the building a toilet flushed loudly. Everyone looked at each other and began to snigger. Jilly resumed her former position. Mrs Green gazed suspiciously around at them when she came back. When she wasn't looking they grinned and made faces at each other.

'Are you ready to apologize, Jilly Turner?'

Jilly rolled her eyes to heaven and adopted the same penitent look that Jesus had worn in her colouring-in picture. 'Yes, Mrs Green . . . sorry, Mrs Green.'

Alec only just managed to disguise his snort of laughter, turning it into a cough.

'Alec, use your handkerchief, else you'll spread germs around. Jilly, you may pick up the paper and resume your seat. We'll say a prayer for our brave fighting men before you all go home.'

They bowed their heads and pressed their palms together.

Outside, the day was bright with sunshine. Alec hunched into his jacket and strode on ahead, with Jilly trying to keep up. 'Stay behind me,' he said over his shoulder, 'I don't want the others to think I'm friends with a girl.'

'What's wrong with girls?'

'They're daft, that's what's wrong with them. They don't like anything but dolls and giggling.'

'I've got chocolate.'

'I don't believe you. Let me see.'

Jilly felt in her pocket for the two small squares. She dusted the fluff from them and handed him a square. 'If you suck it, it lasts longer.'

'Thanks,' he grunted. 'You're all right for a girl.'

They sucked in silent bliss until the last vestige of melted chocolate disappeared, then Jilly told him, 'I like planes better than dolls. I counted them when they flew over last night.'

'How many were there, then?'

Jilly pulled the largest number she could think of out of her head. 'At least twenty-three.'

'There were more than that. Hundreds.' He climbed over the stile and waited for her at the other side. 'We can't go on the beach because of the barbed wire and mines. We'll have to go through the woods. Stay on the path and keep a look out for rabbit traps.'

'We're going through the woods?'

'That's what I said.'

'What if we get lost?'

'We won't. And keep quiet in case the Home Guard are there – though I know where they've dug their trenches, and since it's Sunday they'll be at home gobbling up their dinners.'

Jilly had never been inside the woods before. It was dark and exciting and smelled of damp things. The ground was criss-crossed with mossy tree roots and the breeze made the leaves on the trees rustle and shush. Beams of sunlight shafted down through the trees, and the branches caused dappled patterns of moving light. Jilly was enchanted.

It took them half an hour to reach the other side. There, the woods thinned into a grassy clearing that sloped upwards towards the other edge of the woods. Marks had been scored into the hill and bits of metal littered the grass.

Awed, Jilly whispered, 'Is it a Jerry plane?'

'No, it's one of ours. It's a fighter. Spitfire,' Alec said knowledgeably. 'I saw it come in low last night and heard it land.'

The Spitfire was flattened against the grass, its propeller and nose crumpled where it had collided with a tree.

'Is anybody inside it?'

'I don't know. I don't think anyone's found it yet but us. D'you want to take a look inside?'

She could hardly breathe for the excitement and danger of it. Dumbly, she nodded.

Alec went up on to the wing first, pulling her up after him. Oily dirt was plastered all over the canopy, but neither of them could reach it to see inside the fighter. The Spitfire smelled of the paraffin Jilly's mother used in the heater to warm the house, when they ran out of coal.

'You'll have to stand on my shoulders. There's a broken bit in the corner of the canopy. If you lean across, you might be able to see something through it. Here, take my hand-kerchief to wipe the dirt away.'

Jilly tried not to wobble as she climbed precariously on to Alec's shoulders. Planting her feet each side of his neck, she leaned against the plane for support. The metal was warm from the sun.

As she gazed through the broken bit of canopy, she gave a small scream of fright, for she saw that most of the canopy had been torn away on the other side. Not far from her own face was another – that of a man. There was a cut on his forehead. Above it, a shock of light brown curls matted with blood were being tossed by the breeze. His eyes were closed.

'What can you see?' Alec hissed.

Jilly was petrified, stuck to the spot, even though her legs wobbled with the effort of staying on Alec's shoulders. She found her voice, a quivering, fearful sound. 'There's a man with blood all over his face. I think he might be a dead hero.'

A pair of blue eyes flicked open. The man's mouth twitched into a grin and his curly moustache wiggled. 'I'm not a dead hero yet, though I think I came close to it last night. What's your name, sweetheart?'

'Jilly Turner.'

'I'm Rick Oliver. Don't be frightened, Jilly Turner. It will take more than a bit of a prang to kill this hero off, though I seem to have buckled my legs a bit. Look, I'm in a spot of bother. Go and fetch me some help, there's a good girl. And make sure nobody lights any matches, else I'll go up like a Roman candle on Guy Fawkes night.'

Two

Most of the village turned out for the rescue operation. Jilly didn't go to fetch her mother, since their cottage was too far away and she didn't want to miss any of the rescue herself.

Eventually, it would take several men to help remove the pilot from the cockpit of the Spitfire. The operation would be officiated by Donald Burns, the publican, who also headed the village Home Guard.

Now, the publican was strategically positioned on the wing, where he could oversee proceedings and bawl out instructions.

Burns nodded respectfully when Dr Andrews, a bowler-hatted, fussy little man nearing retirement age, came into the clearing with his bag.

'We didn't move him. We waited till you arrived,' Burns bellowed, stating the obvious in a rather self-important manner.

Men were swarming all over the plane like ants. Others stood in groups. One lit a pipe. 'Like as not he's out of the base at Warmwell,' he said knowledgeably.

'What are you trying to do, blow the lot of us up? Can't you smell the fuel? Put that bloody thing out!' Donald Burns shouted. 'It smells like horse shit, anyway.'

'You watch your language,' a woman said, her voice shrill. 'You're not in the public bar now, Donald Burns. There be children present.'

'Why don't you shut your trap and go home, Mrs Perkins. Take the children with you. This here is men's business and we don't want no women nagging at us. We get enough of that at home, don't we gentlemen?'

There was a collective chorus of throat-clearing and assenting nods.

Dr Andrews gazed at Burns through the round glasses perched on the end of his nose. 'He'll have to be moved before I can examine him. Can he talk?'

'That he can, Doctor. He says his name is Richard Oliver and his legs are broken. He's eighteen years of age.'

'I'd rather he gave me his details himself,' Doctor Andrews said, gazing upon Donald Burns with displeasure. 'Perhaps I should remind you that a patient's details are a confidential matter. They're not meant for an outsider's ears. Now . . . what's your name, young man?'

'Richard Oliver.'

Dr Andrews wrote it on a pad. 'Year of birth?'

'1926.'

'Good . . . can you tell me what injuries you've sustained?'

'Both my legs are broken, and I think I might have caught a Jerry bullet.'

'Where?'

'In my arse . . . at least . . . I hope it's only my arse. One creased my head and knocked me for six. When I came to I was nearly on the ground. Only just managed to flatten the Spit out and land. Gave my noodle another bit of a crack when I touched down. Luckily I've got a hard skull without much in it. Neanderthal, my wingco calls me, but don't tell anyone.'

The doctor industriously wrote it down, muttering, 'All my consultations are kept confidential, young man.'

Beside Jilly, Alec snorted with laughter. Jilly grinned at him, even though she didn't know what he was laughing about.

'Right, then. We'll have to get you out. I'm afraid I haven't got any morphine to give you for the pain. Be careful of his legs, men.'

'We'll get the young man out,' Burns said confidently. 'Wallace, you're the strongest. Take him under the armpits from behind, would you? And I want one either side, to ease his legs up after him. We'll brace his neck first, then sit him on the side, see. Once he's there we can splint his legs together so they don't flop around. Then we'll lower him gently down. No jolting him, mind. Stretcher-bearers, be at the standby.'

It took half an hour to get the pilot out. He cried out on

several occasions, and nearly passed out a couple of times. When they had finally laid him on the stretcher and the doctor had examined him, he was so pale, he closed his eyes.

'Out of the way, you children,' Dr Andrews said fussily.

Jilly, who'd been holding on to her tears, gave a shuddering sob, followed by another.

'Girls!' Alec said, heaving a sigh. 'What are you blubbering about?'

'I don't want Rick Oliver to be hurt. He's so brave and handsome.'

Rick's eyes fluttered open and he said wearily to the doctor, 'Let me talk to the kiddies before you carry me off. Come closer, you two.'

He shook Alec's hand. 'Thanks for your help, old boy. I'd still be in there if it wasn't for you. My helmet is in the Spit. I want you to have it.'

'I'll get it for the boy,' Burns said officiously.

'As for you, Jilly Turner, dry your tears. My injuries don't hurt much, I promise. You can have the wings off my jacket to remember me by. Perhaps you'd be good enough to give them to her, Doc?'

The wings were embroidered in cream and brown thread, and were the same shape as his moustache, only they had a crown in the middle. It took just a few seconds for the doctor to run a sharp little knife under the stitching and hand it to her. The frayed cotton hung from the edges, as if the badge had sprouted short, untidy legs. Jilly imagined that they might suddenly stretch out. Then the badge would run along her fingers and launch itself from her palm to soar into the sky. She closed her hand gently around her reward, keeping it earthbound. She was enormously proud of it.

'I hope you soon get better, Mr Oliver,' Jilly told him. 'You can have my lucky shell necklace, if you like.'

'Lucky, is it?'

She nodded. 'I made it myself. You can use the shell as a spoon if you're lost in the desert and haven't got one to eat your tinned soup with.'

'You never know when that will happen, and I need all the luck I can get. Did anyone ever tell you that you're a very pretty girl? Just my type.'

She felt herself turning bright red. Pulling the string the shell was attached to over her head, she shyly handed the necklace to him.

His hand closed around it. One of his fingernails was swollen and bruised. 'Thank you, sweetheart. I'll come back and see you one day, when the war is over. I'll soon mend and be up flying again, won't I, Doc?' There was a man with a camera, and the pilot obligingly propped himself up on one elbow and smiled into the lens. 'You should take a picture of the kids,' he said afterwards. 'They rescued me.'

Dr Andrews managed a nod.

'Giddy up then, gentlemen. The sooner I get to hospital the sooner I'll be back on Jerry's tail.' He blew Jilly a kiss as they picked up the stretcher.

'The cameraman took a photograph of them in front of the Spitfire, then asked them some questions before moving off.

Rick Oliver closed his eyes and quietly groaned as the stretcher-bearers bumped him off over the tussocks. Jilly thought he was handsome with his moustache. A door in her heart opened and let him in, her brave pilot hero. She was going to kneel by the side of her bed and pray for him every night – even though there might be spiders on the floor.

'Here, where d'you think you're going, young Ackerly?' Burns shouted as everyone began to follow after the stretcher. 'That there plane is government property. Someone's got to stay and guard it until I've contacted the base and they send one of their own men.'

Ackerly would have still been guarding the Spitfire at the end of the month, if he hadn't acted on his own initiative and gone home for his dinner later that day.

Jilly and Alec became close friends. Alec was moody at times, but Jilly knew he was ill-treated by the Crutchlys. Farmer Crutchly's two ruddy-faced, round-bodied daughters pulled Alec's hair and bullied him constantly. Sometimes he came to school with bruises on his arms and face. Alec was clever and they weren't, so they called him Smart Alec.

'Smart Alec's a sissy Londoner. He went and cried his eyes out when our dad slit the hog's throat last night.'

'I did not!' Alec said hotly.

'Bloody sissy!' Martha said daringly, slapping him around the head with her meaty hands. 'He don't know nuthin' about varming, that he don't. Dad put a strap across his arse, last night. He was caught reading when he should have been doing his chores. *Just William*, the book was. He'll give him *Just William* if he catches him again! He'll send that Smart Alec back to bloody London, you see if he don't.'

'I'll tell my mum on you if you swear again, Martha Crutchly,' Jilly said fiercely.

'I don't care. Your mother is nothing around here, and I can swear if I want.'

Alec scuffed his foot at the dirt. 'If I get sent back to London, at least I won't have to listen to you Crutchlys any more.'

'What did you say about my family, Alec Frampton?' the other sister, Rosemary, screeched, and punched him on the shoulder.

'That you all smell of cow farts!' he muttered under his breath, and took off down the road.

Before they could start on her, Jilly followed after him, giggling at the insult. When she reached the stile and considered they were a safe distance away, she turned and shouted out, 'Cow farts! Stinky old cow fart Crutchlys!'

'At least our mother doesn't go out with American soldiers.'

'That's because she's ugly . . . like you two.'

'Shut up, will you,' Alec said, and took her by the collar. 'They'll take it out on me when I get back. I'll already be in enough trouble for leaving the farm when I still have chores to do. Let's go and play in the Spit.'

'Can I be the pilot?'

'No . . . I've got the helmet.'

'But I've got the pilot's wings. You could lend me the helmet.'

'Only if you lend me the wings for a week.'

'A whole week? That's not fair.'

'Two days, then. I'm going to write a story about a brave fighter pilot and enter it for a competition in the paper. That's if the Crutchlys will allow me to. I want to copy the wings to decorate it with. If I win, the prize is ten shillings, and I'll give you thruppence.'

Her eyes widened. 'Crumbs . . . a whole ten shillings! You'll be rich. What will you do with it?'

'I don't know. Save it up, I suppose, so when my dad comes home from the war I can buy him a present. I've got a tin I keep in the woods with my private things in. The Crutchlys are always sneaking through my belongings to see what I've got. The tin's hidden in a hollow tree trunk, but you have to climb up to get it. I'll show you where it is in case I die. Then you can have all my worldly goods to remember me by. But don't tell anyone else, because it's a secret.'

She drew on her chest with her finger, and, although she didn't want to die, said the sacred oath: 'Cross my heart and hope to die.' She felt sorry for Alec having to live with the Crutchlys. 'I can't remember my dad. Can you remember yours?'

Alec nodded. 'My father was a teacher. So was my mother. Only she died when the house was bombed. I've got a photograph of them in my tin. I'll show you on the way home.'

Jilly squeezed his arm in sympathy. 'I don't know what I'd do if my mum died. You'll always be my friend, won't you, Alec? Even though I'm only a girl?'

'I s'pose so. You're not bad for a girl. You've got nice eyes . . . like a dog. You're prettier than the Crutchlys, anyway.'

'You've got nice eyes too. Like one of those fierce hawks, only grey. You're prettier than the Crutchlys too.'

'Don't be daft. Boys can't be pretty, only handsome.' He grinned. 'You should smell the dung when I'm mucking out the stalls. It stinks something awful and the flies crawl all over everything.'

'I like you better than the pilot, even though he's my hero. You can be my second hero if you want.'

Alec smiled and jammed the helmet on her head. 'You can be the pilot, then, and I'll be the squadron leader. I'll sit behind you on the plane and tell you how to fly it.'

'I'll lend you the wings to write your story with, but I want them back. You'll have to come back to my house to get them.'

'Won't your mum mind?'

'No . . . as long as we don't tramp muck all over the floor.
She might let you write your story at my house, and post it
for you. Then the Crutchlys needn't know about it.'

Alec brightened up at the thought and gave one of his rare
smiles.

She murmured, 'You look nice when you smile; not so
fierce.'

It was nearing the end of September. Mornings found the
hedges strung with dew. The harvesting was over, sheaves
dotted the stubble and the leaves on the trees had become a
fiesta of yellow, orange and brown. Horse chestnuts dropped
glossy brown seeds from their prickly cases, and conker tour-
naments were in full swing.

The blackberries ripened on the bushes. They picked hand-
fuls as they walked, stuffing them into their mouths and
staining purple their fingers and tongues.

Alec showed Jilly how to climb the tree, using the side of
her foot on a knot where a branch had broken off in the past.
The hollow was in the fork of the trunk, where the branches
splayed out. It was just big enough to hide the red tin, which
was wrapped in a piece of oilcloth.

It was crowded in the fork with two of them sitting there,
but the leaves closed thickly around them with an arid
autumn rattle. They took a branch apiece as Alec showed
Jilly the photograph of his parents. It was in a small frame,
and the glass was cracked. He looked a lot like his father,
except the man had a happy face, while Alec hardly smiled.
His father was seated on a bench, his arm around a woman
with a baby seated on her lap. The woman was very pretty,
and gazing down at the child with a soft smile. Tears pricked
Jilly's eyes for what Alec had lost. 'They look nice.'

He nodded. 'The baby is me. The photograph used to be
on the mantelpiece. Mum gave it to me when I was evacuated. I've got a letter my father left for me, too.'

'Will you read it to me?'

'No, it's sealed. I'm not supposed to open it unless . . . unless
I need to. The tin has my birth certificate in it too, and other
important things. Just in case I ever need to prove who I am.'
He closed the lid. Carefully wrapping up the tin, he placed it

back into its hiding place. Casually, he said, 'Perhaps I'll let you read the letter when you grow up.'

'When will that be?'

'When you're eighteen, I expect.'

Disappointment filled her, but all the same, it was nice to share a secret with Alec, and have something to look forward to. 'It's a long time to wait.'

He shrugged. 'That's too bad.'

Along with most of the American troops, Gary Carstairs had gone. Sylvia missed him a lot, and hoped he'd survive the war. She thought she might have been in love with him a bit because she missed him more than going out dancing, and the extra bits and pieces he'd brought for the kids. Though she missed those treats too, since it was hard to make ends meet.

Still, she'd been in love with John Turner when he'd gone off to war. The Red Cross had contacted her, told her he was a prisoner somewhere in Germany. He was sitting the war out in comfort, she supposed, and smiled. That would suit John. He hadn't really wanted to go to war in the first place and didn't have much get up and go to him.

She could barely remember his face, except when she looked at a photograph. Even then he seemed remote, like a stranger. It would be odd when he came home. She supposed they'd just have to get used to each other all over again.

Seated with her feet propped up on a stool, Sylvia was lengthening Jilly's coat, making false cuffs and a hem from an old checked skirt of hers. It should do another winter when she'd finished. Thank goodness the girl was still as slender as a reed.

It was nearly the end of the school holidays. The twins had gone to stay with their aunt and uncle. Although they were nice kids, they were growing fast and were always hungry. Sylvia had to be careful they didn't sneak Jilly's portion off her plate when she wasn't looking.

Like most women, Sylvia was tired of the war, of making do. But she managed on the rations, which she supplemented with the produce from the garden. They always had fresh eggs, and vegetables.

Jilly was bringing her friend back to tea. Alec Frampton was a quiet, polite lad. His face was closed, and sometimes the expression in his grey eyes was defensive. Sylvia had noticed the bruises on him. The brutality he was subjected to had left its mark. She'd mentioned it to the constable, who'd shrugged and promised to look into it.

She'd only seen the boy smile once, and that was when he'd listened to her read his story to them both. It had been a good tale. Now, they watched out for the postman, waiting to see how the story fared.

Her mind wandered to the garden. She'd have to dig over the vegetable patch soon, ready for planting winter beans and carrots. And the apples needed to be picked and stored. She was proud that her children didn't suffer from rickets, which was caused by a lack of calcium, she'd heard, and bowed the legs of children who didn't get their full ration of cheese and milk. Her store of ingredients to make a cake for Christmas was growing, too. Sylvia had heard that soy flour, with almond essence added to it, made a good substitute for marzipan.

Which reminded her, she'd better neck the chicken before Jilly got home. She didn't know how much longer her daughter could be fooled by tales of the animals running back to the wild. She wished Jilly wouldn't get so attached to them. Perhaps she'd get her a kitten for Christmas. That would be cheap because there were so many strays around. But then, that would be another mouth to feed.

A knock at the door brought Sylvia to her feet.

Her face paled when she saw the constable from the next village standing there, and the car beyond. It must be something important for him to use petrol and come by car rather than bicycle. Her hand flew to her mouth. 'Has something happened to Jilly?'

'No, Mrs Turner. I understand that Alec Frampton is playing with your daughter, though?'

'Yes, they'll be in soon for tea. Will you come in? Alec hasn't done anything wrong, has he? He seems to be a nice boy.'

Without answering, the constable stepped into the living room, where she had the table laid with bread and margarine, and the last of the tin of jam that Gary had given her. She'd scraped together the ingredients to make an apple pie with twists of potato pastry on top.

'Can you tell me what's wrong, Constable?'

'The boy's father has been killed in action. I'm to take him to the orphanage.'

'Oh, the poor little devil. Won't the Crutchlys keep him on?'

'Crutchly says that the boy's been more trouble than he's worth. Barnardo's Home has a place for him. He'll be kindly treated there, so you won't have to worry about the lad being beaten any more.'

'So you *did* investigate?'

He gave a bit of a smile. 'It was nothing to make a fuss over – I was given the strap myself when I was growing up. It didn't do me any harm. Not as bad as what some of our lads are going through at the moment.'

'The damned war,' she muttered. 'I'll be glad when it's over.'

'As will we all, Mrs Turner.'

She heard the children come through the back door. Jilly would take this hard, she thought.

'Can't he at least stay for his tea?'

'I'm sorry, Mrs Turner. I have to take him straight back. It makes it easier for them if they don't have time to think. Put a bit of pie in a bag for him to eat on the way, if you like. I expect he'll appreciate it.'

God help the poor little bugger, she thought, as the pair came in. Alec's face closed up when he saw the constable. His eyes rounded and he stood very still, like a rabbit caught in the beam of a torch. It was obvious that he sensed what was coming. Sylvia wrapped up a slice of pie in a butter wrapper and handed it to him.

'Alec Frampton,' the man said, 'I'm here to tell you that your father has been killed in action, and you are required to come with me. I'm to take you to the orphanage.'

'No!' Jilly screamed and flung her arms around the boy. 'You can't take him to an orphanage. I won't let you. It's not fair. He can stay with us, can't he, Mum?'

'Jilly, love, I have the other two to look after as well. We haven't got the room.'

Her daughter held on tight to Alec. 'He can sleep in Peter's bed with him.'

'See to your daughter, Mrs Turner.'

Sylvia grabbed Jilly and tore her away from the boy. Jilly struggled, screamed and kicked at her. Sylvia had never seen her daughter so upset before.

'Come on, boy. Let's go,' the policeman said, taking a grip on Alec's collar.

'Just a minute, sir.' Alec turned a desperate look on Jilly and said, as he was being dragged towards the door, 'Stop kicking up such a fuss, Jilly. I expect Fry the spy will take me in. Just look after my tin. I'll be back for it one day.' The door closed behind them.

Sylvia had to bar the door with her body to stop Jilly following after him. She burst into loud sobs as the car drove away. 'I hate you. I hate everyone!' she screamed, then stomped off up the stairs and slammed the door behind her.

Nothing Sylvia did seemed to comfort Jilly. Sylvia thought her daughter would never stop crying. It nearly broke her heart when the girl finally came to her arms for comfort and whispered brokenly, 'It hurt inside when Alec was taken away. He's my best friend.'

'I know, my love, and I know how sad you feel when you lose someone you care for. You just have to believe that you'll see him again one day.'

A month later a letter came with a cheque for ten shillings enclosed, and the news that Alec had won the writing competition.

Jilly's mother cut the story from the paper for her. Carefully, she folded it, placing it with the letter and the ten shilling bank cheque inside Alec's red tin.

Alec had said he'd be back for it one day, and her mother had told her to believe he would. He could have the cheque then. It would be a surprise for him.

Three

Alec found himself at the nautical school. On the first day he was bathed and had his hair cut short. Shivering with apprehension as the realization of his predicament began to sink in, he tried to appear grown up, since he only had himself to rely on now.

He and another boy were escorted to the tailor's shop, where they were measured before being handed a uniform and boots.

'You're an orphan too, then,' the other boy said with a sniff. 'My dad copped it in Africa. What about yours?'

'France. My mother was killed in the London blitz.' Alec held out his hand, like his father had taught him. 'I'm Alec Frampton. What's your name?'

'Robbie Green.' His companion, a small, wiry looking chap with muddy skin and eyes, hesitated for a moment, then shook Alec's hand and volunteered, 'My mother has a new bloke. She didn't wait until my old man was cold in his grave before she put me in here. Said she's getting married again and he doesn't want me.'

'I'm sorry.'

'I'm not,' he said fiercely. 'My mother's a tart, and I don't want to see either of them again. They used me as a punching bag.'

'I know what that's like. I was evacuated to a farm. They were always hitting me and I hated them.'

'You talk a bit posh. I expect they were jealous.'

'Not really. My parents were teachers and I'm going to be one myself when I grow up.'

'I'll know where to come when I can't figure out what the words are then. My ma said I'm stupid, like my dad.'

Alec felt sorry for him. 'Can't you read, then?'

Robbie shrugged. 'I expect I could if somebody showed me how to learn it properly. My teacher used to whack me around the head with a book, as if she was trying to hammer the words in, the silly old cow. So I didn't go to school much.'

'As soon as we find out what the routine is here, I'll see if I can help you with it. It will be practise for when I'm a teacher.'

Robbie shrugged. 'Don't bother. The first chance I get, I'll probably run away.'

'What for? At least we'll be fed here. And it'll be winter soon. You'll die of the cold.'

'Nobody will care, so why should I?'

'I'll care,' Alec told him. 'We're new here. We should be friends and look after each other.'

'Aw, you're only saying that.'

'No, I'm not. I haven't got any friends, except for a girl I knew in the village. But we won't be able to see each other now and she'll probably forget all about me before too long.'

Despite his defiant stance, Robbie sobbed himself to sleep that night, until somebody told him to shut up. He did, giving a long drawn-out sniff now and again.

Long after his new friend had fallen asleep, Alec was still awake. Grief for his father nearly overwhelmed him and he didn't know how to handle it. He felt so alone, despite the other boys around him in the dormitory being in the same boat. Eventually he pulled the blanket over his head, allowing tears to run unchecked down his cheeks. The thought that his parents might be watching over him gave him some comfort. 'No matter what, I'll do my best to make something of myself, so you'll be proud of me,' he whispered quietly.

A feeling of peace crept over him, and his tears dried. He knew he'd have to be strong to survive, and it was the one and only time he allowed himself the luxury of tears.

It was a strange feeling, wearing long trousers. Stranger still was the system of flags and whistles, and the odd names given to the corridors and various rooms. Alec soon learned about the heroic seafarers and their achievements, like the brave Admiral Horatio Nelson and the Battle of Trafalgar.

It didn't take long to get into the routine set down by the home. They rose at six o'clock to the sound of a bugle. Most of them still half-asleep, they fell out of bed to wash and dress themselves. Breakfast was served at seven thirty. There was plenty of bread and dripping, which they washed down with tea or cocoa – more food than he'd had at the Crutchly farm.

After breakfast they fell in for inspection. The morning was spent either hard at their lessons or playing sport. They also learned nautical skills, such as tying knots or signalling. Midday, and they fell ravenously upon their dinner. There were no complaints from Alec. Two hours after tea at five thirty, they said their prayers and went to bed.

Each day merged into the next. He was kept too busy to feel sorry for himself. He made himself responsible for Robbie Green, and felt pride when his friend finally began to absorb a word or two.

A few weeks after Alec moved into the home he was summoned before the executive officer. He stood to attention in front of the man's desk. The officer finally looked up from his file. Clearing his throat, he smiled. 'How are you settling in, Frampton?'

'Very well, sir, thank you.'

'Good . . . good. I'm receiving favourable reports about you, especially in the academic area. Your behaviour too is exemplary. I'm pleased with your progress. Keep it up.'

'Thank you, sir. Yes, I will.'

'You have no complaints?'

'No, sir. I like it fine here.'

The officer tapped the file on his desk with his forefinger. 'Odd really . . . I understood you to be a troublemaker. You were evacuated to a farm, weren't you?'

'Yes, sir.'

'Did you like it there?'

'No, sir.'

'Hmmm . . . your honesty is laudable, lad, but we can't have everything our way, can we?'

'No, sir.'

The man unfolded a piece of paper. 'We've received a letter from a Mr Reginald Fry. Your only relative, I understand?'

'Yes, sir.' Fry the spy, he thought, and remembering Jilly's giggle he grinned to himself. 'Will he take me in, sir?'

'I'm afraid he's unable to. I'll read you his reply to my letter. I hope you won't be too disappointed.

> *'Re: Your query regarding Alec Robert Frampton (aged 9).*
> *Sir,*
>
> *I am a man who holds a position of importance in the war effort. I have discussed the matter with my wife, who works as a nurse. Our working hours are lengthy and we have concluded that we're unable to take my cousin's child under our roof. Quite simply, we do not have the time to properly supervise and discipline the boy at the moment, or, with consideration of our ages, the inclination to do so in the foreseeable future.*
>
> *As Alec's only living relative, I heartily endorse your suggestion that he be considered for migration to the Australian colony, where he can enter one of your training schemes and make something of himself.*
>
> *Should he show academic aptitude, consideration will be given to setting aside a sum for his further education and training, at an amount agreed between us. I will, of course, take an interest in the lad's welfare, and endeavour to keep in touch with him.*
>
> *Yours sincerely,*
> *Reginald G Fry.'*

Alec wasn't disappointed at all by the letter. He wasn't unhappy in the home. Although he and the other boys were well-regulated, and disciplined when needed, he knew what each day would bring and felt secure. He was also decently clothed and well fed.

There were boys of his own age to play with in the home, though he preferred his own company, or that of Robbie, for most of the time.

Alec did miss the green countryside of Blackbriar Caundle, though; the damp smell of the woods and the sea seemed to have become part of him while he was there. Mostly, he missed his friendship with little Jilly Turner. She came into his mind at odd times. But he was old enough to know her memory would eventually fade, as had the memory of his parents. He regretted not having their photograph to look at now and again, and wondered if Jilly had rescued his tin.

There was great delight to be had in knowing his school-work had improved and he was eager to learn as much as he could. His brain seemed to absorb everything and crave for more – so he learned a great deal.

'You have a good mind, Frampton. Don't waste it. Have you applied any thought to your future, and what you could apply your learning to? Has the school whetted your appetite to go to sea? If so, we'll push you to the limit, since we think you have the potential to become an officer.'

Alec didn't think he'd like to spend his life confined to a ship. 'Thank you, sir. I thought I might like to become a teacher, like my mother and father were.'

'I'm sure they'd be happy to know they set you such a fine example while they lived.' He flipped open the file. 'An excellent idea, Frampton. I'll mention if to Mr Fry when I write, since he's generously offered to sponsor your further education. And I'll mark it on your records. Australia needs good teachers, and it's been decided that you, along with others, will be going there as part of the migration programme, when this war ends. You'll be expected to take advantage of every opportunity offered to you.'

'Yes, sir. I will.'

'We've noticed that you're doing a good job coaching Green. But he'll never amount to much, you know.'

Alec saw now what Robbie had always been up against. 'I'd be obliged if you didn't tell him that, sir. It's not his fault he can't learn as easily as other boys. He tries hard and needs to be praised for that.'

The man gave him a measured look. 'How sensible you are for your age, Frampton. You'll go far. Off you go, now. I'll watch your progress with interest.'

At the end of the year, Alec watched with pride when Robbie was awarded a book prize for the most improved student.

The war in Europe ended. It was the eighth of May 1945. The sun shone as brightly as the daffodils. Smiles were brighter.

The siren that usually screamed out a warning of coming destruction was now mute. The thundering planes no longer flew overhead. Jilly missed them.

A party was held in the village street. Bunting festooned the hedgerows, Union Jacks were hung from cottage windows to flutter in triumph.

The music teacher, Miss Eckersly, had her piano wheeled into the street. She sat at the instrument on a round stool covered in green velvet – a stool, as Jilly knew from experience, that corkscrewed higher or lower, depending on which way you spun it. Pink-faced, she was playing with one hand while taking sips from a glass of port and lemon in her other hand.

Donald Burns beamed jovial smiles over everyone. 'I've been saving a bottle or two of port and sherry for just this occasion,' he said, and raised his glass. 'God save the King!'

'Cooking sherry,' Mrs Henry whispered with a sniff, but drank to the King anyway, then held her glass out to be refilled.

There were games and races. Jilly, her skirt tucked into her knicker legs, won a red, white and blue garter for coming second in her race. The much older Martha Crutchly won it and crowed as triumphantly as the cockerel in her father's hen house.

All the children were dressed in their best. Jilly and Audrey wore ribbons in their hair.

Peter ate as many sweet things as he could stuff in his mouth. And he drank a glass of sherry and some beer that was left on the table. After a while, he began to look a bit pale.

Jilly tugged at Audrey's skirt. 'I think Peter's going to be sick.'

'Serves him right, the greedy pig,' Audrey said self-righteously and pushed Peter in the back. 'I'd better take him home and look after him, I suppose, since your mother is talking to that awful Michael from the farm.'

Martha Crutchly giggled. 'Michael thinks she's got nice you-know-whats. He said he wants to put his hand up her skirt and do her.'

'Don't be so common,' Audrey told her.

'Oh, listen to Miss Perfect, then. It's a wonder you mix with the rest of us, or breathe the same air.'

'I do, because I have no choice, Martha Crutchly. I don't like this party much anyway. Grown-ups act so stupid when they drink. Your father is kissing everyone, and his stomach hangs over his trousers like that fat old sow of yours. We're going home. Come along, Peter, get moving. Uncle Derek doesn't want us to mix with the likes of her.'

'Be careful you don't trip over your hoity-toity madam nose,' Martha called out as Audrey moved away.

It was getting dark, and candles were lit. Somebody began to play an accordion. The publican was charging for his wine now. Everyone was smiling though, and the women began to dance and sing.

'They all think they sing like Vera Lynn,' Sylvia said, joining Jilly. 'Look after the torch, would you? I'm just going to have a dance or two, then we'll go home. Where are the twins?'

'They've gone home. Peter felt sick.'

'Serve him right for stuffing himself.'

Her mother began dancing with the Crutchly farmhand. She had a big smile on her face and was singing softly in his ear. The farmhand kept sliding his hand on to Sylvia's bum, and she kept pulling it away. But she was laughing about it all the same, in that teasing way she had about her.

Two of the village women were staring at them and whispering behind their hands.

Tired out now, Jilly leaned her head on the table, her fingers still clutched around the torch. Presently, the noise around her faded away to nothing.

When she woke it was dark and she was on her own. The breeze made whispering noises in the trees and the clouds kept covering up the moon, making the darkness seem dense and menacing. 'Mum?' she cried out. 'Where are you?'

A light came on in the nearest cottage and a window was thrust open. A man called out, 'Who's making all that noise?'

'It's me, Jilly Turner. I can't see my mum.'

'It's Jilly Turner. Poor little thing, her mother must have forgotten her.'

'No wonder. That Turner woman needs reporting. She only had eyes for that Crutchly farmhand earlier.'

'Hush, Jessie. The girl might hear you.'

'You hush. Get yourself dressed, Bert. You can take the girl home. Anyone who leaves a little kid alone in the dark to go off with a man isn't a fit mother. She's no better than she ought to be. When John Turner comes home from the war I'm going to make sure he knows it.'

'You keep a still tongue in your head, Jessie.'

'Says who?'

'I do. And I'm not asking you, I'm telling you. John's put up with enough these last few years without you adding to it with your vicious tongue.'

Just then Jilly's mother's voice came through the gate of the field opposite. 'I'm here, Jilly, and if I hear you say one more bad word about me in front of my daughter, Jessica Selby, I'll come up there and smack you right in your ugly gob.'

Jessie stuck her head out of the window and shouted, 'What was you doing behind the hedge, then?'

'Having a pee, if it's any of your business. I was caught short.'

'Will you lot shut up,' somebody yelled from the next house down. 'It sounds as though world war three's going on out there. Some of us need to get some sleep.'

Jilly felt safe when her mother's arms came around her and a kiss landed on her face. 'Have you still got the torch, Jilly love? You can turn it on and show us the way home.'

They'd just got out of the village and were walking through the dark rustling night, when the beam of the torch fell on a man standing in the road. It was the farmhand. Open bottle in one hand, he swayed back and forth.

Jilly gave a little scream as they came to a sudden halt.

'What d'you want, Michael?' Sylvia asked him.

He grinned. 'I thought I'd make sure you got home safely.'

'Well, you needn't bother. I can see my cottage from here, and there's nothing dangerous before I get to it, 'cepting for you, of course, so clear off.'

'I thought you might invite me in, like, since you allowed me to have a feel.'

'You thought wrong, and you're a liar. I didn't allow you to do anything, so don't you go talking dirty to me in front of my daughter. You deserve to have your face smacked, you do. Get away home with you else I'll scream blue murder and have you charged with assault.'

He took a step closer. 'Why don't you scream then? Nobody would believe you, anyway, since you went out with the American soldiers. Come on, Sylvia. I just want to feel you against me, that's all. You're nice and soft.'

'Do you, now? Well feel this,' Sylvia said softly, and she kicked out at him.

As he doubled up with a shriek of pain, she said, 'If you make a nuisance of yourself again I'll go to the police and report you, just see if I don't.' Her mother's hand tightened around Jilly's as the man began to show signs of recovery. 'Come on, Jilly, let's go!'

They pounded along the road and were soon indoors, breathing heavily. Her mother locked both doors, then checked the windows. She made sure Peter and Audrey were in bed. 'Go to bed now, Jilly.'

'What if he breaks in?'

'He won't. He'll be too frightened I'll tell the police.' Jilly was given a hug and a kiss. 'I'm sorry I gave you a bit of a fright. I was talking to Miss Eckersly about her giving you some more piano lessons. Then I had to go for a wee. The trouble is, I haven't got a piano for you to practise on, and I don't think we can afford to buy one.'

'I didn't like piano lessons, anyway. Miss Eckersly used to smack my fingers with a ruler when I got a note wrong.'

'Cruel cow, and her looking as though butter wouldn't melt! We won't bother with them again, then.'

'Will our dad be home soon?'

'Any day, now the war is over. That'll be nice, won't it? We'll be a proper family again. I just hope the Crutchlys don't keep Michael on and your dad gets his job back. Into bed now. Sweet dreams, Jilly girl. Remember, you're the sunshine in my heart.'

As Jilly drifted off to sleep she wondered what her father was like. A little knot of excitement gathered in her stomach as she remembered the Spitfire pilot. Her dad was probably a handsome hero too.

*   *   *

Demobbed in September, John Turner felt strange in his civvy suit.

The train from Waterloo Station in London was crowded, and was hot and humid, ripe with the smell of humanity. John had sat on his suitcase in the dirty corridor, unable to get a seat until they reached Southampton. It was nearly dusk when he was dropped off at Wool in Dorset. He knew he wouldn't get a bus at this time of night. Walking didn't bother him, though he wouldn't get home until after midnight.

He was lucky. He managed to hitch a ride on a motorbike before he'd gone a mile. He threw his bag into the sidecar with relief.

The driver dropped him off on the main road, where the turn-off to the village was. The Dorset countryside seemed unchanged, as if the war hadn't touched it. Resentment filled him. He'd only been home once in the early part of the war. He hadn't seen much fighting. He'd been captured, and had spent most of the war in a prisoner of war camp.

He'd received a couple of letters from Sylvia in a Red Cross parcel. It sounded as though she'd enjoyed the war, working at the telephone exchange to make ends meet. She'd hardly mentioned the kids. But recently, he'd had news of his older children from their uncle. Audrey and Peter had both started at their various grammar schools, and lived with Derek and his wife during the week. John had flared with pride at the thought of his children being clever enough to pass the grammar school exam.

Derek had written:

> '*I do think this arrangement should continue when you return home. Their mother would have wanted them to have a good education, and I pulled a few strings. Who better to care for them but their own kin? Blanche and I feel that Sylvia, although a friendly and pleasant woman, is unable to lavish as much affection on the twins as she does on her own daughter. Far be it from me to cause trouble between husband and wife, but the children have told me of American soldiers visiting the cottage on occasion. Of course,*

it was probably quite innocent . . . all the same, chil-
dren need to be set a good example by their parents
if they're to succeed later in life.'

John wondered. Sylvia was the type who attracted men. She
was beautiful, kind-hearted and friendly. A good laugh. She'd
enjoyed the physical side of things, and had certainly attracted
him. He recalled that she'd kept him fully satisfied in the
short time they'd been together. The baby she'd dropped
with a minimum of fuss had amused her. She'd taken to
mothering in a casual, unfussy manner, catering to the baby's
needs when the infant demanded instead of sticking to a
strict routine, like Rose had done with the twins.

Rose had been the opposite in nature. He still couldn't
understand why she'd married him – a common farm worker.
Her money had attracted him, and he'd told her he was the
farm manager in order to impress her. Rose had turned out
to be a controlling woman, strong and morally upright. She'd
never allow anything to be out of place, and prided herself
on her service to those less fortunate than herself. His first
wife had soon been on every committee in the district.

After the twins had been born Rose had refused to engage
in further relations with him. A tedious woman, she'd been
unattractive, obdurate and not very clever. It had been a relief
when she'd died unexpectedly, a weak artery in the brain
giving way. As was expected, she'd left her house in order.
The unexpected – she'd outsmarted him in the end.

As well as the cottage, Rose had possessed a private
income, money her father had left her. All her worldly goods
belonged to her children now. Derek had gone to great pains
to explain the will she'd made under his supervision, and
he'd been appointed trustee.

'It's what she wanted, old boy,' he'd said. 'It was family
money, after all. The cottage has been willed to the twins,
as well. Though you be won't be turfed out, you might need
to make provision for yourself when the twins come of age.'

John had expected something, so the will had come as a
shock. He felt as though she'd married him simply so she
could produce the children – something that Derek hadn't
managed with his own wife.

'What if I decide to contest the will?'

'By all means do, old chap, but there's not much point in doing that unless you have money to pay the legal fees. I shouldn't think the court would look too kindly on a man who tried to take money from the inheritance left to his own children. Blanche and I would be happy to take the children, of course. The twins will be better off with a mother to look after them.'

Shortly afterwards John had met Sylvia. Although she was reluctant to take the twins on he'd put her in the family way, so she hadn't had any choice. The kid had arrived early, and the war had started a few months later. He couldn't remember clearly what Sylvia looked like now. He just remembered her tits.

Now he'd been away from the village John didn't really want to return to his former life. But he didn't know what else to do. He had no skills except his knowledge of general farm work. He didn't learn easily either. He felt a bit of a failure in that regard, since he liked tinkering with engines, and thought he might have become a good mechanic if he'd been given the chance.

He shifted his case from one shoulder to the other as he reached the village. Curtains were drawn back. Squares of light painted the road surface with a patchwork pattern. The smell of cooking made his stomach rumble. There was a bit of a breeze up and the pub sign creaked as it swung. Rumbles of laughter came from the building's interior.

John felt in his pocket and encountered a coin, wondered if he still had a slate. When he pushed open the door, heads turned. The laughter stopped.

Donald Burns stared at him for a moment, clearly shocked. He recovered quickly, a broad, over-jovial smile appearing on his ruddy face. 'If it isn't John Turner! I nearly didn't recognize you. Welcome home, John.'

There came that moment of resentment inside him again, that Donald Burns – a man just a few years older than himself – had escaped the war unscathed, while John wore a scar on his face where a bayonet had laid him open.

Donald pulled a pint and set it frothing on the bar. 'Your poison was bitter, as I recall. Here you are then, John. A pint of the best for the returned hero, and on the house. He won't pay for anything in here tonight, will he chaps?'

There was a chorus of assent and the men began to pat their pockets.

John threw his case on the floor, stepped forward and pulled a smile on to his face, though he felt like a stranger. 'Just a couple, then. I've got to get home to see my missus and the kids. I take it they still live here?'

There was a moment of awkwardness, when the men avoided looking at each other, then Donald swiped a dishrag over the bar. 'Yes, they're still here, John.'

The ale went down his gullet like a yard of cold silk, washing away the grey taste of imprisonment that seemed to have settled there. Some returned hero he was. He'd hardly seen anything of the war.

Two hours later John banged at the cottage door and stood back, a grin on his face as he swayed back and forth. He'd surprise them, all right.

The door was opened by a small girl in a pink nightdress. Her eyes widened with fright when she saw him. She gave a piercing scream and slammed it shut again. He heard her shout out, 'Mum, there's a Jerry at the door!'

'Oh, don't be so daft.'

John's stomach began to sour. He fingered his scar as he peered through the letter box. 'Let me in, Sylvia.'

'John?' he heard her say. The door opened, the smile she wore faltered a bit. 'John . . . it's you.' She stood to one side. 'You'd better come in, then.'

As if he was a visitor in his own home . . . a bloody stranger! Beyond her stood the twins, staring at him. How they'd grown. The pair of them looked like Rose. Sylvia's child peeped at him from behind them. He couldn't remember her name.

'You remember me, don't you kids?'

'You're our father,' the boy said. 'Can I fetch you a cup of tea, sir?'

Sir! Anger filled him. 'No, you bloody well can't! You can give your father a hug, the lot of you.'

They all looked at Sylvia, who nodded. 'It's all right.'

The twins were stiff and reluctant. The young girl held back.

'Hug your father, Jilly,' Sylvia told her.

The girl's bottom lip stuck out and her hands went to her hips. Emphatically, she said, 'No!'

Sylvia tossed him an apologetic look. 'Jilly, do as you're told.'

'No. He's ugly and I hate him. I don't want him for my father and I'm never going to hug him. Not ever!' Bursting into tears she ran up the stairs. A door slammed shut.

The spoiled little tyke needed a strap around her arse, John thought. He said, 'Leave her, Sylvia. She'll come round in a day or two. She'll have to, since I'm here to stay.'

They all stood there awkwardly, looking at each other for a moment, then he said, 'What about that cup of tea then, Peter?'

'I was just going to bed,' Audrey said.

Peter faked a yawn. 'Me too.'

He tried not to glare at the pair as he said distantly, 'Don't let me stop you,' but he sent a hard stare after them as they hurriedly went off up the stairs.

'See to Jilly, would you, Audrey?' Sylvia called up after them. 'I'll be up to say goodnight later on.'

'Some homecoming,' John muttered.

'They'll get used to you, John.'

'They'll have to, because I'm not going away.' He followed her through to the living room. She was wearing a patterned dress in navy blue and white. It was a little tight under the arms where her full breasts surged into the bodice. Her nipples were round, pushing against the material like buttons. Her buttocks rolled under the material, like those of a whore he'd had at the beginning of the war. She had the same female smell about her.

She turned to face him, said, 'Tea, wasn't it, John?' as if she was the vicar's wife entertaining a guest.

He felt the urge to claim possession of his former life, to force this woman into surrender. His testicles nudged against his pants. 'Aren't you going to kiss your man, Sylvia?'

She was about to peck his cheek when her glance fell on the scar. She shuddered.

The surge of anger he experienced sent heat rushing to his face, and he wanted to hit her. 'It was a bayonet. You'll get used to me too, Sylvia . . . later, I expect.'

She shrugged, said coolly, 'Not tonight, John. You're drunk, and I've got my period.'

The smell of blood rose into his nostrils and he nearly gagged on it. Ball-breaker, he thought savagely as his desire fled.

Just over two years later, on a cold day in December, and only a couple of weeks before Christmas, Alec boarded a ship at Tilbury Docks, along with several other boys. It was a new ship and this was her maiden voyage. A band played on the docks and people threw streamers and waved as they said goodbye to relatives and friends who were migrating to a new life in Australia.

There was a great sense of adventure and excitement about them all as they crowded against the rail to watch England fade into the horizon.

'Let's wave,' Ronnie said. 'We can pretend we've got family to see us off, too. That woman over there looks like my mum.' Ronnie smiled and waved at her. The woman waved back.

Although Alec thought it a stupid game, he singled out a man hunched into a dark raincoat. He had a hat pulled down over his forehead. Fry the spy had come to see him off, Alec thought, and waved to him.

Disinterested, the man turned away and jostled his way through the crowd.

Alec wasn't at all sure he wanted to leave England, but he had no choice in the matter, since his only relative had signed the paper that would send him away without consultation.

Alec felt bound to England. His parents were English and his father had died defending the country for his son to inherit. They'd told him the sun always shone in Australia, that he'd be well looked after and trained. It was a great opportunity. Still, he knew he'd miss England and would come home again, one day.

Drawing his jacket around him, Alec shivered. 'Come on, Robbie, let's go down and find our cabin before the others pinch all the best bunks.'

'It's a daft game, anyway,' Robbie said sullenly. 'That

woman looks nothing like my mum. She hugged the child with her, too. My mother never hugged anyone in all her life, especially me.' There were tears in Ronnie's eyes as he turned. Blinking them back, he snarled as he pushed past Alec. 'I hate her,' he spat.

Alec tried to remember if his own mother had hugged him, but as the sea lengthened between himself and the land of his birth, he remembered most a small girl called Jilly, fiercely hanging on to him as the constable had tried to take him away. She'd had big brown eyes and untidy braids. He wondered what she was doing and felt sad that he'd lost her friendship. Alec hadn't said so at the time, but on the day they'd rescued the pilot, he'd been too scared to look in the plane when he'd first set eyes on it, in case he saw a dead body inside. But Jilly hadn't been scared. The pilot had become her hero. And his. He'd wanted to be like him . . . become a pilot. Now he wondered if the man had survived the war.

And what had happened to his tin of treasures – the letter from his father that he'd never had time to open? One day he'd go back and see if it was still concealed in the tree trunk. Or had Jilly rescued it, perhaps?

When they got to their cabin, which was reached by going down several flights of stairs, Robbie's moan caught his attention. 'I think I'm going to be sick,' Robbie muttered.

His friend's initial excitement at going to sea was fading rapidly, as his stomach grew increasingly queasy.

Alec sighed as he pulled the chamber pot out from under the bunk.

Four

> *. . . My family migrated to Australia when I was five years old. By then I had a younger sister. I can't remember much of my early childhood, except the beach figured a lot in it. The weather here in the west is warm for most of the year. We moved house when I was eleven, to one with a view of the sea and a swimming pool in the back garden. As a teenager I enjoyed playing sports, cricket in the summer and Aussie Rules football in the winter. My father had a boat, and we often went camping or fishing together at weekends – still do, in fact.*
>
> *I seem to be rambling on a bit, I know, but I hope I'm giving you some idea of what my life has been like, rather than boring you . . .*

Boring her? As if he could!

Because she was a stranger – because it had taken a great deal of courage for him to approach her, not knowing what to expect – she sensed he'd been battling to find things to say in this all-important initial letter. The sad thing about it was she hadn't received it until a year after Neil had written to her.

She'd just found it hidden under the carpet. The letter, addressed to Jilly, had been opened. Read, no doubt. She was saddened by the thought – but not surprised that her mother had kept it from her.

She wondered what Neil must have thought of her when he didn't receive an answer. Had he watched for the postman, like she'd once watched, waiting for news of Alec's competition entry? Did her son regard Jilly's silence as indifference?

Anger steamed inside her. By deliberately holding the letter back, Sylvia may have damaged any future relationship between Jilly and her son. She'd had no right to make such a decision. At forty-seven, Jilly was old enough decide her own course in life, especially about something as important as this was to her. But she was thankful her mother hadn't destroyed the letter, for then she'd never have known.

'Well, I do have a say now, Mother,' she said. 'I feel like shouting it from the rooftops!'

As the clock struck three Jilly put the kettle on the stove and began to set the tray for tea. She'd made scones, plump golden cushions spread with home-made gooseberry jam. They'd eat it in the conservatory, the dog at her feet, surrounded by the glorious autumn. She'd tell her husband about the letter, then. He'd listen to her in the way he always had, his head cocked to one side, his attention all hers. And if she asked him for it, he'd offer his advice.

It occurred to Jilly that the life Neil described in his letter was nothing like the one she'd have been able to offer him. It seemed as though she'd grown up in houses filled with tension – that the adults in her life had been combatants.

After her father had returned from the war it had soon become clear that John Turner and his wife had differences. Jilly hadn't fully understood what they were as the family began to be torn apart.

Then, she discovered she was one of them . . .

Blackbriar Caundle, 1947

Jilly's father was in one of his bad moods again, and his staring blue eyes were fixed on her face over breakfast.

Trying to be invisible, Jilly ate her boiled egg and toast as quickly as she could, but the tension inside her made her aware of the noise she made when she swallowed. Her throat closed up and she choked on the crumbs.

'Serves you right for eating it so fast. Drink your milk.'

'It's on the turn.'

'Drink it!' he exploded, making her jump.

She grimaced as she took a mouthful, then placed the cup back on the saucer.

'And the rest.'

She stared at him, silently hating him. He was as mean as Farmer Crutchly's old drake this morning, and she knew he'd hold her nose and *make* her drink it if she didn't obey him. She picked up the cup and swallowed the contents quickly, trying not to gag – banging the cup back on its saucer as hard as she dared.

Her mother came through from the kitchen, snatched Jilly's satchel off the newel post in the hall on the way through and slipped an apple inside, saying, 'What's all the shouting about?' Without waiting for an answer she hustled, 'Come on then, Jilly girl, else you'll be late for school. You can walk with me as far as the bus stop. Hurry up, I don't want to miss the bus and be late for work.'

'Do as you're told,' her father snapped.

Sylvia offered him a dirty look. 'Give her a chance, will you, John?'

When they got outside Jilly's stomach began to feel queasy. 'The milk was sour and I feel sick.'

Her mother gazed sharply at her. 'Why did you drink it, then?'

'*He* made me.'

Her mother tut-tutted. 'It was only just on the turn. I had some in my tea. It probably won't do you any harm.'

Her mother was mistaken. A couple of moments later Jilly's breakfast was deposited into the hedge.

As the bus trundled down the road towards them her mother gave Jilly's mouth a quick wipe with her handkerchief. 'You'll feel better now. Eat your apple, it will take the taste away.' A light kiss on the forehead and she was gone, heading for the bus stop at a trot, with her arm outstretched for the driver to stop.

Jilly wished she could go on the bus as well. She couldn't remember ever leaving the village. Now the evacuees had gone, the school only had a few pupils left, so they'd joined up with the children from Cranston Cross, the next village. The parents of her new friend, Gloria Duxbury, owned the general store there, and ran the post office that served the two villages.

Gloria told Jilly that her mother was trying to arrange a school excursion to Poole, where they could go into the pottery and learn how they made china. Afterwards, they'd eat their lunch beside the lake in Poole Park, then come home. Jilly's stomach was full of butterflies at the thought of seeing what was outside the village. She'd be glad when she was old enough to go to big school.

As she walked past the bus shelter somebody punched her on the shoulder. She'd forgotten about the Crutchly girls! She was punched back and forth between them, then one of them kicked her, and the other one pulled her hair ribbon off and threw it into the hedge, too high for Jilly to reach.

'Your dad's an ugly coward,' one of them shouted out.

'No he's not. That scar was where he was nearly killed in the war,' Jilly said hotly, even though she thought he looked ugly too. 'He's a hero.'

'He's not. He was captured by the Germans and went to prison camp. He's mad. He talks to himself and our dad said there be something wrong with his head, that's why he gave him the sack. He should be locked away in the loony bin before he hurts someone.'

'My dad said your dad is a coward too, then. Your dad didn't even go to war. He was a scaredy-cat.'

She received a kick in the shin for her trouble.

'That's all you know, clever clogs! He's got a bad back, hasn't he? Besides, somebody has to grow food. He got his bad back from slaving on the land, milking cows and hauling bags of seed on his shoulders, so people like you can eat. Somebody has to grow food.'

'That's enough of that mean talk, you Crutchly girls,' Butcher Hadly roared from the doorway of his shop, and waved a cleaver in the air. His blue-striped apron was blood smeared. 'You should be ashamed of yourselves, picking on a little tiddler like Jilly Turner. Get off to school, the lot of you.'

About to say her father had a bad back too, Jilly thought better of it. He'd told her he'd tan her backside if she talked to anyone about his business – and having already been at the painful end of a couple of his beatings, she wasn't about to risk it again.

'Cow farts,' she muttered as the two girls ran off, laughing. The postman was coming up the slope. He smiled as he heaved his bag from his shoulder and took a slip of cardboard from it. 'I've got something for you, Jilly.'

'For me?' Puzzlement filled her. She couldn't remember getting anything from the postman before. 'Is it my birthday?'

The postman smiled. 'I don't think so, love. This is a postcard of a ship. It's from that evacuee lad who used to live up at Crutchly Farm. He's gone to Australia.'

It took her a moment or two to remember Alec's name. She hadn't thought of him in a long time. 'Where's that?'

'A long way away, nearly underneath the world. They call it down under.' He gave a bit of a laugh that turned into a rattling cough, and thumped his chest with his fist to ease it.

'I had a cousin who went there during the war. They escaped from Singapore on the last ship. They were given a wooden house to live in, and reckoned the sun shone all the time. They got fed up with it after a while.' He glanced up at the sky, where clouds were forming. 'We could do with a bit of sunshine ourselves, better than grey old Britain. You'd better get off to school before you get into trouble, girl. I just heard the bell ring.'

Jilly slipped the postcard in her pocket and began to skip off down the lane – getting into the classroom just as Miss Morrow had reached the end of the register.

'Jillian Turner?' Miss Morrow said.

'Here, Miss,' she said breathlessly and clattered into her seat.

Miss Morrow placed a tick against her name, then looked up at her. 'Try to get here on time, in future, Jilly.'

'Yes, Miss. I felt sick this morning.'

'Well, don't be sick in class. Your mother shouldn't send you to school if you're unwell. And make sure your hair is braided neatly, otherwise it encourages nits.'

'I wasn't unwell. The milk was sour.'

'Then you shouldn't have drunk it, you silly girl. Right, children, open your books at page eighteen. We're doing a fractions test this morning.'

A collective groan went up as the teacher began to chalk figures up on the blackboard.

It was lunchtime before Jilly was able to look at her

postcard. She and Gloria stood behind the bicycle shed out of the wind, while they looked at the picture. Jilly shared all her secrets with Gloria. The ship was very big. She tested the name tentatively. '*Orcades*. What a funny name for a ship to have.'

'It says *Orient Line* underneath, so I expect it's a Chinese ship. Your dad would go mad if he knew you had a boyfriend.'

'Alec isn't my boyfriend. He's just a friend.' She gazed at Gloria in alarm. 'You'd better not tell him.'

'I wouldn't dare. Your dad gives me the frights. I heard him shouting at your mum the other day. He said he didn't think you were his daughter.'

Jilly's eyes widened. 'Of course I am!'

'He said you didn't look anything like him.'

'That's because I look like my mum. What did she say?'

'That he was being silly, and he'd better stop saying that because people might believe it, when it wasn't true. There's some writing on the back of the card. What does it say?'

Jilly felt like telling Gloria to mind her own business after what she'd just said. Instead, she decided to barter. 'I'll tell you if you give me a bit of that sherbet in your pocket.'

Gloria sighed as she reached into her pocket and brought out a yellow tube with a liquorice straw sticking out the top.

After her tongue had rasped the last of the sherbet from her palm, Jilly turned the card over, reading the scribbled pencil message on the back out loud to Gloria.

'*Dear Jilly Turner,*
    This is the ship I came to Australia on. I hope you're well.
    Yours faithfully, your very best friend,
    Alec Frampton.
    PS. It's very hot over here.'

Gloria glared at her. 'I thought *I* was your best friend?'

'You are. Alec was my best friend a long time ago, before you were.'

Alec had pencilled a kiss on the bottom, but must have though better of it because an attempt had been made to rub it out, and it was more of a grey smudge than anything. Jilly felt a moment of envy, and wished it was hot here, too. Then it would be the long school holidays, and she could go to the beach, lie on the sand and get a tan.

'That wasn't much of a letter. He sounds stupid.'

'He wasn't stupid, he was clever,' Jilly said hotly. 'I liked him.'

'Better than me at schoolwork?' Gloria challenged.

Jilly didn't know what to say, except the truth. She wasn't about to deny Alec, who had sent her a postcard from down underneath the world. 'He was cleverer than anybody. He won a story competition in the newspaper.'

Gloria scowled and skipped out into the playground, singing at the top of her voice, 'Jilly Turner's got a boyfriend . . . Jilly's got a boyfriend . . .'

Catching Gloria up, Jilly yanked her pigtail so hard that her head jerked back. 'I won't be your friend and go on the pottery trip if you don't shut up.'

Gloria gave a bit of a smirk. Her voice was offhand. 'You're not coming anyway. Your father hasn't sent back the form and money for the coach, and it's full up now. That's because he doesn't think you're his daughter.'

'How can I not be his daughter, when he's married to my mother?'

'I don't know. Perhaps your mother really did find you under the cabbages. Anyway, you're the only one in the class not going. And I don't care if you're my friend or not. Anne Webster has invited me to her birthday party, and she hasn't invited you, so I'll be her best friend instead.'

Jilly retaliated. 'Alec's always been my best friend. He's better than you.' She didn't care if John Turner wasn't her father, but she'd been looking forward to going to the pottery. It just wasn't fair. 'I hate you,' she muttered, close to tears. 'You're just jealous because you didn't get a postcard.'

Gloria suddenly sprang at her, and the pair wrestled and smacked each other before Miss Morrow pulled them apart and told them off.

And that was the end of their friendship.

The car drew up outside Rose Cottage early in the afternoon. From it stepped Derek Fowler and another man.

Sourly, John invited his brother-in-law and his companion inside. He hadn't got much time for the man. 'What do you want? I'm busy.'

Derek gazed at John's unshaven chin and the table with its unwashed dishes, an expression of distaste on his face. 'Yes, I can see you have work to get on with. I take it you haven't found employment yet?'

'With this face? It's not through lack of trying,' John said aggressively, though he hadn't done much trying of late. He felt constantly tired, and spending money on bus fares all the time didn't seem worth the effort.

Derek picked up the milk jug and sniffed it. 'This is sour. You shouldn't drink this, especially if it's farm milk. It can give you consumption.'

'A fat lot you'd care.'

'I'd care if my niece and nephew caught it. You should clean this place up a bit. It smells.'

'Damp creeps up the walls and smoke blows back down the chimney. The place is old, what do you expect? It needs painting right through, too.'

'I'll provide you with some distemper for the walls, if you like.'

'And I'll have to supply the free labour, I suppose. Forget it. And what about the kitchen sink? It's cracked.'

'Peter said you hit it with a cleaver when you were in a temper. *You* damaged it, so *you* can replace it at your own expense. Are you still taking those pills your doctor prescribed for you?'

'Sod the pills. They make me feel depressed.'

'They'll help to keep you calm. Perhaps you should see a psychiatrist, John.'

'Like hell! I'm not seeing a head shrinker. I'm not mad.'

Derek sighed. 'I didn't say you were.'

John moved a pile of crumpled clothing waiting to be ironed from a couch to the floor. 'Take a seat.'

The two men exchanged a glance, then Derek said, 'We'll stand, I think.'

'Please yourself. Don't say I didn't ask.'

Damn Sylvia, John suddenly thought. She was slovenly. She'd had time last night to do the ironing, but no – she'd rather play snakes and ladders with that kid of hers. His hands began to tremble as anger filled him.

She'd said when he'd reminded her of it, 'I'm tired after working all day. I've already cooked the dinner and washed up. You can do the ironing, surely.'

He'd given her a bit of a slap. Not much, just enough to show her who was boss. Not that it worked. She'd grown up in the slums and knew how to defend herself. He could only think to shame her. 'Rose wouldn't have kept the house in this state.'

'Bugger Rose,' she'd said.

'She was twice the housewife and mother you are.'

'Thanks for the kind words, John. I imagine I wouldn't have to look far to find a man who's ten times the husband and father you are – especially with regard to marital relations.'

He slapped her harder. 'That's your fault. You just don't attract me in that way any more. You married me under false pretences. That girl's not mine, I know it. And what about the Yanks during the war? Ouch—' She'd slapped him back. A stinger.

As he nursed his sore cheek, she said, 'Get off that subject, will you? You're completely wrong, and I'm tired of listening to it. And keep your bloody hands off me else I'll brain you with the frying pan when you're asleep.'

He believed her. 'As far as I'm concerned you can give up your job and stay home.'

'And who's going to provide us with food? If we wait for you to find a job we'll all starve to death.'

Trust her to rub it in, he thought. Wasn't it enough that he'd risked his life to fight for his country and had been forced to spend most of the war in a bloody prison camp? His glance went to the two smartly-dressed men standing in his sitting room. Didn't they realize they owed their existence to people like him? He'd be dead if he hadn't shot his adversary at the very moment he'd lunged at him. The shot had shattered the man's head.

A quick vision of blood and brains splattering over him nearly made him gag. He began to sweat. Closing his eyes for a moment, John felt a shudder of disgust run through him. The man had lost his life trying to take John's, but all John could feel was guilt. He'd curled into a ball and had begun to cry until someone had found him. His captors had taunted him, called him a coward, humiliated him. The man he'd killed sometimes spoke inside his head, and he saw him in his dreams. John wished he'd died on that day.

He caught an expression of repugnance mixed with pity on the face of the man Derek had brought with him. John knew that look only too well. 'Who might you be?' he asked.

Derek said, 'This is my solicitor, Malcolm Metcalf.

Metcalf's handshake was limp and flabby. John began to suspect that the visit bode him no good. He moved to the window, gazed out into the gloomy afternoon. 'What are you here for, Derek?'

'I want custody of the twins,' his brother-in-law said calmly.

John turned to stare at him, feeling at a disadvantage in his corduroy trousers and an old cardigan worn over his stained shirt and braces. 'No. Definitely not.'

'Mr Fowler has a good case to put before the court,' Metcalf told him.

'Court? What the hell are you talking about? I'm their father!'

Metcalf pulled some papers from his briefcase, an expensive piece of cowhide with a silver lock. 'My client and his wife supported the children over several years. They have provided them with a home, clothing and food, supported their schooling and taught them their manners. From the goodness of their hearts they have acted as a steadying influence, a balance to your wife, a woman who has, by the children's own testimony, been neglectful of their welfare, and who, in your absence, has exposed them to harmful influences in their formative years.'

'What the hell are you talking about?'

The papers were laid on the table. 'I'll leave them there for you to peruse, Mr Turner. Until this matter is resolved, Audrey and Peter Turner will remain under the care of their uncle and aunt.'

'I'm sorry, John, old chap,' Derek said awkwardly. 'It's what Rose would have wanted, you know.'

'Sod Rose!' John exploded. 'And sod you, too. I want my kids back, d'you hear? And I want them delivered on Friday. What's more, they won't be going back with you on Monday.'

'I'm afraid that's not going to happen, John. It will be best for you if you cooperate and sign the papers. I'll allow you to remain in the cottage. You will have to pay a nominal rent, of course. When the children reach their majority it will be up to them to decide whether they intend to sell it.'

Something snapped inside John's head. 'Get out, you buzzard!' he screamed. Fist raised, he stepped forward, but before he could hit his brother-in-law the solicitor hit him with his briefcase. One of the locks caught John across the bridge of his nose and blood began to flow.

He was pushed into a chair. 'Violence won't get you anywhere,' the solicitor said sternly.

John tried to staunch the blood with the antimacassar from the back of the chair. 'We'll see about that. Get out of my house before I fetch my pistol and shoot the pair of you as dead as doornails.'

He sprang to his feet and headed for the cupboard under the stairs, where he kept his guns hidden. When he worked on the Crutchly farm he'd used them to kill foxes, stray dogs and cats.

'Bloody vermin the lot of you,' he muttered, his mind going to Jilly again. She was a stray – a runt some tomcat had planted inside the slut of a woman he'd taken under his roof. Only God knew who her father was. He'd been studying Jilly day after day, but there was nothing of himself in her. Along with her mother, he'd like to put her down one day. They should take her instead. Teach her some manners.

'Vermin, I'll kill you all!' he shouted, and, taking the pistol from the hidden compartment he'd made for it, he fumbled the bullets into the chamber.

The front door slammed shut before he finished loading the weapon. He heard the car engine burst into life as he headed after the men. There came a squeal of tyres as he reached the garden gate. The car zigzagged crazily on a wet patch as he took aim. He began to laugh.

They were running like rabbits. He took a high aim and pulled the trigger, clipping a twig from the tree. It dropped on the car, which picked up speed and disappeared around the corner.

'Cowards!' he yelled after them.

He went back indoors, sobbing out loud. The voice inside his head taunted him.

'Cry baby. Why didn't you shoot them like you did me?'

'It was an accident,' John screamed.

The blood was still flowing from his nose, but he didn't care. He didn't want to kill anybody. He just wanted his kids back. Jilly came into his mind again. He shuddered at the thought of what he'd intended to do to her and her mother. He took some of the pills the doctor had given him and washed them down with some bourbon he found in a bottle under the kitchen sink.

The police came for him an hour later.

'Mr Turner,' one of them shouted, 'we have your house surrounded. Throw out your gun.'

John had begun to doze, but his head jerked up at the sound of the voice. The pistol was nestled on his lap. His shirt front was covered in dried blood. He must have hurt himself.

'Come on, John. We know you've had a hard time of it lately. Give yourself up. We'll take you to the hospital where you can get some treatment. They'll give you something to calm your nerves. You can rest there and be looked after.'

Rest! That's what he needed. He was so tired, and his head ached. Everything he looked at seemed blurred. He couldn't see to empty the gun. He managed to rise from his chair. Placing the gun back in its hiding place, he staggered to the door.

On the other side of the glass he could see the outline of the constable's helmet against the frosted glass. He wouldn't have lasted two seconds at the front. John giggled. He could have blown the man's stupid head off.

'You wouldn't have had the guts,' the voice in his head told him.

Opening the door he stood there, swaying back and forth, a wide grin on his face. 'I'll come quietly, Constable, just like I did with the Germans. I feel sick. I think I swallowed too many pills.'

'Where's the gun?' the policeman asked him.

Did they think he was daft? 'There wasn't a gun. It was just a piece of bent pipe. I threw it in the Crutchlys' stinking slurry pit. If you want it you'll have to find it first.' Buckling at the knees, John slumped forward. The constable called loudly for help and soon his two burly companions were ranged on either side of John, hauling him up by his arms. His wrists were manacled behind his back.

'He's drunk,' one of them said in disgust. 'I can smell it on his breath. We'll throw him in the lock-up and let him sleep if off before we charge him.'

'He mentioned pills. According to Dr Fowler, Turner is mentally unstable, the poor bugger. Take him to the car while I have a look around to see if I can find a gun. We'll need it as evidence, and we might have to take him to the hospital first.'

The constable looked under the stairs but didn't see the compartment screwed into the back of one of the risers.

As the car drove through the village John saw Jilly coming home from school, the satchel bobbing on her back as she skipped along. She stopped, her eyes widening when she saw the police car – mouthing the word 'Daddy' when she saw his face at the window.

John scowled at her. Jilly wasn't his, he was certain. She was a cuckoo his wife had brought to his nest. Sylvia had tricked him into marriage. As he turned his head to stare at the girl she began to run after the car. Suddenly she tripped, to sprawl on her face in the middle of the road.

The high-pitched giggle he gave surprised him. He'd just realized that the constable had secured the cottage doors behind him. Jilly would have to sit on the doorstep until her mother came home from work.

Five

It was dark when Sylvia got off the bus. She said a cheery goodnight to the driver, and began to hurry off up the hill towards the cottage. Despite her aching feet she felt good. She'd just been promoted to supervisor, and the extra money would come in handy.

It was beginning to drizzle. Curtains were drawn. Head hunched into her collar, Sylvia hurried through it.

She remembered her daughter's essay, the one she'd got ten out of ten for the previous week. Jilly had written, 'The reflection from the cottage lights shone on the rain patches and ran like rivulets of moonlight down the slope.'

Sylvia grinned, and, lifting her eyes, saw that the description was apt. Jilly saw beauty in almost everything, even the blessed rain. But she was too sensitive. Luckily, she was a good kid who didn't take much looking after and didn't cause any trouble.

Behind the curtains people went about their business. The women in their aprons stood over steaming pans, even though they were still making do with rations. There was a sense of hope about England now, despite the shortages. Soon rationing would end, and things would be back to normal.

Sylvia's smile faded. She just wished her own household was happier. She and John did nothing but row. Now he'd started hitting her. And he'd beaten Jilly for practically no reason. The last time she'd found her daughter whimpering with pain in the garden shed, where she'd run to escape her father. Her eyes had been wide with shock, and drowning in tears. The poor kid could hardly breathe without John jumping down her throat. And he was sarcastic to Jilly, making a disparaging remark rather than praising her when she did something that deserved it.

Sylvia could protect herself, but she couldn't always be there to do the same for Jilly.

The girl would just have to toughen up.

She frowned, and lengthened her stride when she saw there was no light in the cottage window, her feet clattering on the road. The gate squeaked as she pushed it open.

'Is that you, Mum?' a quivering voice said from the porch.

'Jilly?' Sylvia could just make out her daughter's form in the darkness, a forlorn figure on the doorstep. She fumbled in her bag for her key. 'What are you doing sitting there all alone? Where's your father?'

'The police came and took him away.'

'The police! What on earth for?'

'I don't know. I fell over and my knees are scratched.' She gave a sniff as she followed her mother inside. 'I was scared.'

Jilly's face was pinched with cold, shivers wracked her from head to toe. Sylvia switched on the light and gathered Jilly up in her arms, hugging her tight. 'You don't have to be scared now. Let's have a nice cup of tea.'

'There's blood on the lino,' Jilly said, her voice high with tension. 'What if he's killed someone, Mum?'

'Nonsense. I expect he fell over and banged his head or something, and the police came to take him to hospital. I'll clean this up and bank up the fire while you make the tea, then we'll walk down to the phone box and ring Dr Fowler. He'll be able to find out what's going on. See if there are four pennies in the tin for the phone box. I don't want to have to come all the way back home again.'

She opened her shopping bag and took out a paper bag. 'Here. Somebody at work had a birthday and brought in a jam roll. I kept a slice for you.'

Jilly knew it was her mother's slice. She cut it in half so they could eat it with their tea.

Her mother's eyes lit on it and she said softly, 'You're not daft, are you?'

'I'm looking for John,' Sylvia shouted down the receiver. 'Jilly told me some tale about the police taking him away . . . What do you mean, he shot at you? Where is he? . . . Oh my God!

Tell me what happened . . . He didn't hurt you, did he? There was blood in the house. . .'

Jilly cuddled against her mother while a muffled voice came from the other end of the line. Sylvia's face grew paler and paler and tears began to trickle down her cheeks. There came a metallic sound of the pips going. The money had run out. She scrambled in her pockets for pennies, saying, 'But . . . no, wait, Operator. I can't find any more money, but I work for—

'Sod the cow! I'll have her guts for garters tomorrow,' Sylvia muttered as the line went dead. Outside the phone box she lit a cigarette and exhaled the smoke in a long blue cloud. 'Now what are we going to do?'

'What's wrong, Mum?'

'They've put your father in the asylum, that's what.'

'What's an asylum?'

'Where mad people go. They say he's depressed. I could have told *them* that.' She heaved an aggrieved sigh. 'Don't you go telling anyone, Jilly. People will pretend they feel sorry for us, but they'll be laughing behind our backs and whispering behind their curtains, the hypocrites!'

Jilly nodded. She didn't want anyone to know that her father was mad.

'Come on, let's go home. I'll take the day off tomorrow, see if I can find out more. Damn it! Just when I get a promotion and a raise, I have to shell out on a minder for you. Perhaps the Crutchlys will have you after school . . .'

Jilly folded her arms over her chest. 'I'm not going to the Crutchlys'. They hate me. Martha and Rosemary keep pulling my hair and punching me.'

'Well, you're going to have to learn to hit them back. Beggars can't be choosers, and if I give up my job we won't have anything to eat.' Grinding the cigarette end under her heel, her mother took Jilly's hand and pulled impatiently on it. 'I haven't had time to think yet,' she muttered. 'There's something going on I don't know about. Why would John try and shoot someone? He hasn't even got a gun, as far as I know.'

The police turned the cottage upside down the next day, but the gun wasn't found.

'If you're hiding it, Mrs Turner, you could get into serious trouble,' the burly sergeant told her.

'You don't have to tell me that. I've never seen John with a gun – not ever. I hate the things, and wouldn't want one in the house. I think Dr Fowler might have been mistaken. Where is my husband?'

'He's being treated at St Agnes's, the hospital for the mentally unstable.'

'Can I go and see him?'

'I wouldn't advise it.'

She disliked his hectoring tone. 'Wouldn't you, now? I didn't ask for your advice.'

The sergeant raised his voice. 'I suggest you keep a civil tongue in your head, Mrs Turner, else I'll have you arrested for obstruction.' He looked over her head. 'Have you found anything, Constable?'

'Nothing, sir. In my opinion he probably disposed of the weapon, probably in the farm slurry pit, like he said.'

'Ah, if that's your opinion I'll give you the chance to prove it by going into the pit and searching for it.'

When the constable's face fell the sergeant gave a mirthless grin. 'Turner wouldn't have had time to get over to the farm and dispose of it before you arrived to investigate the crime, you fool.' He turned back to Sylvia. 'If you come across it you'd best let me know, and at once, Mrs Turner.'

Sylvia shrugged. 'I've got other things to bother about, like finding someone to look after my daughter after school. I can't take time off from work indefinitely.'

Still, she thought after the police had departed and she was gazing ruefully at the mess they'd made, at least there would be one less mouth to feed.

To Jilly's relief, the Crutchlys refused to have her after school.

Jilly argued her case. 'I'm old enough to look after myself until you get home. You can trust me, and I'll do some housework, so you won't have to do so much when you get home.'

Reluctantly, her mother agreed. 'You're to come home straight from school. Don't tell anyone you're here by yourself, and don't open the door to anyone.' Taking her face between her hands, Sylvia kissed Jilly. 'You're a good girl, Jilly.'

'When're Audrey and Peter coming home?'

'They're not. They're living with the Fowlers now.'

'Because our father's sick?'

'That's right.'

'When will he get better?' Not that she wanted him to come home. It was nicer living alone with her mother.

'I don't know, love. We'll have to wait until the doctor says he's well enough.'

John was considered well enough two years later.

While Sylvia paid the taxi driver, John shuffled into the cottage, then lowered himself into his old armchair and stared out of the window.

Sylvia fussed around him. 'Let me know if you want anything, John. I'll put the radio on for you, shall I? Jilly, fetch your father's slippers so we can make him comfortable.'

His blue eyes turned Jilly's way and she froze, feeling as nervous as a mouse under the unblinking gaze of a cat. Her fingers curled into her palm as a remembered tension tightened inside her again, as if someone had wound her up with a spring. Her father frightened her.

He muttered something under his breath and turned away.

'Jilly has made some scones especially for you. She's turning into a good little cook. I'll fetch a couple for you to eat with your tea.'

'Get her out of my sight.'

'Now, now, John, don't start that all over again. Jilly's a good girl. She's learned to do a lot of things, and has the dinner all cooked ready for when I get home from work. So you won't have to do anything, just rest and relax.'

'Just keep the brat away from me; I want nothing to do with her. Where are the other two?'

Sylvia sighed. 'Derek and Blanche are looking after them. They went to court and were awarded custody. Just as well, really. I wouldn't have been able to cope with the twins, what with working as well. Derek drops in from time to time to let me know how they're getting along. Their school reports are in the drawer if you want to read them. The twins are getting average marks.' Jilly smiled proudly when her mother smiled and said, 'Our Jilly won a book prize for English this year.'

Once again, those unblinking eyes turned her way, as cold as ice. 'She would have been doing easier work than if she'd been at the grammar school. She doesn't look like the other two.'

'Of course she doesn't. They have different mothers. Jilly looks like me.'

'I can't see anything of me in her.'

Sylvia's voice was laced with impatience. 'The twins don't look like you, either.'

'They have the same eyes as Dad,' Jilly ventured.

Her father ignored her, his chin sinking on to his chest. 'Wake me when dinner's ready. Just keep her out of my sight. The less I see of the sly little madam, the better I'll like it.'

Resentment pulled at Jilly. She'd done nothing to deserve such treatment. A knot of hatred took up lodging in her and words burst out of her with some force. 'The less I see of you the better, too. I wish they'd kept you in hospital!'

She fled the room and up the stairs before she said more, her misery a tight and painful animal in her chest. Sinking on to her bed she hugged her hurt as tears trickled down her face.

Her mother came in and took her in her arms. 'Don't let him upset you. He's been through a lot. He never used to be like this, you know. It was the war. It affected lots of soldiers badly.'

'I hate him,' Jilly said with passion. 'He always blames me for everything that goes wrong.'

'Yes . . . I know.' Her mother smoothed the hair back from her head, saying ruefully, 'To be honest, my love, I don't like him very much, either. But I'm married to him. The doctor said your father will improve in time, if he stays on his medicine.'

'Couldn't we go and live somewhere else? Everyone talks about us here.'

'Not at the moment. We don't have to pay much rent here.

Perhaps when your father finds work, or when you're ready for big school. Stop feeling sorry for yourself. There are others worse off.'

To Jilly, that next school year seemed ages away. But her mother was right: there were others worse off. At least she had someone who loved her – someone she could turn to in times of trouble, and who would love her, regardless of what she did.

She remembered the boy who'd been her best friend when she was young. He'd been a better friend than Gloria Duxbury, who never spoke to her now. She wondered what had happened to him.

When her mother left, Jilly pulled from the depths of the wardrobe a canvas bag she'd embroidered at school in cross stitch. Removing the pilot's helmet she pulled it over her head, then prised the lid off the red tin it had been wrapped around.

At the very top was the newspaper cutting of the boy called Alec Frampton, and herself. They had saved a pilot from a plane wreck. 'Village Children Rescue War Ace', the headline stated. Jilly could barely remember the event, though the broken spine of the plane was still there in the woods.

The cutting had turned yellow.

She vaguely remembered the plane's engine being taken away on a truck trundling through the village, followed by a second one carrying the panels, tail and wings. The leather seat had remained, but that had disappeared one day, too.

Her mother had told Jilly that the publican had the seat and bent propeller mounted and hung on his wall – with the news-paper account of the rescue, and a letter of thanks from the pilot. 'He hasn't pinned up the bit about you and that lad you used to play with. Donald Burns makes himself out to be the hero of the rescue. He tells the tale to any stranger who walks in, the great big show-off. If it hadn't been for you and that evacuee boy, he'd never have known the plane had crashed.'

'What happened to that boy?' Jilly had asked, and her mother had shaken her head.

'I don't know, love. He might have stayed in the chil-dren's home, or somebody might have fostered him.'

'What does fostered mean?'

'It means that some kind-hearted person might have taken him into their family, and will look after him until he's old enough to look after himself.'

Jilly hoped that had happened to Alec Frampton, and although she couldn't remember him unless she looked at the contents of his tin, she wondered if he remembered her.

She carefully replaced the cutting. Looking at it made her feel sad, as if part of her was missing. Removing the flying helmet, she put everything away and went downstairs to help her mother with the dinner.

December 31st 1950

Dear Jilly Turner,

I've recently celebrated my fourteenth birthday. The lads where I live tossed me up in the air in a blanket fourteen times.

I've won a scholarship, and in January will leave the boys' home to go to the Anglican grammar school. I was lucky to be accepted into such a good school for my final years, and I'm expected to work hard, do well and make Barnardo's proud of me. Remember my great-uncle, Fry the spy? He has agreed to pay my boarding fees.

Eventually, I hope to get into the university here, then train to be a teacher. I'll need to find somewhere to live and a part-time job to support myself then. As soon as I'm qualified and have saved up my fare I'll visit you in England.

My friend Robbie has run away to become a sheep shearer with a man he met at the agricultural show. I'll miss him because he made me laugh, but I wish him luck.

I hope you had a nice Christmas. Here is a present, a magpie feather. Sometimes, I pretend you're my family. It would be a fine thing if you sent me a letter, but you don't know where I live, and anyway, you've probably forgotten me.

Happy New Year from your best friend,
Alex Frampton.
PS. Do you like Nat King Cole? I do.

* * *

That done, Alec slipped the black and white feather inside the envelope, sealed it and placed it in a tin box designed to hold money for household bills. It was company for the other four letters he'd written to Jilly.

His heart gave a jump as he noticed that the coins he'd so carefully hoarded over the last couple of years were missing.

Robbie was the only one who'd known where he kept the key to the box. As Alec scrabbled through the box to no avail, he was saddened to think that the boy he'd befriended had stolen from him.

He closed the lid, turned the key in the lock, then, after looking round to make sure he wasn't observed, hid the key back inside the spine of his hymn book. There were three boys sharing his room and several others living in the house. Doors were left unlocked and you had to be careful.

He hadn't expected his best friend to steal from him, though. If Robbie had asked him for the money, he would probably have lent it to him, he thought angrily. Still, it was gone and it was no good worrying about it now.

Taking a small piece of cardboard from his bedside drawer, Alec crossed off the square with 1950 on it a day early, and smiled. There were only seven squares left before he was twenty-one. Then he could please himself what he did.

But first, he intended to make the most of the education he was being offered so he could make his way in the world. He looked forward to his transition to grammar school, though he suspected that boarding there would be pretty much the same as he was used to.

It was Sunday afternoon, late enough for some of the heat to have fled the day. The sun was low and the shadows lengthening. They were going down to the Swan River to picnic on the bank, swim and practise their life-saving. Afterwards, they were going to celebrate the New Year of 1951 with a barbecue and fireworks.

Alec took out his bathing suit and towel and went downstairs. The air was still as they climbed into the bus. The summer sun had already burned their skin and they all wore a tan.

It would be freezing cold now in England, Alec thought, as the bus bumped over the uneven ground. Jilly wouldn't believe they swam in December.

The river loomed closer. The banks were lined with gum trees that drooped towards the river in the limpid air, peeling bark that littered the ground like thick layers of tissue paper. Magpies carolled among their grey-green leaves, and a kookaburra was startled into giving a raucous song before flying off to join its wide-beaked, equally garrulous mate.

The bus stopped. The doors opened. A heap of the younger boys tumbled out to go racing off towards the water, giving whoops and hollers of delight as they flopped into the shallows and boisterously splashed each other in the lustrous afternoon.

There was something magical about the summer river, molten gold in the lowering sun. It reminded Alec of autumn in England, and the glorious fall of leaves.

The droplets the boys tossed upwards spun in the air like liquid coins, as though King Midas himself had touched a finger against it.

Coping with her father's unpredictable behaviour after he returned from the hospital was a test for Jilly. Although she tried to do nothing to incur his anger, his sarcastic barbs were hurtful. She cheeked him back too much. She was sly, stupid, ugly, deceitful, a liar . . . a bastard with no manners.

She tried to dodge his cuffs and pinches, and once, when she was home late from school, he was waiting for her behind the door, a wooden coat hanger in his hand. Covered in bruises, she was forced to stay home for three days leading up to the Easter break.

Her mother had cuddled away her hurt when she'd arrived home from work. 'I don't want the teachers to see that. They'll report it to the authorities, then they'll take you away and we'll never see each other again, Jilly girl. I'd never live down the shame.'

The possibility of being taken from her mother was frightening. They might send her far away, to Australia where that

boy Alec had been sent. She'd put up with her father's beatings rather than have that happen.

But even the thought of that was insignificant when set
against what happened after the visit of Blanche and Derek
Fowler with the twins.

Six

A t the age of seventeen, the Turner twins were reserved, but confident.

'Peter goes to university in a year or two, and intends to eventually become a pharmacist. Audrey has obtained her secretarial diploma and has secured an office position at Brights Engineering,' said Blanche, with an air of self-congratulation.

Jilly smiled at her brother and sister, but she felt shy. She hadn't seen them for a long time and they looked grown up. Peter was so tall he had to stoop to come in the door. He was already dressed like a student, in a ginger corduroy jacket with a long scarf draped casually around his neck.

'Hello, Father,' he said, his voice sounding rather posh to Jilly's ears. 'It's nice to see you looking so well.'

Their father grunted.

Audrey's hair was fashioned like her aunt's, blonded and back-combed with the ends flicked up. Her small breasts were thrust against a baby-blue ribbed sweater. Blanche's twinset was blue as well. She wore pearls with it. The pair could have been sisters, and they looked really pretty.

'Father,' Audrey trilled, her eyes avoiding his scar as she pecked his cheek, 'how lovely to see you again.'

Their father acknowledged the overture with a grunted, 'Is it?'

Disconcerted, Peter turned towards Jilly. 'Hello, squirt. Long time, no see. You haven't changed much.' He pulled a bar of chocolate from his pocket and handed it to her. 'Here, I've brought you this.'

'Thank you.' Pleased to be remembered, she slid the chocolate into the depths of her pocket. 'You've grown so tall, Peter.'

Audrey tittered. 'You didn't expect him to be the same

size, did you? Honestly, Jilly, you do say some stupid things at times.'

'Lay off her, Audrey. She hasn't seen me for ages, and I have grown tall.'

Audrey didn't look pleased by the reprimand. 'Do you still wet the bed?'

A blush seeped under Jilly's skin at being reminded. 'No, of course I don't. Not for ages. I'm going to big school in January.'

'The secondary school, I imagine.'

'There's nothing wrong with the secondary school,' Sylvia snapped, all prickles.

'I didn't say there was,' Audrey said hastily.

Sylvia gave Audrey a hard look, then sniffed. 'You didn't have to.' She turned to their brooding father. 'I'll make some tea, shall I? John, you should have taken those pills an hour ago. Don't forget them.'

'Sod the pills. There's nothing wrong with me, never has been. Jilly, go and help your mother. Better lay out the best china for Lord and Lady Muck and the baby mucklings, since they've honoured us with a visit.'

The strain in the air had taken a turn for the worse. Jilly was on tenterhooks as she bustled around with plates and cutlery. She'd been really pleased to see her brother and sister. Now her father was going to spoil it all.

But he wasn't going to have it all his own way. Dr Fowler was saying, 'No need to take that tone, old boy. It's not the twins' fault you were unable to look after them. It was just sheer hard luck that you had a breakdown. Nothing to be ashamed of, you know.'

'I'm not ashamed, but you should be. I wasn't given the chance to look after my own children. I managed well enough with Jilly.'

'Jilly has her mother. The twins didn't.' Blanche gave an exaggerated sigh. 'I told you it was a mistake coming here, Derek. Honestly, you wonder why you bother to be nice to *some* people.' She subsided into a seething silence.

Sylvia pleaded, 'Please don't start, John.'

'What do you expect? This pair stole my children when my back was turned, and look at them. They're a pair of patronizing snobs, just like their mother was. It's a wonder they can lower themselves to speak to me. One visit in two years – not even a visit when I was in hospital.'

Derek said reasonably, 'It was hardly the place to take impressionable children. I kept Sylvia fully informed of their progress. Didn't I, dear?'

'That's true, John. He did.'

Jilly walked in, carefully carrying the teapot, just in time to hear her father say, 'As far as I'm concerned you can all bugger off. You'll be getting no tea in this house.'

Audrey looked offended as she said to nobody in particular, 'This is the last time I'll visit here.'

Flushing to her parting of dark roots, Blanche rose to her feet with great affront. 'Come along, you two. It's obvious we're not welcome here.'

'You couldn't have any kids of your own, so you had to steal mine,' John threw at her. 'And you've ruined them . . . turned them into a couple of snobs.'

'It wasn't like that.' Blanche gave Sylvia a hard look. 'We did it for their own good when we heard what was going on in this house. What with the soldiers coming and going and the beatings the children were subjected to.'

'What soldiers and beatings?' Sylvia shouted.

Blanche ignored her. 'Not to mention Audrey having to sleep in a wet bed and Sylvia trying to poison the children's minds against us—'

A great knot of misery settled like a lump in Jilly's chest and she felt like running upstairs and hiding under the bed. Although she tried not to, she began to quietly grizzle.

'That's enough, old girl,' Derek said mildly. 'It's in the past and we agreed it would never be mentioned again.'

'The ungrateful liars!' Sylvia shouted. 'How dare you come in here and accuse me of such things! I never laid a finger on those children, and they know it. It was you who tried to poison them against me . . . you jumped-up little *cinema usherette.*'

'Actually, I was a *cashier.*'

Audrey had edged around the room to where Jilly stood, and now put an arm around her shoulders, whispering, 'I'm sorry, Jilly. We shouldn't have come.'

'As for the soldier, he was a friend of mine. If it hadn't been for his generosity, those two would have starved to death. The greedy little brats ate their own rations, then stole Jilly's food if they could, when my back was turned.'

'Please stop, Mum,' Jilly pleaded. 'All this shouting is making me feel sick.'

'Yes, for everyone's sake, enough!' Derek Fowler howled. 'Out to the car, you three. At once!'

After they'd gone, Derek took an envelope from his pocket and threw it into John's lap. He gave Sylvia an apologetic look. 'You've been living in this cottage for next to nothing for several years, John. I need the rent money to save for the children's future.'

Sylvia paled. 'I can't afford to pay more rent.'

'I'm sorry, Sylvia. I've got other tenants who can. I need to tidy the place up first. John, you haven't kept the cottage in good repair, nor are you looking for work. This is notice to quit the cottage. You have one month in which to move. If you're not out by then I'll seek an eviction order. Apply for a council house. I'll give you a medical certificate to say you have special needs.'

John stared hard at him. 'This cottage belonged to my first wife.'

'Who was my sister, and the twins' mother.'

'Who are my children, whether they like it or not. The only way any of you'll get me out of this house is to carry me out in a pine box. Now, get out. Close the door behind you, else I'll give you the same as you got last time. Only this time, I won't miss.'

Derek blanched. 'I warn you, John, if you keep this up you'll be sorry. You'll end up back in hospital – or worse, prison!'

John rose to his feet and moved to where Derek stood, saying quietly into his face, 'I don't think you quite understood what I said. I'll never go back to hospital. Never! I'd rather swing first. Do you understand?'

Derek didn't back down. 'One month, John,' he said, and turning, headed for the door.

John slammed the door after him and began to laugh.

The high-pitched noise frightened Jilly and she stared at

him. The laughter stopped abruptly when he caught sight of her. 'What are you staring at?'

'Leave her alone,' Sylvia said.

The backhand was casual, swift and effective – as if he'd been swatting a troublesome fly. Jilly fell over.

Her mother gave a little scream of anger and helped her up. 'Leave her alone.'

'Shut up,' he said. 'I've got a right to discipline my own kid – assuming that she is my kid, that is.'

Sylvia slid in front of Jilly. 'Who else would have fathered her?'

'Any of a number of men, from what I hear.'

'You heard wrong.' A tiny, conciliatory tone entered her voice. 'Go and sit down, John. I'll bring you a nice cup of tea and you can take your medicine. And I'll put our names on the council's housing list.'

'We're staying right here,' he said stubbornly.

'Jilly, be a dear, take some money from the pot. Slip down to the shop and buy me a packet of Woodbines.'

Jilly was old enough to realize that her mother wanted time to quiet her father down – to persuade him to take his pills and wait for them to work. The situation was becoming hard for her mother to handle, and having to leave the cottage would make things twice as hard.

It wasn't the first time her father had hit her for no reason. He also hit her mother on occasion. But her mother wasn't frightened to hit him back. Jilly wouldn't dare. She hated her father with a passion – hated the way he muttered and ranted, and the frightening way he stared at her.

'Buy yourself a comic with the change,' her mother whispered in her ear as she left.

Now her mother was working longer hours, she had to catch the earlier bus.

Many of the house chores now fell on Jilly's shoulders. Her mother had made her a weekly roster. Every Monday morning she changed the bed sheets before going to school. Tuesdays she cleaned the bath and sinks. Wednesday, she dusted the bedroom furniture. The carpet sweeper was run over the rugs on Thursday. For her efforts she earned her shilling pocket money. Though sometimes, when there was a bill to pay, her mother might not be able to afford it.

Jilly had opened a post office savings account, and tried to save most of her money. But the shop was beginning to get sweets in now, and sometimes she couldn't resist buying herself a quarter of dolly mixtures, or some sherbet.

'Saving money is a good habit to get into,' Mrs Duxbury had said approvingly. 'I do wish Gloria was a bit more careful with hers. Now, since you are underage, you must take these forms along to your mother or father to sign. Every time you put money in your account, or take it out, I'll write the amount you have left in the post office in this line here.'

Sylvia had grinned when she saw it. 'I'll have to open an account up myself. Not that there's anything left over to save at the end of the week. What are you saving up for?'

'A rainy day,' Jilly answered, but really, she was saving up to buy her mother something nice for Christmas. It was exciting to watch the amount get bigger and bigger, and she now had eleven shillings saved – although she couldn't take any of it out without her mother's signature.

Friday came. Things had calmed down since the Fowlers' visit. The doctor had come to visit and had put Jilly's father on stronger medication. But the cottage was filled with tension. Jilly tried to stay out of her father's way. The way he muttered to himself, as if someone else was there with him, gave her the creeps.

Today, she swept the front path. She'd just finished the task when the postman came.

She made her father some toast and tea for breakfast, then carried the tray through with the letter for her father. He was listening to some music on the radio.

For once he didn't stare at her, but down at the letter. His hands trembled as he ripped it open. 'Damn them!' he roared. 'They won't get this cottage!' And he swept an arm over the table, knocking the cup of tea from the tray into the grate. The grate hissed like a cat as liquid splashed on to the hot surface. The cup shattered.

Jilly jumped back, pleading, 'Please don't start, Dad.'

Jumping from his chair, he yelled, 'Don't start? I'll do something better than that before I'll allow them to chuck me out of my own home! I'll burn the cottage down, and myself with it!' His eyes fell on her. 'This is all your mother's fault. She drives me mad, and so do you. If she hadn't gone with soldiers . . . We'll see how she feels when she finds out what's happened to her precious daughter, when she comes home from that damned job of hers!'

Fear clutched Jilly by the throat. 'What do you mean?'

'You'll see.' He went into the kitchen and came back with a can of paraffin. 'Get upstairs with you,' he yelled.

Scared to death by the wild look in his eyes, Jilly fled up the stairs, where she grabbed up the bag containing Alec's red tin and her savings book. She wasn't going to stay here and get beaten again. She climbed out of the upstairs window, dropped on to the coal bunker, then down into the long weeds that had once been a lawn.

She hid behind the bunker as a shout went up. 'Jilly Turner, you can get back in here!'

His voice stopped her in her tracks. She peered around the bunker to see him at the upstairs window. He had a gun in his hand. He was going to kill her!

She gave a shuddering scream of terror as her eyes met his. Bursting into sobs she fell to her knees, pressing her hands together. She was shaking all over as she silently prayed, 'Please, God, don't let him kill me. I didn't do anything to hurt him and I don't want to go to heaven yet.'

Her father's eyes were full of menace. He stared at her for a few long moments, then he shut the window and dragged the curtains across.

Jilly fled along the side of the cottage towards the front garden. She could hardly breathe for the fright she felt. When the gate squeaked she squeaked with it, in case her father heard and came after her. Dropping to her knees she crawled through it and cowered behind the safety of the stone wall, her face buried in her knees, which were hugged against her chest.

Afterwards, Jilly couldn't remember which came first, the fire or the shot.

Inside the cottage, the soldier in John's head was talking about the hospital.

'If you go in there they'll try and get me out of your head again,' he said.

'Why did you make me let the girl go?' John asked him.

'She's only a child. You don't like killing, remember.'

The soldier began to fade. 'Don't go,' John said.

'I'll wait if you intend to prove you're not a coward. You'd better hurry, else the girl will fetch the police and you won't be able to escape them. They'll lock you up for good, and put you through that awful shock treatment again.'

'I'd rather burn in hell,' John whimpered as he trickled the paraffin down the stairs, up the hall and across the threshold.

The soldier laughed.

The fumes stank to high heaven, clogging John's throat and making him dizzy as he breathed them in. There was a feeling of chaos inside him. His heart pounded blood through his ears, and his mind was tormented by the fact that he was a failure. All he wanted was some peace and quiet . . . but was this the right way to get it?

'If you want peace, it's right here,' the soldier told him. 'You'll never have to worry about anyone again.'

In the living room, the coal fire sensed the fumes and sent little blue flames leaping out towards the fuel. The multi-coloured rug in front of the fireplace began to smoke. A flame licked at the paraffin, caught and ran swiftly out into the hall. In the space of a heartbeat he was surrounded by fire. It was magnificent in sound, colour and fury. Breathing was agony and he could feel his lungs shrivelling.

John managed a wry grin as flames licked painfully at his feet. He hoped hell wasn't as painful. He gazed at the photograph of Sylvia and Jilly on the mantelpiece. They were both laughing. The heat made the photo blister. Their mouths contorted, as though they were in pain. Jilly began to look like him as heat scarred her face.

Flames suddenly whooshed upwards in the hall. The air around him was red-hot, his trousers were on fire, his legs were melting and it was hard to breathe.

'Now,' the soldier said, 'prove you're not a coward.'

John smiled and lifted the revolver. Gently, he squeezed the trigger.

*　　*　　*

Butcher Hadly was still closed when Jilly pounded at his door, her heart hammering and her eyes wide with fright.

The blind on the door went up and the butcher gazed out at her, looking none too pleased.

'Help me!' she screamed hysterically.

Quickly, he unlocked the door. 'What's happened, girl? Are you being bullied by—'

'The cottage is on fire . . . my dad's in there.' She burst into tears.

The butcher's wife came through from the back room. 'What's going on?'

'There's a fire at her home. It's probably nothing much.' The butcher whipped off his bloodied apron. 'Look after her while I rouse Donald Burns. And ring the fire brigade; we'd better be on the safe side.'

'Poor little thing,' Mrs Hadly murmured. 'I told you John Turner would do something stupid one day. They should never have let him out of hospital.'

He gave her a warning look. 'Hush, woman. You don't know he did anything. If there's a fire it was probably caused by a spark jumping out the grate.'

Wracked by sobs, Jilly was trembling all over.

'You come through the back with me, Jilly,' Mrs Hadly said kindly. 'I'll warm you some milk and tuck you up on the couch while this is sorted out.'

They walked through a back room, where a couple of animal carcasses hung from hooks in the ceiling. Several live rabbits were in a cage in the corner. A pair of dead ones lay on the chopping block, half-skinned, their lustrous eyes dull. A tiny rivulet of blood trickled over the chopping block and dripped into the sawdust on the floor.

Jilly averted her eyes as she walked through to the parlour. How terrible to be a rabbit, and caged up waiting your turn to die. The woman gave her milk and a biscuit, then tucked a blanket around her. 'Now, you stay there until we sort this out. I'm going off to finish skinning the rabbits, and to make some sausages. Try and sleep, dear.'

Mr Hadly came back later, poked his soot-streaked head around the door and gazed at her. 'Somebody's sending for your mum, dear.'

Ducking back into the shop he held a muffled conversation with his wife. 'Like an incendiary bomb hit it . . . fire engine . . . too late . . . nothing left . . . not a sign . . . I'll talk to the girl.'

He came back through. 'I'm not going to ask you what happened back at the cottage, luvvy, but if anyone else asks, tell them you were in the garden, saw the smoke and came running to me for help.' He tapped the side of his nose and winked at her. 'That's in case there's a bit of insurance to collect.'

Dumbly, Jilly nodded.

'We're going back up to the cottage in case there's something we can salvage. Will you be all right by yourself, Jilly?'

Jilly nodded. As soon as they'd gone she went to the room behind the shop, opened the door to the rabbit cage and took the rabbits to the field behind the shop, where they hopped off into the long grass.

Sylvia arrived in a police car. Ashen-faced, she drew Jilly into her arms. 'Thank God you're safe. I should never have left you alone with your father.'

'Now, now, Mrs Turner,' the policeman said. 'Let's not jump to conclusions. I haven't questioned the girl yet.'

'She told me she how it happened,' Mrs Hadly said loudly. 'Said she was in the garden, when she turned and saw the smoke.' Turning to Jilly, she continued, 'You came running down here to fetch my husband, didn't you, luvvy?'

Jilly nodded. She felt numb, and tired. Her eyes began to droop.

'There's your answer,' Mrs Burns, the publican's wife, said. 'No need to question her at all then, Constable. The poor little lass has been through enough already, I reckon.'

'Of course, it might have been gypsies that set fire to the cottage. Somebody walked into the shop as brazen as you please while we was out. Stole a couple of rabbits.'

'I might have to ask the girl in the morning when she's over her fright, just so it's official, like. We'll need a statement for the coroner. I'm sorry about your husband, Mrs Turner. If you need any help sorting things out, please let me know.'

Sylvia nodded.

Mrs Burns said, 'You'll need somewhere to stay tonight. I can manage a room for you and your daughter.'

'Thank you, Mrs Burns.' The tragedy beginning to sink in, Sylvia gazed at the constable. 'You'll let me know when . . .?' She shrugged. 'You know.'

'Probably tomorrow – the fire was a fierce one and we'll have to wait until it's cooled down. It's going to rain tonight and that will help. I doubt if there's much left.'

'Dr Fowler will have to be informed. The cottage belongs – *belonged* – to John's other children. They live with the doctor. He's their uncle, and it might be best if he breaks the news to them.'

'I'll see to it, Mrs Turner. I'll telephone him from the station. You just worry about yourself and the girl. You'll need somewhere to live and some clothes to wear.'

Outside, the air was heavy with the acrid stink of smoke. Mrs Burns's nose wrinkled 'I daresay the villagers will chip in with some clothing. A big pile was handed in for the church jumble sale. We'll go through it and kit you both out. There, there,' she said, when Sylvia burst into tears. 'Don't you worry about anything – excepting perhaps finding some accommodation for yourself,' she added hastily.

They found very little of John Turner's body to bury. The authorities didn't probe too far as to the cause of the fire. A beam had fallen and crushed his skull during the conflagration.

Most of the villagers turned up to pay their respects, and Derek Fowler paid for some sandwiches and wine at the pub.

Mrs Burns nudged Blanche in the ribs with her elbow, and said loudly, 'I imagine you'll be offering the Turners a home at your place, then.'

Blanche looked horrified by the thought. 'I'm afraid that's impossible. We'll continue to support the twins, of course, but really . . . we have such a small house. Now John has gone I feel no obligation whatsoever towards his widow and offspring, since they're not related to us.' She gave a light, tinkling laugh. 'I really think that Mrs Turner will be more comfortable with her own kind, don't you?' Ushering the twins before her, the three of them made a beeline for the car.

Sylvia turned to Mrs Burns. 'You don't have to worry. I'll be catching the bus out tomorrow morning. Once John's insurance pays out I might be able to afford a little house of our own.'

Derek Fowler had been lingering nearby. Taking her arm he led her into a quiet corner where they couldn't be over-heard. 'I'm afraid not, Sylvia. The life insurance was taken out by my sister Rose, and the twins were named as bene-ficiary on his insurance. I've been paying the premiums since she died. The house insurance will be used to rebuild the cottage. Of course, he may have other insurance . . .'

'You don't miss a trick, do you?' she said with some bitter-ness. 'What about Jilly? She's his daughter too. Isn't she entitled to something?'

'She would be if John had anything to leave her.' Derek took an envelope from inside his jacket. Glancing over his shoulder, he thrust it swiftly into her hand. 'I don't want to see you and Jilly on the street. Take this. Inside is the address of a bedsit I use on occasion, and the key. There's also some money to tide you over, since you'll need clothing and things. There are some new council houses going up and I might be able to get you one of those later on. We'll see.' Her mouth nearly fell open when he kissed her cheek. 'As soon as I'm able, I'll drop in on you to see how you're getting on.'

The envelope contained a generous amount of money. The gesture surprised Sylvia. Oh, she knew Derek had always fancied her, but she hadn't imagined he'd be quite so helpful and sympathetic to her needs, when John had despised him.

'Thank you, Derek, that's kind of you. I'm sorry about the cottage. If there's anything I can do in return . . .'

His glance dropped to the swell of her breast. He cleared his throat and smiled. 'It's quite possible I might think of something,' he whispered, and strode off without another word.

So he's finally found the courage to make a move, Sylvia thought. You're going to bear watching, Derek Fowler.

Seven

. . . I certainly have no complaints about the way I was brought up. I've always known I was an adopted child and I became curious about my background in my teens, when I befriended another boy at school who'd also been adopted.

In the way of teenagers, I'm afraid we were inventive about our parentage – both of us were rather keen on the idea that we were fathered by aliens from outer space and were first cousins to Superman. Even with cloak and mask I found it impossible to fly, so eventually that notion was abandoned in favour of a more sensible career . . .

Although Jilly smiled at his nonsense, she thought it sad that she'd been the cause of a boy having to invent a past for himself. Her conscience stabbed her. She parried it. This was not the time to explore her regrets.

. . . I attended a school where I received a good education, was accepted by the university here and scraped through my studies with a hard-earned science degree. I then pursued an accountancy and business management course, and now work for a stockbroker. Eventually, I hope to become a partner . . .

It sounded as though Neil had gone to a good home where he'd been given every opportunity to make something of himself. Jilly was grateful for that.

But . . . Neil? It was not the name she'd given him. She'd given him his father's name.

The official had pushed the point for his birth certificate.

'The name of the father?'

She'd been in a bitter mood. 'I'd rather not have it on the certificate.' It was the one part of the transaction she'd had any control over. But she was hurt and the decision came straight from her churning emotions. Her youthful wisdom told her that if his name wasn't on the certificate, the father would never be able to have a claim over his son – would never know him.

Her mother would have told her she'd cut off her nose to spite her face, if she'd been able to discuss it with her. The reasoning sounded childish now, but now she was blessed with hindsight. Then, she'd hardly left childhood behind.

A disdainful stare had come her way. 'You must know who the child's father is?'

Of course she knew, but she could be obdurate when she wanted. She hadn't intended to acknowledge a man who'd slunk off without a word – offering only the means to dispose of the inconvenience.

How tempting that had been. Though how sordid the back-street alternative. She didn't even want to admit to considering such a course now, but of course, she had, as others before her had. She couldn't condemn them, since she'd learned that desperation makes any avenue attractive.

'I don't want his father on there.'

The man wiped a blot from the nib of his fountain pen, then wrote on the entry in bold black letters '*Father unknown*'! She didn't realize then how damning that might seem to another's eyes.

Over the years, on the occasions when she'd been able to peel back the pain of parting and deliberately bring herself to think of her son, Jilly had always hoped he'd been loved by his other mother – and with the same intensity she'd felt for him herself.

Her love for her infant son had been bittersweet, coloured by the fact that she knew she'd lose him. She'd tried to keep some emotional distance between them in the six weeks between his birth and their parting, but it had been to no avail – not when her son had suckled from her breast, his little dark-capped head snuggled within reach of her kisses.

He'd been such a small, trusting parcel in her arms on that day of parting, his face flushed with sleep as he'd snuggled against her, unaware.

But, no . . . she still couldn't bear to think of that day when she'd betrayed him, or even remember it. Just snatches she allowed herself. That last Judas kiss pressed against the soft skin of his forehead, the door closing in her face with her son on the other side. There had been a yawning space of a heartbeat when he'd stopped being her son and had begun to be Neil James – leaving her behind, a part of his past he might never want to see again, or know about. Despite the welfare officer with her, Jilly had found herself isolated in this action, unbelievably bereft. She'd hurt so badly she'd thought she might die from it, so the word broken-hearted took on a new meaning.

She'd wanted to scream out to them to bring him back – wanted to tear a hole through that dark door panel separating them. Such a thin two inches of door panel – such a long and solid barrier of time to pass between herself and her son.

Others had convinced her she wasn't worthy of keeping him. How neat and clean this solution for everyone concerned. She had no money, no job and nobody to support her. Her baby would have somebody better . . . somebody married . . . a father to guide him. He'd be loved.

As if she hadn't loved him beyond reason herself. But love could be such a nebulous emotion, she thought. It had deserted her when she'd been at her most vulnerable, and at a time when she'd needed it most.

She'd grown a scar over that particular wound. Neil's letter had now weakened it. A tear fell on the paper. Since then, she'd learned that real love could never be turned off.

The bedsit was a nicely furnished room at the top of a large, red brick house in Parkstone. It had a sloping ceiling and large living area. The sleeping section was sliced off by folding doors. Jilly slept on the large, comfortable settee, while her mother used the bed.

It was warmer than the cottage had been, since there was a gas fire. The kitchen was small, little more than a cupboard, but, although the bathroom was along the hall, they didn't often have to share it, since the bedsit was situated right at the top of the house, and apart from the others.

'It's a bit on the cosy side,' her mother said, then brightened. 'At least it's not costing us any rent. It's convenient for work and school, and doesn't need much cleaning. We'll enjoy living here.'

Derek Fowler became a regular visitor. He bought Jilly a new duffel coat for winter, and some shoes, and kitted her out in the navy blue school uniform.

One cold day he gave her some money to go off to the cinema. '*The Wizard of Oz* is showing at the Regal. You'll enjoy it,' he told her.

After her daughter had gone, Sylvia smiled at Derek. 'That was nice of you. Would you like some tea?'

'Not at the moment, my dear.'

She was not surprised when he seated himself beside her on the settee and took her hand in his; she'd been half expecting it. 'Have you heard something about the council house, Derek?'

He smiled. 'I don't want to talk about council housing yet, since I have a bit of a problem. I think you know what it is.' And in case she didn't, he placed her hand over it. 'I've always admired you, Sylvia.'

Pushing him away she said shortly, 'I'm surprised to see you act like this. It's unexpected. You're a doctor.'

'You're not in the least surprised, and I'm also a man. Allow me to put this into perspective for you. If you want that council house you'll cooperate. In fact, if you want to stay here in this flat, you'll change your mind. I'm not paying your rent without having something in return.'

'And if I tell Blanche?'

'I love my wife, Sylvia, but she's not what she seems. None of us are, are we?'

'I'm not sure what you mean.'

'My dear, I'm well aware of your past, which, although I didn't reveal it at the time, was one of the reasons I didn't want you to bring up my sister's children.'

Was he bluffing? She gazed at him, her throat constricting. 'What are you talking about?'

'Your time on the streets. Your arrest and your stay in the reform school.'

'It wasn't by choice. I was forced.'

'By the woman who called herself your grandmother. Yes, I know, Sylvia, and I understand. I'm not blaming you for marrying John Turner.'

'Why are you mentioning it at all?'

'Inducement. Come on, Sylvia, if you can do it for American soldiers you can do it for me. I'll make sure you're protected, and guarantee you'll enjoy it.' He reached out to gently trail his fingers over her breasts, and they reacted to his touch straight away. 'How long is it since you've enjoyed the attention of a man?'

'John's only been dead—'

'Forget your scruples. John wasn't any good to you. The pills he was prescribed would have made sure of that. You know, there's a dangerous excitement attached to an affair that heightens sensation. Look on this as a game. Blanche would really punish me if she found out.'

It would serve her right, Sylvia thought.

A thrill of excitement ran through her as he began to undo the buttons on her bodice. He leaned forward, gently breathed across her raised nubs. 'You have lovely breasts, my dear. I've always admired them.' He took her hand back and placed it against his hardness. He was big. Desire flooded warmly through her. It had been a long time.

'Be wicked, Sylvia. I like wicked women.'

She looked up at him. 'Promise you'll use protection.'

Derek didn't waste any time. He smiled, and, pulling her up from the settee, led her towards the bed. Pushing her down he lowered himself next to her and his mouth closed over hers.

Despite her initial reluctance and the thought that Derek had deliberately put her into a position where she couldn't refuse, he turned out to be a surprisingly inventive and satisfying lover. She began to look forward to his visits, but couldn't help wondering how many other women he'd enjoyed in the bed she slept in.

Being Derek's kept woman wasn't bad, because he never made her feel like one. He was generous with money, most of which she saved, and bought her gifts of exotic lingerie to wear for his visits, black lace.

They met mostly on weekdays. But Sylvia persuaded Jilly to join the Girl Guides, so they wouldn't be disturbed. Then he came on Saturday too, when he could.

Their affair ended abruptly six months later, when Sylvia opened the door to find Blanche on the other side. Her heart sank as the woman pushed past, gazing around with a sneer on her face. 'How utterly sordid.'

'It's all I can afford,' Sylvia said, blustering a little. 'I'm on the council waiting list.'

Blanche looked her up and down. 'Don't bother lying. I know who pays the rent on this place, and what my husband gets up to. You can get out!'

'If I don't?'

'You'll be cited as the other woman when I divorce him. Now, wouldn't your daughter be mortified? I've always considered Jillian to be such a sweet, polite little girl.'

Sylvia shrugged, knowing she had no argument left now. 'How did you find out?'

'I followed him last week. The trouble with Derek is that he likes the game too much. I thought this one had gone on too long, so decided to investigate.'

'What if he refuses to give me up?'

Blanche laughed. 'Derek's very establishment. He has a position in society to maintain, and he wouldn't like the scandal of divorce. You have a month to leave, Sylvia.'

'Does he know you're here?'

'He will soon.' Blanche's eyes were merciless as they flicked over Sylvia's black negligee. 'You need to be taught a lesson, so I thought I'd wait and we can tell him together. He can be such a fool sometimes.'

Derek's face crumpled when he set eyes on Blanche. 'Hello, old girl. You found out then?'

'As you see, Derek. I know we've enjoyed the occasional *ménage à trois* in this sort of situation before, but not with this woman. And I'm going to punish you hard when we get home.'

'Yes, dear,' he said meekly.

Blanche smiled when Sylvia looked shocked, turning from

one to the other. 'I've given her a month's notice. In the meantime, you'd better consult with your friends and make sure she has somewhere else to live. Your life will suddenly become very messy if you continue seeing her.'

'All right, m'dear,' he said meekly.

'Good.' She rose to her feet, immaculate in her baby blue suit, her hair blonded to perfection. 'Then I'll say no more. Be home on time today, dear. We have guests coming for dinner. It's Audrey's engagement party. Remember?'

Without another glance at Sylvia, Blanche swept off in a cloud of chypre perfume, and quietly closed the door behind her.

'I'll be damned!' Sylvia exclaimed, amused by the situation despite being caught up in it.

Derek grinned. 'Well, that's the end of that, I'm afraid. You were good, Sylvia – the best. In fact, I nearly took you into my confidence. A pity Blanche didn't appreciate the irony of it. I'll see about that house for you. Something in the new Bourne Estate, perhaps.'

They moved within two weeks.

Sylvia missed her cosy little bedsitter, and she missed Derek's attentions even more. But at least he honoured his promise. And he gave her a parting gift: enough money to furnish the place in reasonable fashion.

Kissing her gently on the cheek, he said, 'You've always attracted me, Sylvia. Don't tell Blanche about the money, else there'll be ructions.'

It was Christmas. Jilly had bought her mother a pair of nylons and a bottle of Evening in Paris in a pretty blue bottle.

Jilly was presented with a tabby kitten. 'Somebody brought them in to work, looking for homes, the poor little things. What are you going to call it?'

'I don't know, yet.' She cuddled the purring little creature close. 'Nellie, perhaps.'

Her mother laughed and lifted his tail. 'Can't you tell the difference between a male and female yet?'

Jilly blushed, because she hadn't thought of looking. 'I'll call him Johnnie Ray, then, after the singer.'

'*Crrrrrry while my tart is baking*,' her mother sang out, making a parody of the singer's hit song. Jilly laughed.

The house had been decorated with paper streamers and there was a small Christmas tree with an angel on top – a fallen angel, Sylvia called her. It had been a Kewpie doll in a former life, won in November at the fairground in Poole. Jilly had tied a frilly lace doily with a ribbon at her back, for wings – and had decorated the branches with cotton wool snow and silver bells.

'D'you think we'll have any visitors?' she said.

'Like who, Jilly? Everyone celebrates Christmas with their family, and we've only got each other.'

'I have a brother and sister. It would be nice to see them occasionally.'

'They couldn't be bothered to even send a card.'

'Dr Fowler sent me ten shillings though,' Jilly said. 'That was nice of him. I do wish he'd start visiting again. I wonder why he stopped.'

Sylvia didn't.

They roasted a stuffed chicken, ate Christmas pudding and custard, then pulled a cracker each and drank some port and lemon.

Next door had several children and there was a large party going on, with music and laughter.

'It would be nice to be part of a large family,' Jilly said wistfully. 'D'you suppose Audrey is married yet?'

'I ran into Dr Fowler in Sainsbury's the other day. The wedding is to be early in April . . . something to do with tax.'

'Do you think she'll ask me to be her bridesmaid?'

'No, love. I doubt if we'll even get an invitation. She's marrying the boss's son, I believe. We weren't asked to the engagement party, and the wedding invitations would have already gone out.'

'But I'm her sister.'

'Her half-sister. Audrey has learned a few lessons from her aunt Blanche, who has always thought she was too good for the likes of us.' Sylvia drew in a deep breath and grinned. 'Though I must say she surprised me. We'll go to the church, anyway.'

'It would have been nice to have been a bridesmaid,' Jilly said wistfully.

'If I ever marry again you can be my bridesmaid. And when you marry I'll be yours. If you want to be part of a large family you'll just have to have several children of your own when you get married. Just make sure you get the right man, Jilly girl. Some of them can be pigs once they get a ring on your finger.'

'How can you tell the difference between a good one and bad one?'

'You can't. The nicest ones can fool you when you least expect it.' She sighed. 'I'd have liked another child. I'm not too old, you know. I was only twenty when you were born, Jilly girl. You're the best thing to come out of that marriage, and the best thing that ever happened to me.'

Jilly hesitated for a moment, then said, 'Dad didn't believe I was his daughter, though.'

Her mother shrugged. 'Your dad was sick, poor sod. It was just one of the weird ideas he got in his head. John was definitely your father. I'm just thankful he didn't harm you that day. All right? And I don't want you to mention it again, especially to outsiders. People always like to think the worst, and they use it against you when you least expect it.'

Jilly nodded. 'Do you think you'll ever meet someone nice and marry again?'

Her mother's eyes slanted towards her. 'I might.' She took a sip of her third glass of port since dinner, and sighed. 'This is a good drop. Christopher Stainer gave it to me for Christmas.'

'Who's he?'

'The new manager at work. He's a widower, and I'm going to the New Year's Eve ball with him.'

When her mother fell asleep, Jilly stoked up the fire and listened to the wireless while she cuddled a purring Johnnie Ray in her lap. She wondered whether her mother was joking about getting married again, or not. Jilly didn't think she had a boyfriend, but she was good-looking and her boss had given her a Christmas present.

Sylvia was friendly with lots of people at work. Most Saturdays they went out dancing together as a group. She never invited anyone home, though she was driven home in a car by a man from time to time. Had the driver been Christopher Stainer?

A week later Sylvia was getting ready for the New Year's Eve ball she was going to.

She looked lovely in a full-skirted, ballerina dress of blue satin, gold sandals and a filmy stole to wear around her bare shoulders. Sylvia's hair was shoulder length now, and was pulled back behind her ears in a smooth style. She dabbed some Evening in Paris behind her ears, then picked up her gloves and evening bag, saying nervously, 'Do I look all right? I want to make a good impression.'

'You look lovely. Just like Cinderella.'

'Before or after midnight?' Taking Jilly's face between her hands, her mother smiled as her glance roved over her face. 'You're growing up to be beautiful. I love you, Jilly girl. I want to give you more than I ever had.'

'The last time I saw you dressed up you were going dancing with Lieutenant Carstairs.'

A smile of remembrance lit her mother's face. 'You remember Gary? He was a lot of fun to go out with.'

'And the planes flying over, and the day I found the Spitfire—'

'With that evacuee lad . . . what was his name? Alexander?'

'Alec Frampton. His mother was killed in the London blitz and his father died in the war.'

'Poor little sod. Fancy you remembering that.'

Jilly wouldn't have remembered if it wasn't for the red tin she had upstairs in her wardrobe. It contained Alec's life – and part of hers, come to that. A sudden idea came to her. 'If I wrote to him care of the orphanage, do you think they'd pass on the letter?'

'They might. There's no harm in trying.'

Jilly laughed as a horn tooted. 'It sounds as though your Prince Charming has arrived.'

Her mother dropped a kiss on Jilly's cheek, released her face and picked up her stole. 'Don't forget to lock the door behind me, and don't wait up. I've got my key. And make sure Johnnie Ray has a pee before you go to bed. You forgot last time, and I trod in some piddle with my bare feet,' she said over her shoulder, just before the door closed.

After her mother had gone, Jilly fetched Alec's tin, and propped the photo of him with his parents against it. Curiously, she picked up the sealed letter from his father and turned it over in her hands, wondering what he had written to his son.

She tried not to remember that her own father had wanted to kill her. Alec's father wore a happy smile. His mother's expression was loving as she gazed down at her baby son, unaware they'd soon all be parted by death.

> *Dear Alec,*
>
> *I hope you are well. Do you remember me, Jilly Turner? I'm a teenager now, nearly fourteen. I go to secondary school in Poole. My teacher told me I'm good at English and art, but not very good at arithmetic. I could have told* her *that!*
>
> *Rose Cottage burned down and my father died in the fire. Mum and I now live on Bourne Council Estate. Mum hates it here, but I don't mind it.*
>
> *You'll be pleased to know I still have your red tin. I'm looking after it until you return, like you asked.*
>
> *I do hope you get this letter.*
>
> *Your friend,*
>
> *Jilly Turner.*
>
> *PS. You probably don't know, but your story about the brave pilot won the competition. I cut the story from the paper and have put it in the tin, as well as the cheque for the ten shillings prize. Mum and I felt really proud of you.*

The letter was one of several that was sent to the head office of Barnardo's. It was stamped received, then sent to the archives, where it was slipped into Alec Frampton's file.

It was a nice day for a wedding. The air was soft, the breeze a whisper, and the sun shone in a spotless blue sky.

They stood amongst the daffodils outside the church walls

and watched Audrey alight from the car in a froth of white. Her tulle veil was kept in place by a pearl tiara and she carried a bouquet of pink carnations.

A flare of envy filled Jilly when Audrey was greeted by her bridesmaids, all gowned in pink satin. Her sister took her uncle's arm, who looked like a splendid lord in his top hat.

'Audrey!' Jilly called out, smiling as she waved frantically to catch her attention.

The bride turned and caught her eye. She smiled apologetically, then her eyes washed over her former stepmother as if she didn't exist. Audrey turned away, whispering something to her uncle.

'Snob,' Sylvia said, loud enough for Audrey to hear.

'Don't, Mum,' Jilly said, trying to hide her disappointment, even though being excluded hurt. 'It doesn't matter.'

'It does matter. She's your sister. I'm going to stay here until it's over, and so are you. I'm going to give her a piece of my mind when she comes out. I don't care who hears it.'

For the first time in her life Jilly refused to do what she was told. 'No, I'm not staying,' she said as the church door closed behind the bridal party. 'It will spoil Audrey's wedding day.'

'A lot you should care, after what she's just done to you.'

'I *do* care. She's my sister, and it will make me feel bad as well as her.' Jilly choked out a laugh, lest she cry. 'Perhaps I'll marry a prince when I grow up, and I'll invite them to my wedding. That'll show them that we're just as good as they are.'

Her mother swatted her with her glove. 'You're a queer one, Jilly Turner. A prince, eh? Where do you intend to dig him up from?'

'I'll know him when I see him.'

'That's what I thought.'

Now her mother was in a better mood, Jilly threaded her arm through hers. 'I've been saving up my pocket money to buy Audrey a present. Now she won't get one. Instead, we'll go to that cafe on the way home and I'll buy you some lunch. They do nice sardines on toast. Audrey did look lovely though, didn't she?'

'It was mostly make-up. She's always been pasty. Blonde hair doesn't suit her. I thought her aunt Blanche looked like a skinny hag,' Sylvia said as they strolled off arm in arm. '*You're* growing into a real beauty, and you're pulling the glances of the men, as well as lads. You'll have to be careful, Jilly girl, not like me. I always picked the wrong men in the past. That bloody Derek Fowler. I wish I hadn't—'

'Wish you hadn't what?'

'Nothing, love – taken your father's side against them, I suppose. We'd have been better off making friends of them.'

'It's not too late to make friends.'

'Yes, it is. There's too much water under the bridge. I'm just thinking out loud. It's no good regretting the past. You have to look to the future.' Casually, she added, 'By the way, what did you think of Christopher Stainer then?'

He'd seemed pleasant enough, the times Jilly had met him, but he had cold eyes. 'I suppose he's all right,' she said cautiously. 'Why?'

'Oh, nothing. He has a house in Westbourne, and quite a bit of money he inherited. Probably more than Derek Fowler has. He has a son, a quiet lad, a bit younger than you. Chris is a bit stuffy at times, though.'

'Are you going to marry him?'

'He hasn't asked me yet. But one thing's for sure: if I marry again I'm not going to marry a poor man.' She shook her purse, grinned and changed the subject. 'Guess what? I might be able to afford a couple of doughnuts for us for afters.'

The church bells stopped ringing as they walked away.

Eight

In 1953 Jilly was in her last year of school.

They'd been informed at assembly that the old Queen Mary had died. There was a picture of her on an easel, stern-faced and wearing a diamond tiara.

Bowing their heads, the pupils said a prayer.

'To give her soul a good send-off,' Sylvia later said irreverently.

So solemn was the occasion that the girl standing next to Jilly gave a huge, gulping sob, which caused Jilly to giggle. When Mrs Jones's eagle eye fell on her, Jilly became nervous. So she giggled again. As soon as the assembly ended she raced from the hall to the cloakroom, where she began to roar with laughter.

'This is not funny, Jilly Turner,' Mrs Jones said, stalking in after her. 'I expect better behaviour from a prefect. What were you laughing at?'

'I don't know, Miss,' Jilly said between giggles. And she really *didn't* know. Sometimes she felt as though she was filled to the brim with laughter, like bubbles in a bottle of lemonade. And sometimes it just fizzed out, as if somebody had released the cork.

'Very well, you can go and stand outside the headmistress's study. See if you can explain your frivolity to her.' Miss Jones had the glimmer of a smile herself, as she walked off.

'Well, Jillian, what now?' the headmistress asked, beaming her a smile.

'I laughed during assembly, Miss Harding.'

'That's a serious misdemeanour indeed. Was it something I said?'

'No, Miss Harding. I just needed to laugh. It happens sometimes. I can't explain it.'

'Then I won't ask for an explanation.' The headmistress slid a plate with a ginger nut on it towards her. 'Eat that while I think of a suitable punishment.' She found Jilly's file and opened it. 'Yes, you've done well this year in English and art. Top of the class, in fact. That's what's keeping you in the "A" stream. Your history has picked up too.' She heaved a sigh. 'Geography is woeful, and I'm afraid we'll never make a mathematician out of you. What do you intend to do when you leave school?'

'I work in a cafe in Bournemouth on Saturdays for pocket money. They've offered me a full-time job when I leave school.'

'I see. Well, as long as you enjoy it. You could probably do better, you know, Jillian.'

'I like cooking. I thought I might learn enough to have my own cafe one day.'

She smiled. 'So, you're going to be a businesswoman in the future, then?'

'Yes, I suppose I am,' Jilly said with some surprise as she slipped the biscuit in her pocket for later. 'I never thought of it that way.'

'You should. I like to see my girls do well for themselves. Finished your biscuit? Good. I won't inflict punishment on you today, since today we're in mourning for the old queen. Do try and save those giggles of yours for a more appropriate occasion in future, though.'

'Yes, Miss Harding, I will,' she promised.

Early in June, Queen Elizabeth the Second was crowned. They were invited to Christopher Stainer's house to watch it on his new television set.

'I want you to be on your best behaviour, Jilly girl. Just because we live on a council estate it doesn't mean that we have to act common.'

It was a gloomy place. Her mother smiled self-consciously at Christopher Stainer and crooked her little finger in the air slightly when she sipped her tea.

An uneasy feeling settled in the pit of Jilly's stomach, even though she grinned at the sight of her mother.

'Anyone would think you were Lady Turner,' she teased her afterwards.

'Well, you never know. I just thought I'd get some practise in.'

Jilly left school when they broke up for August holidays – and went to work full-time in the cafe.

'Just in time for the summer rush,' her boss said. 'And it will save me employing someone I don't know, though I might have to get another part-timer later on.'

The cafe did a steady trade all round, and as the days passed quickly, so did her bank account build up, though she spent some money on something to wear for best – a permanently pleated grey skirt that she could wash easily, and a candy striped blouse to wear with it.

'You have good taste,' her mother told her. 'You can wear something like that anywhere.'

February in Australia was the hottest month of the year.

Alec had received notification that there was a place at university for him, and had spent the previous several weeks working on a farm, trying to save some money to help him through his degree.

He'd been called to head office.

'You're one of the lucky ones who have been singled out, Frampton. Your great-uncle has decided to pay for your books. Not everyone gets this opportunity, so make the most of it. And no slacking, mind. And the ladies' committee has decided to give you a bursary, enough money to buy yourself some new shoes and a Sunday suit for going to church in. Don't forget to show some manners and write them a letter of thanks. I'll give you the address.'

'I will, sir. I'm very grateful.' Alec meant it. He'd watched boys sent out to perform menial jobs at an early age. He was lucky he'd been born with an exceptional brain and capacity to learn quickly.

In 1954 Alec started his first year at university. He intended to work as hard as he could, and convert to a teacher training course when he'd got his degree.

At university he slept in the dorm with several farmers' lads. At night he had to help with college chores, but he was provided with a meal, so he wouldn't starve.

Luckily, Fry the spy had also thought to provide him with a small amount of pocket money to help him through his learning years.

He'd sent his great-uncle a letter of thanks via the orphanage, giving a glowing account of how he was getting on, so the man wouldn't think his money was being squandered on a ne'er-do-well. He'd received no reply.

To eke the savings out he worked in a public bar at night. Cleaning up after the drinkers was not a pleasant job. Fag ends stuck to spilled beer and other liquids, so he had to sweep and scrape the floor first. The carbolic-smelling suds quickly became a beery smelling dark grey brew. But Alec sectioned the floor and worked fast.

Sometimes he worked all day on Saturday, the landlord conveniently overlooking the fact that he was underage. He was paid in cash – mostly from the money forgotten and left behind on the bar by the heavy drinkers who frequented the place.

Burning the candle at both ends became a habit he got used to, as did being permanently, physically tired. But he relished the academic work, especially the maths, history and sciences, which proved not to be as testing as he'd feared. The physical work kept him fit. In fact, he was enjoying himself as he absorbed more of the outside world than his institutionalized life had previously allowed.

Alec didn't have many possessions – the minimum of clothing, and his personal items in the accounts tin. He'd grown a beard, and had adopted the scruffy look by necessity rather than choice.

Today was Sunday. He'd skipped chapel that morning, borrowed a bicycle and headed to the beach, where he was seated in the shade of a Norfolk pine, writing a letter to Jilly Turner.

'How silly this activity is,' he said out loud, and not for the first time. Jilly would have forgotten him long ago. He could hardly remember her, though he had a picture in his mind of a small child with brown eyes and dark pigtails. She'd be at least . . . he calculated her age swiftly in his head. Getting on for sixteen, he supposed. Just a baby, still.

He wondered what Jilly looked like now. Not that he had

much time for girls – especially one as young as Jilly – though one or two temporary barmaids had thoughtfully and enjoyably taken it upon themselves to teach him the facts of life.

Dear Jilly,

Sometimes I consider myself stupid for writing to you at all, as though you're someone I imagine instead of being real. Writing to you has become a habit, though.

I hope you're well, Jilly Turner. Apart from Fry the spy, you're my only link to the past and I think of you often. I expect you've grown into a pretty girl, with those big brown eyes of yours. I wish I could see you again.

I'm in the middle of my studies, and working hard. Another two years and I should have a science degree followed later by a DipEd. Then I can obtain work as a teacher. I daresay that sounds like I'm bragging, but it's what I hope to achieve rather than what I've already achieved – and I like to have a goal to work towards.

Once I start work I'll begin saving up to return to England, though I'm undecided whether I shall stay there, because this country I was shipped off to is a pretty decent one, all round . . .

Alec gazed at the expanse of Indian Ocean stretching in front of him, at the vastness of sky. Surfers were astride their boards, waiting for waves.

It was already hot and a faint haze rose from the water. Seagulls floated, and a swimmer cut through the heave and swell, his arms churning like propellers to cut splashy slices from the cobalt ocean.

Soon, it would be too hot to stand in bare feet on the sand. The bathers would lie on their towels. The girls, attired in next to nothing, would toast their already tanned flesh.

Now and again one would rise, to dash into the water and cool off, returning, covered in little goose pimples and tiny shivers. And their wet-slicked hair would be tossed and towelled, and would lighten to a honey-streaked sweetness as it dried.

A small plane droned across the sky, the sound giving him a moment of nostalgia for his childhood. Most of it had faded, but he remembered Jilly climbing on his shoulders to look through the window of the Spitfire.

> *... Remember that time when we found the Spitfire? I have a confession to make, Jilly. I was a coward, too scared to look inside it myself. I knew you were braver than I was, so I made you look into the cockpit, instead. That was the day the pilot took my place as a hero in your eyes. I wonder if he survived the war ...*

Alec signed his name with a flourish. Why was he making this young girl his confessor, especially since he didn't have the courage to post the letters? Then he thought, she probably didn't live at Blackbriar Caundle any more, so what was the point?

Writing the letter had made him feel restless, and the sparse remains of the ink rolling from the pen had faded almost to nothing by the time he signed it, as if his name was unimportant.

Abruptly, he thought, I should be studying. He threw the ballpoint into the long grass at the base of the tree, rose to his feet and stretched. He'd reached just over six feet in height, and was now growing his muscles. The sun bit into his arms, already toasted a deep brown, as he walked to where he'd left the bicycle.

It would be frosty in England now, he suddenly thought, and was hit by an unexpected wave of homesickness.

'I'm going to marry Chris,' Sylvia stated.

Jilly didn't like the man much, and found his son to be uncommunicative and sullen.

'Don't marry him, Mum. He's not your type. He's too old and too stern. There's something I don't like about him.'

'You're being ridiculous, Jilly. He's only fifty. He takes life seriously, that's all. Besides, he lives in a nice house in a nice area, and has a bit of money tucked away.'

'You're marrying him for his money?'

Anger came into her mother's voice. 'Honestly, I feel

like giving you a good shaking sometimes. I'm surprised
you think I'd be so mercenary. I'll have to give up work,
though.'

Astonished, Jilly gazed at her. 'Give up work? You've
always worked!'

'I know, and I won't like losing the independence of
earning my own wage. Chris said that head office frowns
on married couples working together, especially in management. He doesn't want me to work, anyway. He thinks I'll
have enough to do, running the house. Besides, he says we
don't need extra money. He's thoughtful like that, you know.'

Suddenly uneasy, Jilly pleaded, 'Please don't marry him,
Mum. We're happy living here, by ourselves.'

'You might be, but I'm not. I can hardly make ends meet
and I hate living on a council estate. Besides, I want a bit
of male companionship. A woman can soon get a reputation
for herself if she doesn't have a ring on her finger.'

Jilly remembered the talk about her mother in Blackbriar
Caundle. She wondered now if there had been any truth in
the rumours. The only American she could remember was
the one called Gary Carstairs. But no – he'd been a friend,
and had a family of his own. Even so, her mother had been
talked about – and it had caused trouble when her father had
come home from the war.

Her mother was saying, 'If we stay here you'll meet the
wrong type of boys. You should take a leaf from young
Audrey's book. She did all right for herself with her husband.
She got a ring on her finger early, has a nice house and a
car of her own.'

Her mother had changed her tune about Audrey. 'Do you
love Mr Stainer?'

'You're not jealous are you, Jilly? You can't have me all
to yourself, you know. In a couple of years you'll fall in
love with some nice boy, get yourself married and leave me.
What then?'

'I'm not going to marry until I'm twenty-five, at least.'

'You're naive, Jilly. You've always been too emotional,
and will fall in love easily. Men will see that in you, and
will take advantage.'

'I'm too young to think of marriage.'

'And I'm too old *not* to, Jilly. There's been a shortage of men since the war. Yes, Chris is a bit older than me, and set in his ways, but if I turn him down my chance of marriage and having another baby will lessen. I'll be stuck on this estate until I grow old and die.'

'You want another baby? But Mum, you're thirty-five!'

'Chris wants one. A baby helps keep a marriage together.' Sylvia gave a bit of a laugh. 'His house is bigger than the one the Fowlers live in. Westbourne is a good area, you know. I'll be the lady of the manor. You'll be Princess Jilly, so you might get to catch yourself that prince you were going on about once. That will be a change for the better. Chris has a cleaning lady who comes in to do the housework. So we'll be la-di-da.'

'I'm not sure I want to be la-di-da.'

'Of course you do, sourpuss.' Catching her round the waist, Sylvia whirled Jilly around the room until they were breathless and laughing.

'There, that's better,' she said. 'We're getting married in the church and you can be my bridesmaid. We'll invite the bloody Fowlers, Audrey's and Peter's families, too. We'll show them. Chris is every bit as good as them. Better, in fact.'

But Jilly didn't share her mother's sentiment, and only Audrey and Peter turned up at the church to witness the nuptials.

The wedding day dawned brightly, but by the time Sylvia was ready for church in a blue wide-skirted dress with a shawl neckline and a big hat, the wind had sprung up and clouds were racing across the sky.

As it was, the church was nearly empty, except for the Stainer grandmother, who squatted like an impassive toad in the front pew, and some friends of them both from the telephone exchange.

Jilly felt awkward in her pale blue strap dress with wide net skirt, long gloves, ballet shoes and head-hugging feathered hat. She looked like a reject from the corps de ballet of *Swan Lake*, and wondered what the reaction would be if she danced on her toes all the way down the aisle. A fit of the giggles threatened her, and she had to talk firmly to herself.

She heard Audrey titter at her outfit as they walked past and threw her a grin. She didn't blame her.

Her lips quirking into an ironic grin, Jilly turned her head in time to encounter the amusement in Peter's eyes. She hadn't seen him for ages, but thought he looked handsome and prosperous. He winked at her.

Audrey whispered, 'Hi, sis.' Her smile and the connection between them being acknowledged sent warmth surging through Jilly.

Christopher Stainer, grey-haired, thin and wiry, waited at the altar. He had a self-satisfied but impassive look on his face and was attractive, in a stern way.

His fourteen-year-old son displayed his usual sulky facade. Willis sniffed just as the service was about to begin, then, when his father turned to frown at him, noisily blew his nose. The end was rubbed red, as though he had a cold.

The vicar cleared his throat.

'We are gathered together in the sight of God . . .'

A God who made his displeasure at the union known by sending a gust of wind and a splattering of hailstones against the stained-glass windows, so afterwards, when the storm really hit, it was too wet to take decent photographs of the bridal party.

The guests crowded together in the cold stone porch as the tempest beat around them, gazing anxiously at the sky. Some broke free, running for their cars or the bus stop, and struggling against a flimsy barrier of black umbrellas held aloft, as if they'd been attending a funeral. Peter was one of them.

Audrey gave her a hug. 'The weather doesn't look too promising, Jilly. I was hoping to talk to you, but Aunt Blanche hasn't been very well, so I think I'll have to go straight home before this gets any worse. If you ever need anyone to talk to, you know where I am. Give me a ring, sometime.'

Squashed in the car afterwards between Willis and his solid grandmother, who reeked of mothballs, Jilly pulled her flimsy stole around her shoulders to keep the chill at bay, and tried not to inhale too deeply.

Willis was sucking noisily on a cough lozenge. She caught him staring at her. The expression in his eyes was a mixture of curiosity and wry amusement.

When she grinned at him he turned to gaze out of the window.

Back at the house, Jilly's mother smiled at her new husband and took possession of her new role as mistress of the house. 'I'll go and make some tea then, shall I, Chris?'

Her new mother-in-law wasn't having that and struggled to her feet. 'I'll do it. I grew up in this house. Most of the things in it belonged to my mother and I know where everything is. There's some good china I keep for special occasions. I know my mother wouldn't want a stranger using it, and I doubt if you'll know which is which.'

Sylvia's eyes narrowed as the battle line was drawn. Immediately she fired her first volley in what was to become a running battle between the two women. 'I can't have an old lady like you waiting on us. I suggest you take your mother's best china with you when you go home – since I'll be needing the space to put my own stuff. Come along, Jilly girl, I'm sure you have brains enough to tell the difference between good china and jam jars, even if I haven't.'

Willis sniggered. Christopher frowned.

It soon became apparent to Sylvia that her marriage was not going to turn out as she'd expected.

The house was gloomy, and full of draughts. Smoke was sent billowing into the room every time a door was opened or shut. Her new husband had got rid of the cleaning lady. He now expected her to keep it spotlessly clean.

'You're not working now, so it will keep you occupied,' he said. 'Jilly can help you after work.'

Chris was tight with his money, and ruthlessly efficient. Everything had to be accounted for, and run like clockwork, including their relationship.

On Monday and Friday nights, he spent a mechanical fifteen minutes satisfying himself. Immediately afterwards, he saw to his hygiene, as if she was a tart he'd visited, then went to his own bed and fell asleep.

His efficiency paid off. Sylvia discovered she was pregnant just two months later. She wasn't pleased. Though she'd talked about having a baby, she hadn't thought she'd fall pregnant so easily.

Christopher gave a self-congratulatory smile when she told him the news. 'Let's hope it's a boy.'

'Perhaps you should hire another cleaning lady,' she suggested.

'Nonsense. My former wife had no trouble keeping the house clean when she was expecting Willis, and you have the girl to help you.'

Sylvia wished he'd stop referring to Jilly as 'the girl', as if she was a maid in the house.

'Jilly works. You can't expect her to come home and keep this mausoleum clean. You don't help.'

'I work to bring in the money, and also do the gardening. Your job is to look after the family and the house. That's how it should be.'

His mother walked in on the discussion. 'You made your bed, now you've got to lie in it,' she said with a complacent smile.

'Who asked your opinion on a private conversation? From now on, please don't just walk into my home, Mrs Stainer. Knock at the door and wait until you're invited.'

The old lady gazed at her son. 'See how she treats me? I told you what she was like, but you didn't listen. She certainly changed her spots when she got a ring on her finger.'

'Mother, please don't upset yourself.' Christopher gazed calmly at her. 'Sylvia, I'd be obliged if you didn't talk to my mother like that. She may come and go as she pleases. It will make it easier for you if I make you out a roster of duties, and also one for your daughter. She has to do something for her keep.'

'I was under the impression that you took half her wages from her for that.'

'It's only fair that she should pay board, since she's working. If she was forced to live on her own it would cost her much more.'

Fear leaped into Sylvia's throat at the implied threat. She said in a slightly defensive manner, 'What about your son. Will he have a roster of duties?'

'Willis is a child, still.'

'He's fourteen, only eighteen months younger than Jilly.

He could pick his own clothes up from the floor and make his bed, for a start. And you might try telling him not to leave his bits and pieces on the floor. I stepped on a cricket bat in the hall and turned my ankle. It's dangerous, leaving things lying around.'

'Have you forgotten what children are like?'

'No, and I haven't forgotten that they have to be trained right from the start. That's why Jilly is so good at helping me. Will does nothing but make work for others.'

He sighed. 'I take your point, Sylvia. I'll talk to Willis.'

The older Mrs Stainer smiled nastily at her when Christopher walked off. 'You won't have things all your own way with *my* son.'

Sylvia glared at her. 'And don't think you'll get the better of me, either. I warn you, stay in your own house, else I'll put a dose of rat poison in your coffee.'

Jilly and Willis were told about the expected baby together.

'Won't that be nice?' said Christopher.

'Not if it's a girl,' Willis screwed his forehead into a frown. 'Girls stink.' He stomped off and slammed the door behind him. Smoke billowed from the chimney.

Coughing, Sylvia gazed indignantly at Christopher. 'That kid needs a strap across his backside. It's about time you took him in hand.'

'It's only natural that he'd be jealous.'

'Piffle! Jilly isn't jealous, are you love?'

Jilly wished her mother hadn't drawn her into the argument as she shook her head, and tried to pour salve on to the wound. 'It will be lovely to have a baby in the house.'

Her stepfather gave a wintry smile and his grey eyes wandered to her budding breasts. 'Why should she be jealous? I imagine the girl is old enough to have babies of her own. Isn't that right, dear?'

Colour flooded Jilly's face at being asked such a personal question. She pulled her cardigan across her chest and mumbled an affirmative.

'Just don't let any young man touch you where he shouldn't, because that will turn you into a tart. Do you understand, girl?'

'As if she would!' Sylvia protested. 'I've brought my girl up to behave herself. Go to the corner shop and buy me a packet of Woodbines, Jilly. I'm gasping for a smoke.'

'You'll just have to gasp,' Christopher told her. 'It's a waste of money, and it makes you smell unpleasant.'

'You smoke.'

'That's different. I'm a man and I smoke a pipe. No more cigarettes, Sylvia. It won't be good for the baby, so I won't have it. And no more alcohol.'

Sylvia flushed. 'I haven't seen the inside of a pub since I married you.'

'You don't have to. My mother marked the bottles in the sideboard. She tells me they've gone down considerably.'

Sylvia's gasp of outrage was followed by a rush of blood to her face. 'How dare you have the old hag spy on me! Your mother probably drank it herself when I was out, and blamed it on me.'

Christopher gave her a hard look. 'I'm beginning to think I made a mistake marrying you.'

'Likewise,' Sylvia retorted.

Jilly edged towards the door when her mother accused him, 'You're a mean-minded skinflint. I should have listened to Jilly in the first place and stayed single. At least we'd have our own place, without you and your bloody mother telling us what to do every five minutes. This place is more like a prison than a home.'

'Enough!' Jilly's heart began to thunder when her stepfather turned to stare at her. 'If you don't like living here, you can always leave, girl.'

'No!' her mother shrieked. 'She won't be able to manage, and I won't have it.'

Jilly enjoyed her job in the Bournemouth cafe, which did a steady trade in winter. It was not one of those genteel cream tea cafes. Rather, it sold solid lunches and robust toasted sandwiches. She'd worked there for two years now.

It was a cheerful place with red leather-look seats and booths with Formica tables that just needed a wipe from a cloth. The walls were covered in adverts for cola and milkshakes. A glass-fronted counter held sandwiches and cakes.

The top supported a chrome espresso machine, which hissed steam from the pipe.

The lunchtime rush was over. Jilly began to clear the tables, and slipped a coin into the jukebox in the corner, which was girdled in blue neon. Bill Haley began to sing 'Rock Around The Clock'. Jilly began to jiggle her hips as she wiped the crumbs from the tables.

Jilly loved her job and liked her boss. Mr Cooper was a genial man, who teased her in front of the customers and made her blush.

A man came in. Blowing on his cold fingers he took a seat by a steamed-up window, smiled at them. 'Not too late for lunch, I hope?'

Mr Cooper handed the man a menu. 'My right-hand man, Jilly Turner, will serve you.'

'Some man,' the customer said, and winked.

Mr Cooper smiled at her. 'I'm off to get my lunch, Jilly. The cafe's all yours. Don't burn it down, and if this customer gives you any cheek, just give me a buzz.'

The young man grinned. 'I wouldn't dream of giving a pretty little thing like her any cheek.'

Finishing the tables, Jilly went to take the man's order. He turned his gaze on her, his eyes expressing puzzlement. He was about thirty, blue-eyed and handsome. He also looked vaguely familiar. Probably a regular, she thought.

'Did he say your name was Jilly Turner?'

She nodded.

'From Blackbriar Caundle?'

'I lived there when I was a child.'

He gave a broad smile. 'Do you remember me?'

She scrambled through her mind and came up with nothing specific. 'You seem familiar, sir. Did you live there, too?'

'I'm Rick Oliver.'

She felt her eyes widen and just stopped herself from blurting out, 'My hero!' Her smile came. 'The pilot of the Spitfire. Of course I remember you. Would you like to order now, Mr Oliver? The cook goes off duty in half an hour.'

'My friend will be along shortly, but I know what he'll order. We'll have two mixed grills, followed by apple pie and custard. I'll have a cappuccino while I wait, if you would.'

She gave the order to the cook, then made his coffee perfectly. Hot and dark coffee in the bottom, she steamed the milk into a scalding froth and set it on top with a swirl of cinnamon and brown sugar. Taking it to his table, she smiled at the thought that he'd remembered her name after all this time. 'Here you are, Mr Oliver.'

His smile dazzled her. 'Call me Rick, would you? We must talk. I'll come back for you after work, pick you up and take you home in my car.' His eyes sharpened as his gaze lingered on her. 'You've grown into a pretty girl – a beauty, in fact. I imagine you've got a boyfriend or three, eh?'

'No, but—'

'Perhaps I could take you dancing at the weekend, then?'

She blushed and stammered, 'I don't know, Rick. My mother and stepfather—'

'What they don't know won't hurt them. Just tell them you're working late.' He gave her a lopsided grin that was totally irresistible. 'After all, you did save my life, so I'd like to repay you. Do you believe in fate?'

'Like the horoscope in the magazines?'

He nodded. 'Today, mine said I was going to meet an old friend. That's come true, so fate must have brought us together again. You can't argue with that, Jilly. Do say you'll come out with me.'

Her heart soared painfully at the thought that her hero had come back to her. She wondered what destiny had in store for them as she nodded shyly.

Nine

Christopher Stainer was not pleased when he found out that Jilly was seeing a man.

'But it's an old friend from the past. Remember that pilot Alec Frampton and I rescued, Mum? It's him. He came into the cafe, and he recognized me.'

Predictably, her stepfather said, 'Only tarts have boyfriends of that age.'

'He's not my boyfriend,' she argued. 'We went out dancing once, and he took me to the pictures last Saturday.' She didn't tell him that Rick had held her hand and kissed her on the cheek when he said goodnight.

'Oh for God's sake, Chris, why do you have to make this out to be so sordid? Jilly saved his life when she was a kid. He's likely just being kind to her. Besides, he's an airline pilot. He can only see her once a week. What's the harm? Bring him home so we can meet him next time, Jilly.'

So she did, though Rick had been reluctant.

To Jilly's embarrassment, her mother flirted with him. 'You know, Rick, when my daughter and that boy rescued you from the Spitfire, I must have been the only person in the village who wasn't there. She was keeping you to herself even then, because she didn't tell me about it until it was all over.'

'I'd certainly have remembered you if you'd been there,' he said gallantly, and stood up. 'Shall we go, Jilly? I bought some tickets for the ballet at the Pavilion Theatre. As you've never been to one I thought it would be a treat for you. Goodnight, Mrs Stainer, Mr Stainer. I'll make sure she's home on time.'

A ballet? Jilly couldn't wait.

*   *   *

'Fancy my Jilly girl going out with an airline pilot,' Sylvia said after they'd left. 'If something comes of it that would be one in the eye for the Fowlers.'

'Nothing good will come of it, you mark my words,' Chris said.

Rick Oliver was one of those men who made a woman feel good. Sylvia wished she'd married someone like him herself. Even though her stomach resembled a Christmas pudding, her legs were blue-veined and her ankles were swollen, that didn't mean she was immune to him. The baby was not due for three more months, but Sylvia was not enjoying the experience of carrying it. Her blood pressure was up the last time she'd had a check-up.

'She must get more rest,' the doctor had told Christopher.

Now, his interfering mother came in to clean the kitchen and bathroom, a martyred expression set plainly on her face. She worked her fingers to the bone for her son, as if trying to prove herself a better housewife than Sylvia. The self-centred bastard took it for granted.

'You should get a cleaning lady,' she told him, the one and only time she'd thought to stick up for his mother. 'Your mother is old and has her own house to look after.'

'She likes to feel useful. That man your girl is going out with must be twelve years older than her or more.'

'So what? You're fifteen years older than me. Does that make me a tart, too?'

Christopher opened his mouth, then clamped it shut again, as if he'd thought better of what he'd been about to say to her. Instead, he turned back to Jilly. 'You could stay in and help your mother instead of gadding about town with a man old enough to be your father.'

'She only goes out with him on Saturdays. What harm can that do? You could help me instead of going off to those silly men's meetings. After all, it's your baby too. What do you do there, anyway?'

'That's none of your business.' His face closed down, making him look sly and secretive, like his son.

Willis was quiet, but furtive, always lurking in the shadows. Jilly thought he probably peered through keyholes. She'd stuffed paper in hers, but somebody had removed it, so when she was in her room she hung a cardigan over the doorknob.

Yet, there was something about Will that made Jilly feel sorry for him. He was not like his father, who appeared jovial and caring in public, but was controlling and sarcastic in private. Will was awkward and reclusive.

Oh, she tried to make friends with him, but the boy didn't attract friends. She'd also made him pick up his marbles a few days ago. He'd been bouncing them down the stairs while her mother was trying to rest. Jilly thought he'd done it deliberately.

'Make sure you pick them all up. Somebody might slip on them.'

'My father thinks you're no good,' Will said contemptuously, 'and my grandmother thinks the same about your mother.'

'At least my mother defends you against your father, which is more than anyone else does around here. She's saved you from a couple of beatings. Anyway, who cares what your grandmother thinks? She's just a mean old hen.'

'If I tell her you said that you'll get into trouble.'

'Then I'll box your damned ears for you,' she said angrily, and shut the door in his face. She waited a couple of seconds, then opened it again, to see if he was spying through the keyhole at her. He wasn't. He was halfway along the landing heading for his own room. 'I'm trying to be your friend, Will, but you make it damned hard sometimes. Meet me halfway, would you!'

He turned, and for once, the spontaneous laugh he gave sounded entirely genuine. 'You should hear what my gran has to say about you sometimes.'

'No, I shouldn't. I don't like mean people. There's a Saturday job going where I work. It's cleaning tables and washing-up, stuff like that. I could put a word in for you if you're interested in earning some pocket money.'

Interest came into his eyes. 'Thanks.'

Tonight, Jilly was going out dancing with Rick and nobody was going to stop her. She'd wear a new dress she'd had put by in the shop while she paid it off. It was the latest style, a black shift with fringes that shimmied as she danced. And she'd bought some really high heels, and had been practising in them.

She bathed in six inches of lukewarm water, though she longed for a deep bath. They had to economize, her stepfather had said. Back in her gloomy bedroom, she began to dress, wondering if there would be enough light from the dim globe to see in the mirror. She intended to wear eye make-up, as well as lipstick, to make herself look older.

She'd just finished attaching her stockings to her suspender belt when the door creaked open behind her. Dropping the skirt of her petticoat when her stepfather walked in, Jilly snatched up her dressing gown and held it in front of her.

'I want to talk to you, girl.'

'When I'm dressed.'

He closed the door behind him and leaned against the panel. 'You can dress now. I want to know if you're doing anything sinful with that man you're seeing.'

'I don't know what you mean.'

He took two steps forward, pulled her dressing gown aside and placed a hand over one of her breasts. 'Does he touch you here?' She'd hardly gasped out a protest when his other hand slid between her legs, roughly fondling her. 'Or here?'

'Certainly not!' She pushed him away from her. 'Get out, before I scream for my mother.'

He smiled. 'You're still a virgin, then. Good.' He turned and left, closing the door gently behind him. Breathing a sigh of relief she turned the key in the lock, in case he came back. She intended to keep it locked from now on. She decided not to let her mother know what had happened. She'd been looking weary lately.

A toot on the horn and Jilly shrugged into her dress and shoes, then picked up her coat. She pulled a gauzy scarf over her hairdo. Rick liked it like this, back-combed to give it height at the crown and gently curving into her jaw line. He said it made her look sophisticated. She waved to him out of the window, then quickly added some blue eyeshadow and black mascara.

When she got into the Anglia, Rick smiled at her, his eyes blue against hers. 'You look ravishing tonight, angel.'

Draping an arm along the back of the seat he leaned across and kissed her.

She felt shy and slightly tense. She loved him so much and wanted to be perfect for him. Remembering her lipstick, she scrambled in her bag in a panic. 'I've forgotten to put my lipstick on.'

He took the tube from her. 'Pucker up then, doll.'

When she did he kissed her again, then drew the pink lipstick over her lips.

His nose wrinkled. 'I must buy you some decent perfume.'

Her confidence crashed. He hated her perfume and she wished she hadn't worn it. Suddenly she could smell it on herself, cheap and harsh, like lavatory cleaner. 'I'm sorry,' she murmured, and gazed down at her hands in an agony of distress.

'Hey,' he said softly, 'I wasn't criticizing. It's not that bad, just a bit cheap.'

He was probably used to more glamorous women, she thought, like the film actress Diana Dors – women who'd experienced life and knew about the theatre, art and drinking cocktails.

He took a box from his pocket and placed it in her lap. Inside was a silver chain with a seashell dangling from it. Jilly gazed at it, her eyes shining. 'You remember it then – the shell I gave you for luck when you were rescued from the Spitfire.'

He looked startled for a moment, then whispered smoothly. 'How could I forget it, Jilly?' Picking up the necklace he circled it around her neck. 'Let me do this up for you.'

His hands were cool against the nape of her neck and raised goosebumps. He placed a small, shivering kiss against her ear. 'Perhaps you'll allow me to give you a proper kiss.'

She desperately wanted him to kiss her properly. 'Not here, Rick. My stepfather will be watching.' Indeed, she could feel his eyes on her from the shadows behind his window. 'Later, I promise.'

He withdrew his arm and started the car. 'Later then, angel. I'll hold you to that.' After a few minutes he tossed casually at her, 'You haven't had much to do with men, have you?'

How could he tell? She was conscious of the perspiration that pricked at her armpits, and died a thousand deaths in case she started to smell of sweat. She suddenly felt skinny and ugly. Her chest was too small, her hips to big. She wondered if her buttocks wobbled when she walked . . . and she hated her nose.

The silver shell fell snugly into the hollow of her neck. Gazing at Rick's profile she began to wonder what being kissed properly by him would be like. 'Rick,' she said in a small, desperate voice, 'I haven't had *anything* to do with men. I'm a virgin. My mother told me it's best to save myself for marriage.'

A laugh choked from him and he reached out to caress her thigh, his hand sliding on her nylons. 'How old-fashioned of your mother! Dare I say she's jealous of you, doll? She's losing her looks while you grow more gorgeous by the minute and she doesn't want you to grow up.'

Jilly wondered if that was true.

'A virgin, eh? The thought is quite a turn-on, actually.' He flicked her a wicked glance, one strangely intimate and approving, then grinned. 'We might have to do something about educating you a little. We needn't go all the way.'

Shyly, she returned the grin. She wouldn't go all the way, of course. Yet she felt breathless with anticipation and there was a little moist patch and a feeling of longing inside her. Later, Rick gave her the kiss she'd always dreamed of, one tender and loving – a for ever kind of kiss.

But it didn't stop there. She held her breath, allowing him the liberty of kissing her breasts through the fabric of her dress. He murmured, 'I like them neat.'

When he took her hand and carried it to his lap, she felt the hardness of him and whispered, 'Do you love me, Rick?'

The eyes that gazed into hers were wholly sincere. 'Sure I do, Jilly. That's why I'm taking you straight home now. You're having a bad effect on me. You could help me out a little, you know.'

She blushed. 'I don't know how.'

'I'll show you.' He opened his trousers and took her hand inside, to nestle himself in it. She didn't know what to do, except blush. 'Take this handkerchief, you'll need it. Just close your hand around me, though not too tight, and let me kiss and touch you. You can leave the rest to me.'

He was silky and thrusting against her palm and fingers, and his kiss went further then the one before, his tongue exploring her mouth. Jilly thought of him inside her, thrusting and thrusting, and gave a shudder of delight when he groaned and bucked against the handkerchief. It was soon over. He adjusted his clothes and smiled at her.

'At least I'll be able to sleep tonight. What about you? It wasn't too awful, was it?'

She didn't think she'd sleep again she was so excited. It must have shown in her face for he took her in his arms again and his hand slid up between her thighs and touched her.

Her half-hearted mew of protest made him chuckle. 'It's all right, sweetheart. I'll only tease you a little bit, so you'll know what it's like. We won't go any further. You're going to have to lose it sooner or later, you know. I've got you reserved for myself, so don't go falling in love with anyone else.'

His touch affected her body so greatly she began to arch towards his teasing.

'That's right, angel, enjoy it,' he whispered against her ear as she shuddered. 'There's plenty more where this comes from.'

'I love you,' she said.

'I love you too, Jilly. Next week I'll have to get us a hotel room so we can be comfortable. The car is so cramped.'

Rick Oliver liked them young and innocent. Seducing Jilly Turner was all too easy. Aided by the fact that she hero-worshipped him he led her swiftly and surely into losing her innocence. And he made sure she enjoyed every moment of her seduction.

After a while she became too clingy, and worried. Her period hadn't arrived on time. She hinted at an engagement. It was time to get out. Girls like Jilly had responsibility written all over them. She was too young for him, and her adoration of him had begun to lose its lustre.

Besides, his business in Bournemouth was all but over.

His wife was beginning to ask why he needed to spend every weekend there when the trainee rep could manage the lesser clients.

He spent one last evening with Jilly in the hotel. She fell asleep and he didn't have the heart to wake her. He kissed her gently on the cheek and left her a note, with the address of a former midwife who supplemented her income on the side.

He left twenty-five pounds with it. After all, he thought, she didn't earn much in that cafe where she worked, and she'd been a nice kid.

> *The money might take care of your problem, if you have one, but I rather doubt that you have. The airline is sending me abroad. Goodbye, Jilly. You're a sweet girl and it's been nice knowing you.*

He walked away without conscience. Jilly was young, but she'd known what was going on and she'd get over him, he thought, as he headed back to Cheltenham, where his wife and two kids waited for him.

Distraught, Jilly let herself in. If she'd expected her overnight absence to go unnoticed she was sadly mistaken.

Her stepfather was waiting for her. 'Where have you been all night? Your mother is worried sick about you.'

'I stayed with a friend,' she lied. 'Barbara, from work.'

Grabbing her by the shoulders he shook her back and forth, screaming, 'You liar! You've been with that man, haven't you?'

'Stop it!' she yelled. 'You have no right to treat me like this. I'm not your daughter!' She burst into tears, not from the shaking, but mostly because she'd been jilted by the man she loved.

Sylvia appeared at the top of the stairs, still in her dressing gown and moving slowly. 'What the hell's going on?'

'I'm trying to chastise your daughter,' he shouted. 'She's been out all night, and someone needs to.'

'I fell asleep on Barbara's couch, that's all.'

'Liar!' he scoffed. 'You've been with that man. That pilot!'

'He's gone,' Jilly said, her voice wobbling as she tried to control her misery.

Her mother must have seen what was in her face because she whispered, 'Oh, my poor Jilly!'

As she took a step forward Sylvia's feet went from under her. The next minute she was tumbling head over heels down the stairs, screaming at first, then moaning as she flopped to the bottom.

There was a moment of silence. Then two marbles rolled and bounced down after her. Blood soaked her skirt, and her arm was twisted awkwardly under her.

'Mum!' Jilly whispered in horror, and tore herself from her stepfather's grasp. 'Oh, God!' She turned to her stepfather who was gazing at her, white-faced. 'Go and ring for an ambulance. She's badly hurt. I think she's losing the baby. She might die!'

There came the sound of a door opening upstairs, followed by a gasp. Will's face was a pale moon looking down from the shadows.

'You caused this, you wretch!' she accused him. 'I told you not to play with those marbles on the stairs.'

Willis began to sob. 'I thought I'd put them all away. I must have missed a couple. I didn't do it on purpose, honest.'

'Of course you didn't, dear,' his grandmother said. 'Come to Granny.'

'You will not go to your grandmother, Willis. You will go to your room,' his father snapped. 'I'll deal with you later, after we get Sylvia to hospital.'

When the door slammed after Willis, Christopher picked up the receiver and dialled emergency.

Jilly held her mother's hand. Tears running down her cheeks, she talked softly to her – though Sylvia's eyes remained closed.

The old lady stared at her. 'It wasn't Willis's fault. It was an accident.'

'Do be quiet,' Jilly said savagely. 'It's about time Will faced up to the consequence of his own actions. My mother is badly injured. She might die. Ask yourself, who caused the accident by leaving marbles on the stairs, despite being told not to.'

Sylvia groaned, and her eyelids fluttered open.

'It's all right, Mum,' Jilly said soothingly. 'There's an ambulance on the way.' She could hear the strident clamour of a bell above her panicky heartbeat. Blood soaked into her mother's clothes. *Hurry up and arrive*, she prayed. *I don't want her to die.*

Sylvia's accident pushed Jilly's heartache over Rick to one side. She wasn't allowed to see her until that evening. Her mother looked pale and exhausted. The blue cover on her bed was curiously flat. Her arm was in plaster cast.

'I lost the baby, Jilly,' she said dully. 'It was a little girl. They had to cut me open to see where the bleeding was coming from. She was dead inside me.' Tears sparkled on her cheeks. 'She looked just like you, when you were a baby.'

Jilly slid her arms around her mother and held her tight. 'Perhaps there will be another one.'

'No, Jilly girl. They took away my womb with her. I didn't really want a baby, you know, not until I saw her. Now I'm sorry I thought that way. Still, Chris has got Will and I've got you.'

'His father punished Will when he got back from the hospital. He gave him a good hiding. It was too severe. He used a strap.'

She didn't tell her mother that the beating had been cold-blooded and Willis had begged for mercy. Jilly had intervened, in case his father had killed him.

'He's had enough,' she'd shouted at him. 'The whole street can hear him screaming. If you don't stop it now, I'll fetch a policeman.'

Her stepfather had given her a hard look, then walked away, saying tersely, 'Let this be a lesson to you both.'

The boy's thin back had been criss-crossed with welts, some bloodied. He'd sobbed as she'd covered his wounds with soothing salve. 'I hate him,' he'd said.

'The poor little sod. He didn't leave those marbles there on purpose. He's a hard man to cross, is Chris.' Sylvia hesitated, then shrugged, wincing as she did. 'I should have listened to you in the first place. We were quite comfy in that council place.'

And hard though it was to admit it, Jilly knew she should have listened to her stepfather in the first place. 'Rick and I . . . we're finished,' she said painfully.

Her mother patted her hand. 'I could see it in your face when you came home. He was too old for you, anyway, love. There are plenty more fish in the sea and you're only seventeen. You'll forget him when a better one comes along. Don't take after me . . . learn from your mistakes, Jilly girl.'

The nurse brought her a vase, and Jilly felt like crying as she arranged the flowers she'd brought with her.

There was worse news to come. The next day, the man who'd been lunching with Rick the first time he'd come into the cafe had returned.

'Do you know where Mr Oliver has gone?' she asked him.

'His job here is finished. He's gone back to central office and to his wife and children. If it's anything to do with insurance, I can help you through it.'

'No, it's all right,' she mumbled, feeling sick at the thought that Rick had lied to her all along.

'Do you feel all right, Miss? You're looking a bit pale.'

She drew in a deep breath. 'I'm fine. I just wondered where he was, that's all.'

Jilly couldn't confide her troubles to her mother now. She had enough of her own to cope with. The next evening, she asked her, 'Did they say when you'll be allowed home?'

'Not for a couple of weeks. Then I'm going to have to rest for several weeks. Chris thinks you should hand your notice in and stay home to look after me. I think it's a good idea, if you don't mind. At least I won't have to put up with his horrible mother.'

Her stepfather would think that. Rebellion roiled in Jilly for a moment. If she refused, Grandmother Stainer would get her foot back in the door – and her mother would hate that.

So she nodded. 'I'll give a week's notice on Monday then. It's always quiet after Christmas, so I won't feel so bad about letting my boss down.'

'That's my Jilly.'

When her mother closed her eyes, Jilly kissed her cheek and left.

Ten

... I have very little left to add, except to tell you that I've been happily married to my wife, Patsy, for four years. We have two sons, Ben and Seb. I've enclosed a photograph of us – one of those studio shots where we all have our hair neatly combed and look as though we're on our best behaviour. Our sons, though, are a pair of rogues, and the household usually operates in a state of chaos.

I'm unaware of your family situation, especially with regard to my existence. A colleague of mine, who investigates such matters, and is discreet, assures me that an approach is best made through a third party, so I've decided to do this through a letter addressed directly to your mother. No doubt she will pass it on to you.

I'm curious about my background, and I do hope you'll bring yourself to answer this letter. But I'll understand if you feel unable to rake over these particular ashes, and will not push the issue if you feel you're unable to.

Sincerely,
Neil.

A photograph! Where? Certainly not in the letter. Turning the envelope upside down Jilly frantically shook it. A piece of card slid out to land face down on the floor.

Heart thumping, she picked it up and gazed at it, trying to find the courage to turn it over.

When she did, the impression she got was of Rick Oliver gazing back at her. Her heart skipped a beat or two, then settled down. Neil's eyes were brown like her own, his hair was unruly and dark, too. She traced a fingertip over his nose and his warm smile, wishing it was his skin instead of the impersonal gloss of a photograph. His gaze was direct and open. The children were like him – their features diluted by their mother's looks, which were quietly attractive, rather than pretty. The boys were gazing at their mother, their eyes filled with mischief. Patsy's mouth was quirked into a grin.

Neil had forgotten to say which boy was which, but he'd probably refer to the firstborn first. 'My grandsons, Ben and Seb,' she said out loud, and was filled with an incredible lightness, as the weight of the past fell from her shoulders.

'Yippee!' she yelled and danced madly around the kitchen.

One of the cats stopped grooming itself, one leg held aloft, to stare at her. He offered her a dubious mew.

'You're not supposed to be on the kitchen table,' she told him, advice he ignored until she flicked a towel at him. He jumped down, but the tea towel decapitated one of the deep red chrysanthemums, a Mother's Day offering from her eldest daughter.

She gazed at the photo again. This woman . . . Patsy, wouldn't have been obliged to give her children away. Times had changed, and for the better. Today, an innocent child born outside of marriage wouldn't be greeted with scorn and loathing. Its mother wouldn't be considered unworthy, or unable to care for it, just because she lacked a wedding ring. The child wouldn't be taken away and handed over to somebody else like a parcel.

But Neil wouldn't have been aware of any of those events. He'd been too small, too precious, unaware that the arms he slept in that day – and the last face he saw before closing his eyes – would not be the same face and the same arms when he woke. She couldn't bear the thought that he might have been distressed.

Tears filled her eyes as something else occurred to her. The man in the photograph was not the six-week-old son she'd given away – the baby she'd pined for over nearly three decades. Neil was a man. A man she didn't know, with a family history that was different from the one he would have had with her.

Slipping the missive into her pocket, she took a deep breath, made the tea, added a slice of Alec's favourite fruit cake and carried it out into the conservatory.

She tried to stop her smile coming when he came to take the tray from her. It seemed to be stuck on full beam, yet her eyes were filled with tears.

He scooped a tear from her cheek and gazed at her, concern in his eyes but laughter on his lips. 'I heard you yell. Don't tell me the football pools have come up?'

'How can they when we don't do them? It's something much better – at least, it is for me. I don't know how you'll feel about it.'

He set the tray on the table, kissed the top on her head and said, 'Try me.'

She waited until he was seated, then took the photograph and slid it across to him.

For a moment he looked puzzled, then his eyes cleared and he gazed questioningly at her. 'Honestly now, were you really uncertain of how I'd feel about this?'

She gazed at him. The wetness of her eyes blurred him, made it look as though he was sitting in the rain. She shook her head. 'No, Alec, I wasn't. How could I be, when you came back into my life and made everything begin to make sense again?'

He grinned. 'So . . . I'm still your hero.'

Her hand slid over his. 'You've always been my hero, and always will be.'

'I love you,' he said softly.

Before Sylvia had time to recover from her fall, Will had been packed off to boarding school.

'What about my Saturday job? I was going to ask Mr Cooper to take me on full-time.'

'It's a dead-end job, not a worthwhile career. You've been lazy at school, and this one will make you work harder towards passing your exams.'

Sylvia protested. 'It's a waste of money. Will doesn't even

get average marks. Besides, he's apologized. He didn't do it on purpose, you know. He thought he'd picked all the marbles up.'

'That child you lost was mine as well as yours. I don't think I'll ever forgive him.'

'You know, Chris, you're a miserable old sod, at times,' said Sylvia, who'd long ago given up the fight to be something she wasn't.

But Christopher wouldn't be turned from his course.

Jilly saw Will off. She gave him a bar of chocolate to eat on the train, and a tin with a fruit cake in it for school. 'Your favourite, I made it myself.'

He brightened a bit. 'Thanks, Jilly. You're a good cook.'

'I'm sorry I said all those mean things to you. I was worried about my mother at the time.'

'I know. But anyway, what you said was true. I do need to take responsibility for my actions. It's just . . . nobody has ever allowed me too. I could have sworn I'd picked all those marbles up. Gran helped me two days before. I'm wondering why someone didn't tread on them earlier, since everyone was up and down the stairs the night before. And Gran came in early the next morning with the milk, because she saw that the birds were pecking at the tops to get at it. She came upstairs to use the bathroom.' Jilly's eyes sharpened when he finished. 'Then you came in and all hell broke loose.'

'My mother doesn't blame you for it, you know, Will. And school won't be for ever.'

'The trouble is, I'm not good at anything.' He stood there glumly, suitcase in hand while the train came into the station. 'I'm glad I don't have to live with him any more. I'll miss your mum. She's always nice to me. Tell her I'm sorry.'

'She already knows that. And Will, you're not bad at everything. You just lack confidence in your ability. Work as hard as you can, so you can make something of yourself.'

He surprised her with a kiss on the cheek before he climbed on to the train. He appeared at a window. 'Don't let my dad get you down, Jilly.'

The whistle blew. Doors slammed. Will was a lonely figure at the window as the train moved out of the station.

Jilly resented having to give up her job. She missed going to work, and being a slave to the big house was unrelenting. She also missed her second period. She looked at the money Rick had left for her, then at the address. Remembering its purpose, she shuddered.

But she was desperate. She took a bus into Poole one evening and found the place, a dingy terrace house in a lane not far from the quay, with mean square windows and a doorstep on to the pavement. It still had blackout curtains up, though light shone through the rips. Feeling soiled by just being there, she turned away, retracing her steps.

Her third period didn't arrive, but she couldn't pluck up the courage to tell her mother or go to the doctor.

It was her mother who noticed her changing shape first, coming into her bedroom without knocking when Jilly was getting dressed.

Her glance fell on Jilly's thickening waistline, and sharpened. Harshly, she said, 'You've got a bun in the oven, haven't you?'

Jilly blushed and hung her head in shame.

Her mother slapped her across the face. 'You stupid little fool! Don't you know any better than to get yourself in the family way? Well, as far as I'm concerned, that damned pilot of yours can marry you.'

The slap had shaken Jilly rigid, for it was unexpected. Her mother had never displayed any violence towards her before. 'He can't, he's already married,' she whispered.

An angry breath expelled from her mother. 'You're a slut if you went to bed with a married man.'

Hands on hips, Jilly threw back a retort that came straight from her instinct. 'I didn't know he was married. Besides, you can talk – what about Gary Carstairs and Derek Fowler?'

Kicking the door shut behind her, Sylvia stared hard at her. 'They were just friends.'

'Were they? My father didn't think so. And whenever Derek Fowler visited I was always sent to see a film. I remember coming home early from Girl Guides once, because

I felt sick. The door was locked, and it was ages before you answered it. When you did, both you and he were rumpled, and the bed was messed up.'

'It was messed up before you went out.'

'No, it wasn't. I made it – like I did every morning.'

Sylvia's eyes narrowed. 'Don't you dare say things like that about me in front of Chris. He always thinks the worst of everyone. I'm your mother and I expect some respect from you. It's you we're discussing, and your behaviour. We'll get rid of the pregnancy and pretend it didn't happen.'

'It's illegal . . . and it's dangerous.'

'I know that, but it's worth taking the risk. How far gone are you?'

'It would be me taking the risk, not you.'

'Jilly, what are you saying? See sense. I won't tell Chris about it. Let's just get rid of it, please.'

'Like a piece of rubbish?' One of Jilly's stubborn feelings overcame her. 'I'm going to have the baby.'

'Like hell you are! You're only seventeen.'

'I've already seen someone.' She didn't say that was six weeks previously, when she'd felt particularly desperate. 'I'm nearly four months gone so it can't be done. Look, Mum, I'll be eighteen when the baby is born. I'll be on adult wages, then.'

'And who will look after it while you're working? Can you earn enough to pay rent and support a kid? I hope you're not expecting help from me. I'm disgusted with you.'

Staring at her mother's set face, Jilly's heart sank.

The door swung open, revealing her stepfather. He had a sneer on his face. 'As far as I'm concerned you can pack your bags and get out – right this minute.'

Colour rushed to Sylvia's face. 'D'you have to sneak around like that, Chris? I would have told you, you know.'

'That's not what you said. I don't like deceit.'

'Is there anything you do like?' Sylvia muttered.

Jilly gazed out of the window. 'It's dark and cold, and I've got nowhere to go.'

'I don't care. You can get out of my house, and you needn't bother coming back.'

'At least you can allow her to stay overnight.'

'No. She can get out now.' He turned and walked away.

'Go to Audrey. She does a lot of charity work. Ask her to help you,' Sylvia said, as Jilly took an old suitcase from the wardrobe. 'I'll try and send you some money in a day or two.'

Jilly didn't have much to pack. Alec's tin fitted nicely in the bottom of the case – she wasn't going to leave his bits and pieces for her stepfather to go through and make comment on. And she still had her post office account, which now had thirty-seven pounds tucked away in it.

Her mother was in tears as she followed Jilly down the stairs. 'I don't know what the neighbours will say when they find out.'

Who cares! 'Perhaps they won't find out.'

'I'm so ashamed. They'll all be whispering behind my back. I'll never be able to look them in the eye again.'

What about me, Mum? How d'you think I feel? Jilly kissed her. 'You'll survive, you always do.'

She was wrapped in a hug. 'I'm so ashamed. What will I tell people, Jilly?'

'Nothing. Then they won't know and you won't have to feel ashamed of me,' she said practically. 'Goodbye, Mum. I love you. Look after Johnnie Ray.'

'I will. Let me know what happens, so I don't have to worry about you.'

She couldn't have her mother worrying. 'All right, Mum.'

Jilly realized she wasn't being fair to her mother as the door closed behind her. Plunged into the murky darkness of the porch, her fingers went to the chain around her neck as she took her bearings. It was a long walk to where Audrey lived.

Her hand closed around the shell. The silver was beginning to wear off. It was cheap and tawdry, like the man who'd given it to her. The trouble was, she still wasn't over him, despite the way he'd trampled on her feelings.

'Let's hope he doesn't come back, then, because I don't like being in love, it's too risky,' she said. Tugging the chain and shell from her neck she threw them down the nearest drain and began to head away from the house.

'We're on our own now, baby,' she said. 'And don't ask

me what the future's going to be, because I don't know. At least you've got a warm home for the next few months, which is more than I've got at the moment.'

Audrey's house was not far from her uncle Derek's. It was situated opposite Branksome Woods in an unsealed road full of stones and potholes.

By the time Jilly got there it had gone eight, and she was exhausted.

'I do wish you hadn't brought your troubles to me – not while Auntie Blanche is sick,' Audrey said, and sighed heavily. 'She's dying, you know. Cancer. They don't know how long she's got – six months, perhaps less.'

'I'm sorry about your aunt. Mum said you'd help me because you worked for a doctor, and did charitable works as well. Had I better leave?'

'I worked for a psychologist for a while, to help him out while his office staff was on holiday. I learned such a lot from him. My uncle gets me secretarial jobs from time to time with his colleagues. It gets me out of the house so I can meet people, and it helps keep my hand in.'

Drooping in the hall, Jilly wished Audrey would shut up. 'Oh, I thought you'd meet plenty of people doing charitable work.'

'Don't be silly, dear. I meant the right sort of people. And I'm not going to turn you away, which is nothing to do with charitable work. You happen to be my sister, and I'm pleased you've come to me. Luckily, my husband's in France at the moment. And as it happens, I do know someone who'll be of use to us. She works for the welfare department, and can make arrangements for you. They have homes you can go to, you know. And they'll look after you until the baby is adopted out.'

A yawning hole appeared in Jilly's stomach. 'Adopted out?'

'Of course, dear. There's no alternative, is there? Now, go upstairs and turn left. There's a little room at the end of the corridor that used to be the au pair's – before I dismissed her. She didn't know her place, and was much too familiar, even though my husband didn't think so . . . You can use that room while you're here. There are sheets in the hall cupboard and blankets in the chest at the end of the bed. Do try to stay out of sight if any of my friends come, and especially if Uncle Derek visits. It will save embarrassment if I don't have to fend off awkward questions. Now, off you go, dear.

'Have you had dinner yet?' she called out when Jilly was halfway up the stairs.

Jilly turned and miserably shook her head. 'I'm too tired to eat.'

'Nonsense. Your baby won't be healthy if you don't eat, and you look all in. I'll make something light but filling. A bowl of soup and an omelette. You can go to bed afterwards.' Audrey dropped her facade for a moment. 'I'm sorry you're in trouble, Jilly, really I am. It will be nice having you here for a few days. Adoption is the only solution, you know. A baby born out of wedlock will carry the stigma of its unfortunate birth for the rest of its life. It's not fair to put it through that. Lots of people want to adopt babies, and they go to good homes – not that I'd take one under my own roof, of course. I wouldn't be able to love a baby that wasn't mine.'

'But I want to keep it.'

'It's only natural you should want that. But it's not possible, surely you can see that? Where would you live? How would you afford to bring the child up? And what if you met someone and fell in love? Very few men would marry someone who's . . . well, you know . . . *had another man's baby*. Go on now, dear. Get settled in. Come down to the kitchen when you've finished. We'll eat there.'

Jilly's three weeks with Audrey were testing. Her sister obviously had troubles of her own on her mind. Even so, Audrey managed Jilly's life. She sat in on the interview with the welfare officer. A form was filled in, questions answered, sometimes by Audrey. A medical examination was required.

Audrey kept the indiscretion inside the family and confided in her uncle.

'I'm sorry to see you in such a predicament at your age,' he said. 'You should have made the chap use protection.' He pulled on his rubber gloves. 'Flop your legs open, there's a good girl.' She winced as he slid his fingers inside her, and gazed at her face, chatting while he felt around. 'Good

job we have the National Health Service now, at least you'll
be looked after. If I were you I'd keep this quiet. Adoption
is best for the baby, and best for you. Understand?'

'Yes, sir.'

'Good girl, Jilly. I knew you'd see sense,' he grunted. He
pulled off his gloves and placed them in a bag before throwing
the sheet back over her. Scrupulously, he washed his hands
in the corner basin, then turned back to her. 'You're healthy,
and everything seems to be in order. You can get dressed
now.'

'Would you let my mother know I'm all right?' she said.

A frown touched his brow. 'I'm here in my professional
capacity to provide you with a medical certificate, that's all.
The welfare will take care of everything and keep her
informed.'

'I'm sorry about Mrs Fowler,' Jilly said awkwardly.

His voice became gruff. 'That's kind of you, Jilly.
Sometimes these trials have to be faced. Mrs Fowler has the
best care money can buy. Take care of yourself, my dear.
You'll know better next time, I hope.'

Jilly was washed along by a very determined tide called
Audrey. She couldn't be bothered to argue, since she had no
alternative solution for the dilemma she was in.

When Audrey wasn't telling her what to do, her half-sister
was nervous and twitchy, and fretted constantly about her
aunt's illness.

'Were you happy living with your aunt and uncle, Audrey?'
Jilly asked her one day.

Audrey's eyes widened for a moment, then she smiled.
'Of course. I adored them and so did Peter. I just wish we
could have gone to live with them earlier. They gave us
every comfort. Uncle Derek asked our father if he could
bring us up after our mother died, you know. He agreed, but
then he married your mother and changed his mind. You
know the rest.'

'I know my mother wasn't as bad as you made out.'

Audrey shrugged. 'Before you pass judgement, let me
remind you that you were too young to understand what
went on. We told the truth when questioned, but the lawyer
made it sound much worse than it was. Your mother did

smack us from time to time, and she often left us by ourselves at night, when she went out dancing at the American base. As for that Lieutenant Carstairs . . . whether you believe it or not, your mother *did* have an affair with him. I saw them doing it once. And look at the trouble you've got yourself into, Jilly. I hate to say this, but your pregnancy may have been unconsciously influenced by your mother's behaviour when you were young.'

Jilly managed to stop herself from laughing at Audrey's observation, since she was entirely convinced that her pilot hero had been the one who had influenced her. And how would Audrey feel about her sainted uncle if Jilly told her what she suspected his visits to her mother at the bedsitter were all about?

'Yes, I was happy. Aunt and Uncle were kind, generous and decent. They never raised a finger to hurt us. Not like . . . our father did. He scared me. I'm glad we didn't have to live with him. I don't know how you stood it, Jilly.'

'I had no choice.' She shrugged. 'He's dead now, so he can't hurt anybody.'

'Uncle Derek said he tried to kill you. Is that true?'

Jilly closed her eyes. It was something she didn't want to recall. 'He aimed a gun at me, and could have killed me if he'd wanted to. Then he looked all sad and changed his mind. I feel pity for him, now. He was depressed. And I'm sorry for Mum, too. I think she regrets her present marriage.'

'She's always been the type who jumps in the deep end without thinking things through properly.'

Jilly ignored the snide remark. 'What about you, Audrey, are you happily married?'

'I've achieved everything I ever wanted from life, except I expected to have a baby by now. We're putting it off – my husband wants us to be in a good position to pay for decent schooling.'

'But are you happy?'

Impatiently, Audrey threw at her, 'Why shouldn't I be? Do stop asking stupid questions. Tell me, when did that woman from the welfare say you'll be leaving for London?'

'On Wednesday. They've found me a place in an Anglican home. It's in East Hackney.'

'Oh good. My husband is due to return from France the weekend after.'

'I'm surprised he hasn't phoned you.'

'He did, when you were hanging the washing on the line this morning,' she said shortly.

'You didn't say.'

'Really, Jilly, I find your interest in my business to be quite intrusive at times. I don't have to tell you everything.'

'Sorry,' she muttered.

Audrey nodded. 'I'll drop in on your mother after you've gone, let her know what arrangements have been made.'

Jilly had a distinct impression that any charitable thoughts Audrey had harboured towards her had now reached a state of dehydration. Still, she was grateful for her help.

'I'm sorry to be such a nuisance.'

Audrey hugged her. 'You're not, really you're not, and I'm sorry if you got that impression. Poor you. It came at the wrong time, that's all. I'm a bit fraught.'

A week later, Jilly's train pulled into Waterloo Station, where she was to be met.

It was a late April day. On the way, rain had chased quickly after the sun. It had splattered against the grimy windows as the train had clickety-clacked over the rails. The fields had been full of long grass sprinkled with daisies, violets and prim-roses, arched over with unexpected and elegant rainbows.

The station was high-roofed, soot-streaked, noisy and grey, for the day had left the sun behind and it had settled into rain.

The crowd spilled on to the platform. People hugged, kissed, laughed and jostled each other, or just strode purpose-fully towards the exit. The steam engine panted and breathed out steam, as though it was about to expire from its efforts.

Jilly stood there, undecided, her suitcase clutched in her hand. The crowd pushed past her and thinned. This was where Alec had been born, she thought. The city of London – home to royalty, criminals, spivs and fallen women. Her child would be born here. Already, she liked the place.

Her baby moved inside her, giving a quivering stretch, as if it were a flower unfolding its petals. *You'll be born in the greatest capital city in the world*, she told it. *But not until September. Be patient, as I must be.*

But then, she didn't know how long her patience would have to last.

She headed down the platform, to where two nuns waited.

They smiled at her as she approached. The older one stepped forward and said, 'You must be Jillian Turner. I'm Sister Anne and this is Sister Frances. We knew you'd find us.'

Six weeks later Jilly received a birthday card from her mother for her eighteenth birthday. It had a picture of two kittens playing with a ball of string.

Thinking of you. Have a lovely birthday, her mother had written. *PS. Grandmother Stainer has died.*

There was a ten shilling note enclosed for her.

Eleven

The convent building that was to be Jilly's home for the next few months faced on to a busy road, and was surrounded by a high wall.

'Come along, my dear,' Sister Frances said. 'I'll show you where the dormitory is.'

Jilly was allocated a bed by the window, which overlooked a garden with a large lawn. There was a vegetable garden and fruit trees, as well as evergreen shrubs. Not far from the window was a silver birch.

'Avril, dear,' Sister Frances said to a girl with a well-rounded stomach, 'this is Jillian Turner. Perhaps you'd show her around after she's unpacked? I'll go through her job roster with her after dinner.'

'Job roster?' Jilly said.

'Oh, we have to keep the whole place clean, do the laundry, cook all the meals and look after the garden. Luckily, there are a lot of us. I don't mind. It keeps us occupied and is good exercise. We're allowed to go out in couples on our days off. Sometimes, we take the tube up the West End, or go to the park. On Sundays we go to church. And we go to classes, and such. Or have concerts. It's OK. It stops you from getting bored and keeps your mind off what's ahead,' Avril replied.

'When's your baby due?' Jilly asked.

'Next month. The head hasn't dropped yet, though.'

Jilly wasn't certain what the girl meant by that, but nodded anyway. 'Mine isn't due until September.'

'It will soon come.'

Before she knew it, Jilly had settled into the routine of the home. She wasn't unhappy there, and was better off than some. At least she knew who had fathered her child.

There was one girl, younger than herself, who'd been raped by a gang of boys on her way home from a youth club. Another was carrying the result of incest around inside her.

Most were like Jilly: taken in by some man when they were too young and naive to have learned better.

Jilly obeyed the rules, cheerfully did her share of the chores and cooking, learned from the chatter and behaved herself.

Friendships were fleeting. Avril had her baby, then moved into the mothers' single rooms. Then one day she and her baby were gone. The emptied cot in the nursery was filled with another baby.

The inevitable was rarely mentioned. One long day crawled into another. Jilly moved up the line, learned what having an engaged head meant. August was hot. She felt heavy and lethargic as she went about her tasks. The baby filled every inch of her. Her head began to ache. Her feet swelled. The doctor was called in.

'She has high blood pressure and toxaemia.'

Arrangements were made for her to go into hospital. Jilly found herself on a table, her legs in stirrups and splayed wide.

A doctor came in, followed by a clutch of younger ones. Several pairs of eyes peered over masks. She wanted to die at being exposed so, and gasped with the indignity of cold fingers probing inside her. There was a gush of warm water.

The doctor patted her ankle. 'It shouldn't be long before you go into labour, my dear.'

She was trembling with nerves, uncertain of what lay ahead of her as the nurse took away the wet pad and put a dry one in its place.

Suddenly, Jilly remembered a street party at Blackbriar Caundle; a woman saying to another, 'When I had my first kid it nearly killed me. Thirty-six hours of unrelieved agony. I thought it would never stop.'

When Jilly whimpered, the nurse gazed at her. She was an older woman. 'Has labour started already?'

'I'm scared,' Jilly said.

A cool look enveloped the nurse. 'I imagine you are. It might teach you to be less free with your favours from now on. The doctor wants you to rest, so I'll be giving you a sedative. The first is often a long drawn-out, painful business, and you'll need to conserve your energy.'

An hour later, Jilly was jerked out of her sleep by a groan. It was her own. What followed was nine hours of considerably hard work and almost unendurable pain. She gritted her teeth. She'd endure it, though; she had no choice.

Although she tried not to make a fuss, towards the end she found herself grunting with the effort and groaning with the non-stop pain of the contractions. Soaked through with perspiration, she didn't think she could go on much longer.

Eventually a doctor was called in. 'A couple more nice big pushes,' he said, 'but not until I tell you.' She found the energy to strain with all her might on cue.

'Good, the head has slipped out.'

Then it was over as the body slithered through after the head. She felt deflated, empty and limp. She couldn't stop shaking. Through a grey haze of exhaustion she heard her baby give a warbling cry as air filled his lungs.

'You have a son,' the midwife said.

The sound he made seemed to revitalize Jilly. With the fierceness of a she-wolf, she held out her arms for possession of her infant – and felt love such as she'd never known as she hugged him close against her.

Time might have crawled before. Now it speeded up. Six weeks was all she had. Five in which to give him the best possible start in life. Two weeks in which to wean him from her breast to accept the milk of the cow.

Each day she fell more in love with him. Each day she grew sadder at the thought of losing him.

Four weeks later, when her mother visited, Jilly took baby Rick with her. She didn't know what to say to a mother who'd deserted her when she'd needed her most, but couldn't find the words to punish her for it. 'Hello, Mum.'

Sylvia stepped forward to give her a quick peck. Jilly smelt alcohol on her breath. Her mother looked smart in a new winter coat with a fur collar. She gazed down at Rick. 'Is this the boy?'

Did she think it was a rabbit?

'He looks like you.'

'He looks more like his father.'

'The least said about that wolf, the better. If I knew where to write I'd let his wife know what he did to you.'

Please, no, Jilly thought as her mother took out a packet of cigarettes.

'I thought you'd given up?'

'Stop nagging, I get enough of that from Chris. I like a fag now and again and I'll do as I please.'

'You can't smoke in here, anyway.'

Sylvia shoved the packet back into her bag with an exaggerated sigh. 'I've been talking to that welfare officer.'

Jilly waited.

A secretive smile appeared on her mother's face. 'Aren't you interested in what about?'

Rick opened his eyes, smiled at Jilly then closed them again. His smile clutched at her heart. The pent-up anger Jilly felt towards her mother became evident in the sharpness of her voice. 'Why are you here?'

'Well, if I can't visit my own daughter—'

'I've been here for over six months, and will be leaving in a couple of weeks. Why did you see the welfare?'

'You know I lost my baby? I've been depressed ever since. Chris and I have discussed it. I've persuaded him to let you bring the boy home.'

This was unexpected. Jilly's heart gave a leap, but still she was uneasy as she thought, Why . . . all of a sudden?

'There will be conditions, of course.'

Jilly thought there might be. 'What are they?'

'He'll be brought up as your brother. He'll be *our* baby, Chris's and mine. He'll replace the one we lost.'

Jilly couldn't believe what she was hearing. Her mother regarded Rick as a spare part, a replacement for the baby girl she'd lost. 'The welfare officer agreed to this?'

'We won't tell her. She won't be able to stop you from keeping the baby, as long as there's a responsible adult to help you. We can make our own arrangement after that.'

By *our* arrangement, her mother meant her own.

Jilly had done a lot of thinking while she'd been away from home. Her eyes had been opened. Instantly, she knew that no circumstance would allow her to relinquish her child into that household.

Her son would never be allowed to forget the circumstances of his birth. Her stepfather had agreed to this as a way to punish and control her, and probably her mother, as well. She didn't want her mother taking over her baby's care, either. The thought brought her protective instinct bristling fiercely to the fore. She wasn't a good enough mother . . . she never had been.

Jilly tried to separate her need to protect her son from the need to punish her mother for abandoning her when she'd needed her most. She couldn't. The resentment would always be there, boiling below the surface, whatever excuses Jilly made for her.

If she did what her mother had planned, Rick would be a bone of contention between them, and he'd suffer for it. 'I need to think about it,' she said.

Her mother looked affronted. 'What's there to think about?'

'My baby's future.'

Sylvia raised her voice. 'I'm your own flesh and blood. You shouldn't have to think about it!'

Sometimes blood ties weren't good enough. 'And I'm *his* mother. *His mother!* My baby's not old enough to have a say. He's a person, not a commodity I gave birth to. I have to do what I think is best for him. Not what others think is best for them.'

There was a short silence while Sylvia allowed her daughter's words to sink in. She rose to her feet, clearly annoyed. 'There's nothing more to be said, then, is there? There's gratitude for you.'

This was a time when sleeping dogs were best left undisturbed. 'It was nice to see you, Mum.'

Her mother measured her ironic remark with a glance, and was suddenly an adversary. Her lips were a tight, mean line. 'I can't say the same for you. You look like the tramp you are. I suppose you'll come crawling home in a week or two – expecting us to look after you.'

'I'll try not to inconvenience you.' Jilly tried to hide her hurt, fussing with Rick when he began to whimper. She dashed away the tears in her eyes and sucked in a breath. 'I must go, it's nearly time for his feed.'

'Jilly, I didn't mean it,' her mother whispered. 'I was angry.'

'It doesn't matter.'

Because of the time they'd spent apart, the self-centred streak in her mother was glaringly apparent to Jilly. Sylvia simply didn't consider that other people might have feelings too.

Her mother shrugged. 'Perhaps it's for the best. Out of place, out of mind, eh?'

'As you say.'

Jilly received the inevitable hug, her baby squashed between them. His wail of protest pushed them apart. Her mother didn't waste another glance on her grandson. 'I'm off then. I'm dying to get outside so I can have a fag.'

'I'll be in touch.'

The door opened and closed. Jilly and her son were alone together.

She looked down at him and whispered, 'One day I hope you'll understand that the decision I just made, and any I make in the two weeks we have left together, will be based entirely on the fact that I love you and want you to have a good life.' And so she took the decision that nearly shattered all her carefully built up defences.

Then came the day when she gave him a last kiss to remember her by.

The door closed between them. Parted! Her heart on one side with her son, her body on the other. Don't think. Don't feel. Solid wood between. Her arms too light.

There was a terrible silent scream gathering inside her. Her legs were automatic, one in front of the other as they carried her away, lengthening the distance between the house and herself, then into the car that had been waiting.

What if she went back, took him? She looked back along the road, seeing houses all the same. Windows and porches, chimneys with smoke curling. Faceless. Formless. She felt panic. Which house was her son in?

The car turned the corner. More houses. Houses all the same. Which street? Which suburb?

She found herself at Waterloo Station, case in hand. Her breasts were hard and hurting. In the cloakroom, her image in the mirror startled. She looked normal, as though she still had something left inside her except the yawing chasm of bereavement.

The train whistle blew. The train left the station without her, dragging the reluctant carriages. What had her mother said?

'You'll come crawling back, expecting us to look after you.'

That was another Jilly. Making her way into town she wandered along the pavements and saw a notice chalked on a board. 'Live-in Staff Required.'

'What can you do?' the man asked.

'Anything that's decent, and honest and pays a wage,' she said, because she needed to keep herself busy.

An hour later she was sharing a shabby basement room with an Irish girl who, like herself, was prepared to do anything from waiting on tables to cleaning bedrooms to support herself.

She sent her mother a postcard. 'I have a job in a hotel and will be staying in London for a while.' She added the telephone number where she could be reached, if needed.

She received no reply.

It was December and the weather was hot and humid.

Not that it made much difference what month it was in the north-west of Western Australia, Alec thought. The weather was warmish, hot, or stinking hot, and not much else between. Unless one counted the wet season, of course, when the whole place was a bloody Turkish bath.

Oblivious to the girl beside him, one of two he'd met the night before who were hitchhiking through the area, Alec stared at a stain on the ceiling, which had been left there after the last cyclone.

A small lizard ran up the wall and disappeared into a track. Alec rolled naked out of bed. The springs creaked as he stood.

The girl opened her eyes, groaning as the light hit her. 'Pull down the blind, would you?'

Her mascara had smeared, but her panda eyes went to his genitals and she grinned. So did Alec, because she'd given them quite a work-out the night before.

'I almost wish I was staying longer,' she said. 'Any tea going . . . and some aspirin if you've got some. What was I drinking last night?'

'Tequila sunrise,' he said.

'Sunrise? It put my damned lights out. What's the time?'

'Ten.'

'Christ, my plane leaves at eleven! If I don't catch it I won't be home for Christmas. Can you give me a lift to the airport?'

'Sure, it's only ten minutes away.' He pulled on a clean pair of shorts and a tee-shirt, then slid his feet into a pair of rubber flip-flops.

The girl was pretty, with clear, tanned skin and light brown hair streaked with gold. Her eyes were the colour of honey. As he filled the teapot with water, Alec wished he could remember her name. Emily . . . Elaine . . . Eve?

'Thanks, Adam, you're a lifesaver,' she said, when he took the mug in to her.

He laughed at the connection. 'It's Alec.'

'Sorry.' She sculled the tea then threw the covers back and padded towards the bathroom on long, tanned legs, her buttocks bobbing.

She came back dripping with water, pulling from her back-pack some flimsy bikini pants and a crumpled burnt-orange sun dress that hardly reached to mid-thigh. It stuck to her wet body and his mouth dried as she darted around the room, picking up her bits and pieces to stuff hurriedly into the bag. Her breasts swelled against the material as she dragged a comb through her wet locks. It would be dry in ten minutes.

Catching his eye in the mirror she grinned when she saw him studying her pert backside. 'I'm ready.'

He leered at her. 'So am I.'

'I've got a plane to catch, so get over it,' she said.

Her friend was already at the airport. 'Liz!' she cried out in relief. 'I thought you were going to miss it.'

'Goodbye, Liz, and thanks,' he called out as she walked off without giving him a backward glance.

His ancient station wagon only just made it home from the airport before steam spouted from under the bonnet. It would need a new radiator if he stayed here much longer, and probably a water pump as well.

He left it to cool down while he collected his mail from the tin box nailed to a wooden pole at the end of the garden. He'd finished his two years' country teaching requirement, and was waiting for a letter to inform him if his request for a transfer had been accepted. The pole was riddled with termites and leaning sideways. He carefully straightened it, building a small cairn of rocks at the base to keep it upright.

There was an electricity bill and a letter from England addressed to Alec Frampton Esquire. It was postmarked 12th December 1960.

Esquire? He shook his head; he hadn't thought such old-fashioned language was still in use. It was from a firm of solicitors. Fribble, Jones and August, Solicitors, Lansdowne Road, Bournemouth.

> *Dear Sir,*
>   *It is my unpleasant duty to inform you that your great-uncle, Reginald G Fry, has recently passed away.*
>   *According to his will, apart from a small amount of money left to charity, his entire estate is legated to you, as his next of kin. The estate comprises of . . .*

'Good grief!' Alec said out loud. 'Fry the spy has come up trumps, after all.' Jilly Turner came into his mind. She'd be twenty-one now. Probably married with a couple of kids hanging on to her skirt. He wondered what she looked like, and remembered a pair of large, brown eyes.

A month later, Alec, radiator replaced, headed south. Between him and the city of Perth were a thousand miles of road through bush country that could accurately be described as a furnace in the summer.

It was a mistake. He'd hardly cleared town when the ageing Holden decided to die on him. He left it by the side of the road, steam hissing from its gizzards, and hitched a ride on the nearest truck.

'Goin' far?' the truckie asked.

'England.'

'I don't envy you, the old country will be bloody cold at this time of year. I can take you as far as Geraldton. You can pick up another lift from there.' He turned to his growling companion. 'Shuddup, you drongo, you've already 'ad yer breakfast.'

'Have you got any water to spare?' Alec asked him.

'Can't say I have. Help yourself to a beer from the cooler, though, mate. Pop me one while you're at it, would you? The heat makes you thirsty. It's like a bloody Turkish bath out there.'

When they reached Geraldton eighteen hours later, Alec could hardly stand up. By the time he reached Perth he was suffering from a hangover. He booked into a hotel, drank several gallons of water to hydrate himself, then slept on and off for two days.

Alec then went to a travel agent and bought himself a ticket on a plane going to England two weeks later. He already had an Australian passport, obtained when he'd taken a party of students to Bali on a trip. His bills had been paid and he'd resigned from the education department, receiving in return the requested reference.

The shops were full of summer gear. He found a decent suit and overcoat in a jumble sale and added a couple of hand-knitted pullovers to his haul before sending it all to the cleaners. Off came his beard, his hair was cut. 'Short back and sides,' he said. A mistake: he looked ten years older when the barber had finished.

He rang the solicitors the evening before his departure, advising them he was on his way. He'd been given directions.

'Someone will meet you at the house and hand over possession of it,' a solicitor-ish voice told him.

England, on a winter's day, was colder than he remembered. The wind was bitter as he made his way to Waterloo Station and boarded the train. He felt his skin contract into a shrivelled mass of goose pimples.

Thank God there was hot coffee to be had on the train, though, however awful the taste.

Alec arrived at the house at about four. He was met by Mr Edgar Jones, a balding man with glasses. 'I've had the services connected, and have lit the fire. There's enough coal to last for a few days in the bunker. You'll need to order more, though. The nearest shops are about five minutes away. Turn left at your gate, then turn right at the end of the road. They should serve your needs for tonight, and close at five thirty. There's also a fish and chip shop.'

Alex smiled. 'That will do me for tonight. I'm quite tired after the journey.'

'If you'd just sign for possession of the key, and provide me with identification of course – I'll be off. I can drop you at the shop on my way, if you'd like. As soon as it's convenient, we'll hand over the rest of the estate. In the meantime, there's two hundred pounds in British currency – which I'll also require a receipt for. If you need more before the estate is settled, do give me a call. My card is near your telephone in the hall.'

'Thank you, that was thoughtful of you. I do have traveller's cheques, but not everyone seems to know what to do with them.'

'Quite,' Mr Jones said.

Later that evening, after a feast of battered cod and chips, Alec stretched his legs out towards the fire and opened a bottle of duty-free Scotch.

He gazed at the dancing flames through the glass and relaxed. He hadn't been over the house yet, but the couch let down into a bed and the room was nice and warm. There was a thick green eiderdown in the hall cupboard to wrap himself in when he wanted to sleep.

He turned the radio on to the news that a contraceptive pill for women had gone on sale in Britain. Raising his glass in a salute, he grinned, 'Go girls!'

Fiddling with the dial he came across some music that suited his mellow mood. He switched off the light and cocooned himself in the eiderdown like a mouldy sausage. The fire crackled and shadows leaped. He felt contented, but also . . . His eyes began to droop with fatigue as he wondered if anyone felt as alone as he did tonight.

'This is Radio Luxembourg,' a voice soothed.

He gave a small grin. 'Funny, I thought I was in the UK.'

But Alec knew he must be grateful for small mercies. 'Thank you Great-Uncle Reginald, for giving me somewhere to call home. I'm sorry we never got to meet.' The empty glass slipped from his hand and his head relaxed into the cushions.

Jilly's stepfather died unexpectedly that winter of 1961. After four years she was going home.

'I miss you, Jilly,' her mother had shouted down the telephone. 'We should show a united front at the funeral.'

It was nice to hear her mother's voice. A flood of love had flowed through her, leaving a lump in her throat.

They'd said hard words to one another the last time they'd met, and hadn't communicated since, though Jilly had sent her mother birthday and Christmas cards. She'd missed her, all the same. It was time to make amends.

'How did you get my number?'

'I found a postcard from you in Chris's desk. And your birthday cards to me and Will. He kept them from us. Will's working in a pottery, cleaning up. I've missed you, Jilly girl. You will come home, won't you?'

Jilly had been reluctant. She liked London, and liked her job. Over the last few years she'd worked hard and had earned her independence. A secretarial diploma had seen her promoted to the reception desk. Then she'd completed a course in business studies and had recently been promoted assistant to the manager.

It was hard to hand in her notice. Her boss was disappointed, because he'd helped her to try and better herself.

'I'm sorry,' she said, tears in her eyes. 'I like working here and am truly thankful for all your help. You've been so kind. But my family needs me now.'

'I'll make sure you have a glowing reference, then.' He smiled and patted her hand. 'While I'm the manager there will always be a job for you here. You're a very capable young lady. And Jillian, you should consider running your own business instead of working for a wage. You're a good manager.'

Now the bare, ploughed fields raced past the train window,

both earth and sky sodden with rain. Tree branches were stark skeletons against the sky and chimney pots left scribbles of smoke against a lowering sky. The last time she'd seen this scenery she'd been seventeen, and going in the opposite direction. Her son would turn five later this year, and he'd start school.

Jilly closed her eyes and allowed herself the luxury of imagining a small boy with a satchel on his back. She added a red duffel coat with toggles, so she could pick him out in the crowd – and gave him Rick Oliver's face. He came running from school, grey socks falling around his ankles, a big smile on his face. She opened her arms so he could leap into her hug. Only he ran past her into another woman's arms.

Her eyes opened, her vision shortening to the image of herself in the train window. How pathetic a creature she was. Since Rick Oliver there had never been a man in her life. A furtive sort of love for him still lingered in her heart . . . a persistent shadow . . . a Miss Havisham love, one that harboured revenge for all men because of the transgression of one.

'Ha!' she said out loud.

The man in the seat opposite, middle-aged and bowler-hatted, lowered his paper and stared at her over his spectacles.

She grinned at him. 'Sorry if I startled you. I was thinking out loud . . . about Miss Havisham, of *Great Expectations* fame,' she explained.

He raised an eyebrow, said gently, 'Ah, yes . . . as one does on occasion.'

When she giggled, he smiled and went back to his reading.

Her mother was waiting for Jilly at Westbourne railway station. Her appearance shocked Jilly. She looked older than her years. She'd lost a considerable amount of weight, her skin looked dry and she had puffy bags under her eyes. Black made her appear haggard.

Jilly hugged her tight.

'It's been a long time, Jilly,' Sylvia choked out. 'I've missed you so.' She suddenly burst into tears, then pushed

Jilly to arm's length and smiled. 'God, just look at you, so beautiful, grown-up and smart. Nobody would know that you'd given—' Her mother clapped a hand over her mouth.

—*birth to a bastard*, Jilly finished for her.

'But I don't suppose you want to talk about that. It's wise to put unpleasant things behind you . . . forget them and get on with your life.'

Out of sight, out of mind. Neat theory, only it didn't happen so easily in practice. Abruptly, Jilly changed the subject. 'Have you put me in my old room?'

Her mother nodded. 'Will is about somewhere. He's no trouble. Keeps to himself a lot. His grandmother left Will everything she had. Chris was annoyed, since he thought he was getting it. Anyway, he had her house converted into two flats before she died, and they're rented out.'

It was only a fifteen-minute walk from the station to the house.

'Will!' her mother shouted up the stairs. 'We're home!'

Will came slouching down in a pair of crepe-soled shoes. He wore a knitted black jumper over grey pants.

'You've grown tall,' Jilly said.

Will grinned like a wolf. 'You haven't.'

'It wasn't through lack of trying,' she said with a chuckle.

'Take Jilly's case up, would you Will? I'll make some tea. I expect she could do with a cup.'

Jilly followed him up the stairs. 'What are you doing with yourself these days, except being a landlord?'

'Nuthin' in particular. I'm cleaning up in a pottery since I did my National Service.'

Jilly's cat, Johnnie Ray, was asleep in the middle of her bed. He stared hard at her for a few seconds, then stood up and arched his back, playing casual, as if she'd never been away, but purring hard. She picked him up and stroked him, glad to see him. 'I'm sorry about your father,' she said to Will, because she thought she ought to.

He shrugged, said awkwardly, 'Dad didn't like me much. He was glad when I went away. Said I ought to stay in the services. I didn't fancy it, though. All I did was peel potatoes and onions, and there were too many people telling me what to do all the time.'

'I'm sure that's not true.'

A cynical expression came to his face. 'You know it's true. Dad didn't like anyone, just wanted to control them. Anyway, he wasn't ill or anything. He just went to bed and didn't wake up. The doctor said he had a weak heart and the strain of losing the baby followed by his mother was too much for him. He didn't tell anyone about his weak heart.'

'That was brave of him.'

Will shrugged. 'The funeral is the day after tomorrow. I'm glad you're home, Jilly.'

'Thanks, Will. Let's go down. I'm dying for a cup of tea.'

Her mother handed Jilly a photograph when she went down. It was of Sylvia's wedding to John Turner. Smiling happily. Her mother was of a similar age to Jilly now, and the likeness was marked. 'You might like to have this.'

'I thought all the photographs had burned in the fire?'

'They did. Then I remembered we'd had a professional photograph taken on our wedding day – and the number was on it. The photographer found the negative and made me a copy. I just thought you'd like a photograph of myself and your father.'

'Yes, I would, thanks. You both look so happy.'

'We were then. Funny how things turn out. The damned war affected his brain. I did my best when he came home . . .'

'He didn't think he was my father.'

'I know. He was, though, Jilly. I told you that once before. The trouble with John was he didn't figure things out too well. He allowed Derek Fowler to cheat him. He should have got something out of his first wife's estate. He just didn't go after it – didn't know how to, I suppose. Still, that's all water under the bridge.'

'I'm sorry you lost Chris too.'

'We didn't get on very well towards the end. Even so, it came as a bit of a shock. You get used to living with people, you know. At least he did the right thing by us. Will and I get to share everything, except for the two hundred pounds he left to you. That was a surprise. It's a lot of money, considering all things.'

Jilly was flabbergasted. But was that a small note of resentment in her mother's voice?

'I was thinking of taking in a couple of lodgers. Will doesn't mind, do you, love?'

Will looked from one to the other. 'We won't have to now Jilly's home. You *are* staying, aren't you, Jilly?'

She nodded. 'I was thinking of starting my own business – a little cafe at Canford Cliffs, so I've got a regular clientele of retirees to carry us over the winter. I'm going out to have a look at the area after the funeral. It was kind of your father to leave me that money. It will help finance it, and I hope to get a loan from the bank.'

'Your bicycle's still in the shed,' her mother said.

'I could come with you,' Will said eagerly.

The premises they found were perfect, and situated at the end of a row of shops. The place was already fitted out with glass counter, urns and kitchen equipment. There was an upstairs room where lunches could be served.

Jilly signed the lease and bought the kitchen equipment.

'I'll serve a three-course set lunch each day. Hopefully, I'll build up a clientele of locals. Downstairs will be a tea room. Cakes, scones and sandwiches.'

Jilly scrubbed the place from top to bottom, and was about to paint the walls a misty blue when Will took the paint brush from her hand. 'I'll do it in the evenings for you.'

He also cleaned the windows and hung pretty cream-coloured half curtains for her. She bought cream damask tablecloths at an auction. They added just the note she was trying to achieve. With a school leaver to work in the downstairs cafe, and a home-based pastry cook to keep the cafe supplied with cakes, Jilly opened for business two weeks later.

After the first day she took orders for the lunches, and soon realized she'd have to have two sittings.

'I'll have to hire someone full-time to help out,' she told her mother.

Although used to hard work, Jilly was soon exhausted. The second week she practically crawled into the kitchen at the end of a busy day, to find Will attacking the mountain of dishes, which she still needed to wash before she cycled home.

'I got my driving licence today, and can drive my father's car – so I came to pick you up. I can peel vegetables, keep the premises clean and wash up. And I've bought you a present – a dishwasher. It's to be fitted tomorrow. Not only that, the girl you hired is inexperienced, and needs supervision.'

Will seemed to have noticed more than she'd thought him capable of. 'You wouldn't consider working for me instead, would you?'

He gave a short huff of laughter. 'Better the devil you know than the devil you don't. I've already handed my notice in at the pottery. As they owe me holiday leave I can start here full-time tomorrow.'

'You're a lifesaver, Will,' she said. 'How can I ever repay you?'

'You can teach me the business, that's how.' He threw a tea towel at her. 'Here. I'll wash, you wipe.'

'This is my cafe and I'll give the orders. I'll wipe and you can wash. Got it?'

'Got it,' he said and they began to laugh – something she'd rarely heard him do before.

Twelve

A lec found England bitterly cold after Australia.
The house he'd inherited was a sensible size, though built with a family in mind. He had an Aga installed in the kitchen, one that kept him supplied with hot water while its radiators spread warmth throughout the house. He still lit the open fire in the lounge, though, because he loved watching the flames leap and dance.

He contacted the head office of Barnardo's and requested his medical records, and other items he might need for a résumé, such as school reports.

A month later they sent him what he'd requested, plus an unopened letter someone had written to him. He laughed out loud. It was from Jilly Turner! Her father was dead – Rose Cottage was gone – he'd won a writing contest he couldn't remember entering, with a story about a pilot he could remember. Jilly and her mother had felt proud of him. He smiled at the thought that somebody had thought of him at all.

If Jilly had still been looking after his red tin when the letter had been written, she must have collected it from its hiding place in the tree. A little glow of warmth centred in him and he said softly, 'Good old Jilly.'

Alec applied for three positions – the best of which was at a private boys' school. They required him to pass a written test and appear in front of an interview panel. He found himself facing a board of three professors.

'You're a Barnardo's boy, aren't you, Mr Frampton?'

'Yes, sir. My parents were killed during the war. Barnardo's sent me to Australia, where I was well looked after. My great-uncle helped pay for my education.'

'Your qualifications tell me they did a good job of it between them.'

'Thank you, sir. I'll always be grateful for their help.'

One of the men leant forward. 'Why didn't you stay in the antipodes?'

He gave them the simple answer he thought they'd like to hear. 'Australia is a fine country with a good future ahead of it. But first and foremost I'm British. I also have past connections here that I need to reacquaint myself with.' That connection was so tenuous that he didn't think they'd be interested by being informed that the connection was a small girl with pigtails and a red Oxo tin.

A bit of throat-clearing went on as the three men looked at each other. One of them nodded approvingly.

'We have another candidate to interview. However, you have an honours degree, and it's possible we may offer you a position as a substitute master. A permanent position will not be opening up until the end of the school year, or when Mr Colfax retires, whichever is sooner. We'll inform you of the outcome of this interview within a day or two.'

Alec tried not to grin. The job was his, and they were covering their arses. Colfax would retire as soon as Alec had proved he could perform in front of the class.

He rose to his feet. 'Thank you, sir. I'd appreciate that.'

The man frowned. 'You're not married, I see, Mr Frampton.'

'No, sir. I've been too busy studying to meet the right girl yet.'

'When you do, marry her. The parents like their teachers to be settled and established. It sets the boys a good example.'

'Yes, sir.'

And what could be more settled and established than his great-uncle's staid, but well-cared-for Austin? he thought as he drove away.

The next weekend, with the frost crystallized on the grass, Alec decided to go for a drive. He found himself in Blackbriar Caundle.

Cruising up and down the street, he passed the mock-Tudor house that had grown out of the Turners' old cottage. It stuck out like a sore thumb, red-brick, half-timbered and with diamond-shaped windowpanes. A red sports car was parked in the front. Thank God this monstrosity was isolated from the rest of the village.

'William Shakespeare would turn in his grave,' he said.

The pub beckoned. The same publican stood behind the bar, twenty years older and a great deal fatter. He didn't recognize Alec as he swiped a cloth over the bar. 'What can I get you, sir?'

'I'll have a lager.'

'There's no call for that German muck around here. There's bitter, light or dark ale. Pint or half?'

'Half of light. Do you do lunches?'

'We can manage a ploughman's lunch.' When Alec nodded, the publican bawled out, 'One ploughman's, Maisie.'

'Do you know what happened to the Turners?' Alec asked.

'The Turners . . . They've been gone ten years or more – a writer lives there now. They built a fancy house on the site after the old cottage burnt down. It shouldn't have been allowed, a house like that. It looks out of place. All la-di-da, and entertains a lot, the new owner does.'

'The Turners?' Alec reminded him gently.

'Oh, them. They got offered a council house after the fire, I hear.'

'I've got a feeling that Turner woman married again,' Maisie said, waddling through with his lunch. 'She used to like the American soldiers. Friends of yours, were they?'

'More like acquaintances,' he said, reluctant to satisfy her curiosity. 'I thought I'd look them up while I was passing through.'

'Your best bet would be that doctor relative of theirs. Fowler, I think his name was. He must be retired by now.' The woman lost interest and turned away, shuffling off in manky grey slippers that resembled dead rats.

While Alec ate his crusty roll, a pile of pickled onions and a slab of Cheddar cheese the size of a paving stone, he gazed at the pilot's seat and propeller mounted on the wall. His eyes sharpened when he saw the framed newspaper account. A photograph of himself and Jilly had been in the original report. They'd been famous for a while, smirking with the pride of being singled out from their fellow students.

'1944,' the publican said, noticing his interest. 'A spitfire came down in the woods and caught fire. I managed to get the pilot out before the plane went up. A nice young man, he was.'

'Very brave of you,' Alec said, robbed of breath by the blatant lie. 'I'm surprised you managed to get the seat out intact before it was burnt. Did they award you a medal?'

'Zackerly what I arsed 'im,' said an old man at the bar. 'If they did, we ain't seed it yet.'

Burns looked disconcerted. 'The seat worked loose in the crash, didn't it? And I didn't need no medal, nor no thanks since I was doing my best for the war effort. I was lucky I didn't go up with it, as a matter of fact. It were a close thing. That pilot did England proud in her time of need, though.'

'I'm sure he did,' Alec said sincerely.

Donald Burns abruptly changed the subject. 'You might like to buy a postcard of the pub. I had them printed especially for the tourist trade.'

About ten years previously, judging by their condition, thought Alec, buying one for old times' sake. He'd just shoved it in his pocket when the door slammed open and two young women, broad of face and bum, walked in. Alec cringed when they shouted out in a raucous duet, 'Two pints of your best bitter, landlord.'

'I thought I told you Crutchly wenches not to come in here with your boots on at lunchtime? You stink the place out,' Burns grumbled.

The women gazed at each other and laughed. 'It would stink a lot more if we took them off. We haven't changed our socks in a week.'

'My Maisie is getting too old to clean cow shite off the floor. 'Sides, it puts my passing trade off.'

Their glances fell on Alex. 'That's what visitors come here for innit – country air? Trouble is, most of 'em don't know the difference between a gust of wind and a good fart.'

I know a couple of weasels when I see them, Alec thought.

Recognition came into the eyes of Rosemary and she screwed them into a narrow, unpleasant scrutiny of him. 'Don't I know you?'

'I shouldn't imagine so.' Alec headed for the door. 'I'm from the Ministry of Agriculture.'

'Be that so, then?' Martha said politely. 'I hope you don't be visiting us, since we don't be at home just now.'

'Then I won't expect anyone to answer the door when I knock.'

'The hell 'ee's from the ministry! Don't 'ee recognize 'im, Martha? It be that evacuee from London, Smart Alec 'is name was. What's he skulking around here for? Hey you,' she bawled when he reached the door. 'It's Smart Alec, isn't it? You come back 'ere, I want a word with 'ee!'

Alec pretended not to hear, and, laughing to himself, closed the pub door behind him and headed for the car.

The pub door opened and Rosemary came out, Martha behind her. Alec cursed when the car wouldn't start. Luckily, the bonnet was pointing downhill.

'They'll rub our noses in cowcake if they catch us,' he warned the stately Austin as he released the hand brake. The engine gave a stricken cough. Firing before he reached the bottom of the hill, it lurched forward as he put his foot down.

'You little beauty!' he said, and forked his fingers at the Crutchlys.

When Alec arrived home he went through the phone book. There were several Fowlers – none of whom professed to know Jilly Turner. There were several Turners, too. He rang them all. None of them owned Jilly.

Darkness came in swiftly, before the day had really spent itself. He put the book aside and turned on the TV set standing in the corner, moving the aerial around until the snow cleared from the screen.

He watched *Maigret* through the hatch leading into the kitchen, while he cooked a couple of lamb chops, chips and baked beans. Feeling oddly unsettled when he finished his meal, he switched the television off, drew the postcard from his pocket and wrote:

> *Dear Jilly,*
>
> *I'm back in England. It was inevitable that I should go back to Blackbriar Caundle. The Crutchly sisters were waiting for me. Don't laugh! As always I had to run hell for leather to escape their clutches.*

Remember them? Remember this place? Remember me?
 Your friend,
 Smart Alec.

Alec placed it with the other letters he'd written to Jilly. Perhaps he should have stayed in Australia, not pursued this particular dream. However much the thought of his early childhood had nurtured him while he was growing up, he was aware that the past was something he couldn't possibly have back. It had remained behind when he'd gone into the orphanage, as if his roots had been cut off when he'd been transplanted.

But a tenuous thread of him had remained planted here, and Jilly Turner had kept it alive.

And now he was in the position to settle down. The great-uncle he couldn't remember ever meeting had given him a home and a bank balance. And he'd just been offered a position too good to turn down. He should settle in one place now – eventually he'd belong.

Why did he need to find Jilly Turner? Perhaps he should have cut himself adrift from her long before. So far his quest had proved a disappointment, as Jilly well might prove to be. She might have moved away . . . married, changed her name? *Died* . . .

And she might not have.

Alec was dogged by nature. She was here somewhere near. He could almost smell her.

Why did he need her? he asked himself

He answered himself firmly: She's my only link to the past, that's why. He needed the reassurance of seeing her.

Thirteen

25th August 1985

Dear Neil,

Thank you for your most welcome letter. You cannot possibly know the feeling of relief, and the joy I felt at just knowing you are well, and happy.

By now, I imagine you might have given up the thought of ever hearing from me. I do apologize for not writing sooner. I've only just received your letter, which I discovered amongst my mother's effects – she died three months ago.

Most people call me Jilly, and I'd be pleased if you would too. I realize how difficult it was for you to write to me. It's not so hard for me to write back since I remember you quite clearly – how could I not? You were too young when we parted to retain any memories of me. No doubt you have changed. At least, I would hope so! There is no need for secrecy to be maintained in this matter. My husband has always known about you – indeed, he knew your father. Both of us were acquainted with him at a young age. It seems odd to confess this now. We first met him during the war when we rescued him from a crashed aircraft. He became a hero to both my husband and myself. Your father was a hero in the greatest sense of the word, since he took part in the Battle of Britain at the age of eighteen.

Although I didn't name him on your birth certificate, I can tell you quite positively that his name is Richard Oliver. I was seventeen when we met for the second time. I didn't know then, that he was a married man

*with children. He left town when he became aware of
my condition – and I have not seen or heard anything
of him since. You look very much like him.*

*Our two daughters were told of your existence when
they reached their teenage years, and will be excited
and intrigued when I tell them you've made contact.*

*Dearest Neil, how strange, though, that you should
live in Western Australia, when my husband spent much
of his youth there. Indeed, he was educated there and
coincidentally, you both studied at the same university
and have the same degree.*

Let me tell you a little about Alec . . .

Her beloved husband, her best friend and lover. Her clever,
funny Alec, a man she still adored after all these years together.

He'd come back into her life again early in the August of
1961, during a wet and windy bank holiday . . .

Alec found Jilly unexpectedly, and when he wasn't looking.

'Jilly's Kitchen. Lunches and Teas' the sign above the cafe
stated in gold lettering on maroon.

Surely not *his* Jilly? There must be a thousand women
who answered to the name, Alec thought as his stomach
twisted into a knot of excitement.

Inside, it was a discreet, classy place, with cream tablecloths and curtains. The bell gave a melodic golden chime
rather than a chrome tinkle when he entered.

A polite young man took his order. His hair was slicked
with Brylcreem into the popular Tony Curtis style and he
wore a chef's jacket.

Alec recognized Jilly straight away when she appeared to
greet some people who'd come in after him. She hadn't
grown very tall, but she was neatly made, and her brown
hair curled about her face in that unruly way it always had.
Her eyes were just as large, and just as brown as he remembered them and she had a ready smile for what must be her
regulars.

'Good morning, Mrs Harris. Your usual table is ready for
you . . . Ah, Reverend Godfrey. Mrs Godfrey is not with you
today, I see. She's well, I hope?'

And Reverend Godfrey smiling beatifically at her. 'Her arthritis is playing up today. It's the damp weather. She's asked me to take her home one of those éclairs. And how are you this morning, Miss Turner?'

So, she wasn't married. For some reason Alec felt both light-headed and relieved by the thought.

'I'll make sure an éclair is put aside for her. I hope she soon feels more comfortable.'

Alec didn't introduce himself, but hid behind a newspaper and observed her covertly.

He enjoyed watching her flit about, and managed to catch her eye now and again without giving her a clue as to who he was. She'd smiled at him once – then offered him an odd, puzzled glance. There had been a cryptic glint in her eyes, as if her memory was working overtime.

Alec hadn't considered what he'd do when he discovered Jilly's whereabouts. Now, he wanted to surprise her.

He'd just got his plan figured out when the young man approached and began to clear his tea things away.

'Was there anything else, sir?' he said, his pencil hovering over the docket.

Jilly watched him go. 'He's got an odd accent. American, I think,' Will thought to pass on to her.

There had been something familiar about the smile he'd offered her, though. She didn't have time for men in her life.

'I think you've made another conquest, I bet he'll be back,' Will whispered to her.

'He's not my type. He looked too academic.'

'He was certainly no beatnik,' said Will, who had definite ideas on male fashion since he'd sacrificed his Teddy Boy look to National Service when he'd been eighteen. He now leant towards the masculine jeans and leather-jacketed look. 'How do you know what your type is when you never go out with anybody?'

'I can't be bothered.'

At the cafe the next morning, Will handed her a package.

'What is it?'

'How do I know? It was pushed through the shop letter

box. It has your name on it.' Jilly turned it over. 'Courtesy of Fry the spy' was written on it. She stared at it, uncomprehendingly for a moment, then her heart gave an almighty lurch.

'Oh, my God!' Giving a laugh she tore the bag from the package and picked up the postcard on top. It was a picture of a man and woman standing on the steps of a country pub. It looked like the one at Blackbriar Caundle. It was!

She turned it over. On the back was scrawled: 'Remember them? Remember this place? Remember me? . . . your friend, Smart Alec.'

Whooping with laughter, Jilly collapsed into the nearest chair, feeling as though she were smiling all over. No, not smiling – damn it, she was laughing! It streamed from her as everything fell into place. She hiccuped, 'I'll be . . . damned. It's from . . . Alec . . . Frampton.'

Will grinned at her. 'Who the hell is Alec Frampton?'

Who indeed? She looked at the door every time it opened that day, expecting him to show up. But the bank holiday was over, and he probably had a job to go to.

He'd left no clues in the package. No address or phone number. She couldn't find him in the phone book. How infuriating he was!

She read his letters to her over and over, was touched by them, shedding tears at the sense of yearning and loneliness they conveyed. This was the vulnerable Alec that she'd never really known – and he'd shown her that side of him in the letters. She placed the magpie feather in her hair. How well he'd done for himself, though. He'd become a teacher, as he'd planned to.

She fetched the red tin from its hiding place and tipped the contents on the bed. She gazed at the picture of Rick Oliver and her heart gave a little twist. The son they'd created between them would be five years old this month – and Rick didn't even know of his existence. She'd been nothing more than a conquest to him, discarded lightly when the time came.

The surge of anger she felt was quickly squashed. The emotion regarding her affair and its outcome was still too raw. If she allowed herself to think about it, anger and despair roiled like hot lava inside her chest and she wanted to die with the grief she felt at losing her son. It was bottled up inside her and hurt like hell when she allowed it to take over.

She was tempted to throw the picture of Rick Oliver away, but she couldn't. He was part of Alec's life as well as her own. Alec's life was inside this tin she'd looked after while he'd been away. It was little enough. She mustn't rob him of it.

Fry the spy came into her mind. Reginald, his name had been. He would probably have been on the telephone, though might not be if he'd really been a spy. She grinned as she went downstairs and pulled out the telephone book. Her finger went down the column of names, then stopped. She dialled the number, her fingers tripping over each other.

'Who are you ringing?' Sylvia asked her.

Will was passing through the hall. 'Jilly's got a boyfriend.'

Her mother's voice was slurred. 'Who is it, our Jilly? Do I know him? Be careful, love, you know what happened last time.'

Jilly's happiness was replaced by resentment. 'It's nobody, Mum, just a friend.'

Nobody and everybody, she thought as the phone began ringing at the other end. It had a hollow sound to it, as though it was ringing in an empty house.

Perhaps he didn't live there. About to hang up, she was startled by a voice, deeper than expected, and slightly out of breath. 'Alec Frampton speaking.'

Tears filled her throat and she couldn't answer. But she didn't have to. After a few moments his voice came again, much softer. 'Jilly . . . Jilly Turner? I know it's you. Speak to me. I've just sprinted up the path to pick up this call.'

'Damn you, Alec Frampton!' she scolded. 'You've made me cry with your letters. Typical of you to sneak back into my life and pretend to be someone else, too. You couldn't spy on a dead donkey, and you deserve to be eaten alive by the Crutchly girls.'

'God forbid, but I knew you'd figure it out and be pleased to see me,' he said, his voice filled with laughter. 'When can we meet?'

'Right this minute. You can come over for dinner.' She gave him the address, said, 'Seven thirty. Don't be late.'

'Since when have you been so bossy—' he was saying as she hung up.

Jilly had left a casserole already cooked, which just needed heating up. While she peeled the vegetables and made dumplings, Will made an apple pie. He was turning into a good cook.

'Custard or cream?' he said. 'He looked like a custard type to me.'

'Custard it is, then.'

'I'll finish up. You should go and get a bath. He'll be here in half an hour.'

'He's only a friend.' She glared at him in case he thought differently.

He tossed her a grin. 'All right . . . if you say so.'

She dashed upstairs, coming down twenty minutes later dressed in a comfortable lime-green sweater over denim jeans.

'Cute,' Will said. 'I could fancy you in that outfit myself.'

'Don't get too cheeky, Willis Stainer. Remember, I'm your boss.'

He leaned forward and kissed her cheek. 'Don't worry, boss. I like my women blonde and stacked, like Marilyn Monroe.'

She laughed. 'You and almost every other man in town. Get lost now, Will. I don't want you hanging around while I say hello to him.'

She saw Alec's shadow on the glass at the door before the bell rang and threw the door open, her eyes registering the grey, rainy evening behind him. 'What took you so long? Come in.'

He grinned. Took one step forward . . . two.

'Alec,' she breathed, feeling more alive than she had in months. 'It's been such a long time.' She couldn't stop grinning at him.

Unexpectedly he swept her up in his arms and twirled her round before setting her on her feet again, her sweater rumpled at the waist. 'Jilly Turner. You've grown up.'

Thank God he didn't know exactly how grown-up she'd been! 'How can I remain dignified when you do that?'

'Why should you want to be dignified?' He mussed her

carefully arranged hair with his hand, then took off his camel-
coloured duffel coat and hung it on the hallstand.

She kicked the door shut and pulled the green checked
scarf from his neck, draping it on top of the coat. Intense
grey eyes gazed into hers. 'How did you get to be so incred-
ibly lovely?'

Alec was tall, well-muscled and handsome in an untidy,
rakish sort of way. His approach stole her breath away. His
smile had a rather devastating effect on her, too. She turned
pink, turned to jelly and turned away, in case he got the
wrong idea. 'Come through and say hello to my mother, and
to my stepbrother.'

Sylvia was in her usual state – not exactly drunk, but not
exactly sober, either. She would be better after she'd eaten
her dinner. Jilly couldn't stop her mother from drinking,
though so far she hadn't tried. She just wished her mother
would find herself a new interest in life – and a job perhaps.
It wasn't as if she was old.

There was tension between them now. Her mother was
often irritable with her, and Jilly had bitten her tongue on
many occasions. Resentment never seemed to be far from
the surface – as if the novelty of Jilly being back home had
worn off.

'Do you remember Alec Frampton, Mum?'

In the gracious, lady-of-the-manor mood that drink always
seemed to bestow on her, Sylvia offered Alec a rather smug
smile that stretched her mouth without showing her teeth.
She said with careful enunciation, 'Of course. How lovely
to see you again, Alec. I thought you lived in New
Zealand . . . or was it New Guinea?'

Jilly offered him an apologetic smile and a shrug. 'Neither,
Mum. You know very well that Alec was sent to Australia by
the orphanage after his parents died. Now he's come home.'

'Oh, you're *that* Alec Frampton! The evacuee lad who
was staying at the farm.' She gave a husky laugh. 'Poor you,
Alec, the Crutchlys were so common. Jilly's father died, you
know. And more recently, Will's father. Such tragedy in my
life to be widowed twice.' She smiled sweetly at Will. 'I
lost a child as well. Ah well, I was obviously not meant to
have another child, was I, Jilly?'

Having dealt a double barb, Sylvia smiled when Jilly exchanged a glance with Will. 'Would you like a sherry before dinner, Alec? Will, stop being so long-faced and fetch our guest a sherry, would you? Fill my glass up too, dear.'

Will rose to his feet and took her glass.

Jilly finished mentally counting to ten. 'You've met my stepbrother at the cafe. Will, meet Alec Frampton. We played together when we were small.'

Alec held out his hand. 'It's nice to meet you, Will.'

After a moment of hesitation, Will took it. 'I'm pleased to meet you, too, Alec. I think the world of Jilly.'

They exchanged one of those looks men reserve for first meetings – looks only they seem to understand the significance of. Alec smiled. 'As it happens, so do I. I always have.'

Oh, for goodness' sake! Jilly thought. Let's not have any mental headbutting nonsense tonight, else I'll bang your heads together physically. She giggled at the thought. Alec gazed at her and chuckled, as if he'd read her mind.

'The sherry,' Sylvia said impatiently. 'Don't keep our guest waiting, Will.'

The evening was pleasant, apart from a slight undercurrent of tension. The food turned out perfectly. Afterwards, Sylvia flirted with Alec. It was as if she was jealous that her daughter was the focus of Alec's attention. Jilly was embarrassed for Alec, and annoyed with her mother. Alec took it in his stride, though, and was perfectly natural and polite.

Will eventually stepped in. 'I expect Alec and Jilly want to talk privately after all this time. I put a match to the fire in the sitting room earlier. It smells a bit damp in there, but the fire will make it feel more cheery. Mum, you're usually watching the TV in the living room by this time. I'll make you some tea.'

The sitting room had warmed up. Jilly didn't apologize for her mother's behaviour. With his looks, Alec was probably used to women flirting with him. She switched on the lamps, then opening the sideboard she brought out his red tin and placed it on his lap. 'Yours, I believe, Alec.'

He gazed at it for a few seconds, several emotions playing on his face, then he gave her a slow, tentative smile. 'You kept it then.'

The intimacy of his smile startled her. The memories of her childhood friendship with him came rushing back. Like warm wine in the mouth, the bouquet of that smile exploded on her palate. She knew exactly what he was thinking and feeling. As for herself, she felt unaccountably teary-eyed. 'Did you think I wouldn't?'

'I thought you'd guard it with your life, and you did. Why didn't you disappoint me, Jilly?'

'Because everyone else in your life did, even though they couldn't help dying. You were so alone, Alec. You needed to believe in someone else, apart from yourself.'

He raised an eyebrow. 'Thanks, Dr Freud.'

'My pleasure. You shouldn't have asked if you didn't want the truth. Aren't you going to open it?'

She sensed the reluctance in him, wished she hadn't pushed him. 'Would you like me to keep it until you're ready? Perhaps it's something better done in private.'

'You might be right. I'll take it home with me. It's my burden now.'

'We all have one.' He'd inflicted a tiny wound in her heart. After all this time, when she wanted so desperately to be trusted with his memories, he was not willing to share them with her.

Then he surprised her by saying, 'I can't look in it without you being there. We'll open it together, when you visit me.'

She wanted to join him on the couch and hug him tight. Instead, she turned the radio on and took the chair opposite him.

'Nice,' he said when the sound of George Shearing filled the room, and he leaned back against the cushions. 'How long have you been in the catering business?'

'Six months with my own cafe. It's hard work, but we're beginning to show a profit.' She hitched in a breath. 'I lived in London for several years. While I was there I trained in a hotel, and did a business course at night. I worked my way up to be assistant to the manager and I came home after Will's father died.'

He gave her a sharp look, but didn't probe further except to remark, 'You were young to be living alone in London.'

'Yes . . . but it was a live-in position, so I was quite safe.

I don't know what I'd do without Will in the cafe,' she said. 'He's very competent, but he could do better for himself if he tried.'

'Send him to night school, then give him more responsibility. He seems to be the sort of young man who will thrive on it if it's offered. He needs to prove his worth to himself.'

Alec was perceptive. Jilly had never really regarded Will as being a man. But since he was only a year or so younger than herself, she supposed he was. 'Now who's being Dr Freud? I take it you're teaching.'

His smile lit up his face. 'I love it. I managed to get a relief position at a good school, and have just been appointed to a permanent position as science and maths master.'

She made a face. 'The most I can do is manage my books, though sometimes the columns don't add up as they should and Will has to check them for me.'

'You should send Will to do a bookkeeping course, then. He can lighten the load for you.'

Will knocked at the door and brought the coffee tray in. He placed it on the table between them. 'I'm going to the flicks to see *The Guns of Navarone* and will be back about eleven thirty. Goodnight, Alec. I hope we'll meet again.'

'I'm sure we shall, Will. Enjoy the film.'

'I've got something to tell you,' Alec said after Will had gone.

'What is it?'

'My great-uncle wasn't a spy at all. He was an accountant who managed a bank branch.'

Jilly giggled. 'How disappointing. Perhaps he was a spy in his spare time. Thanks for the letters. They made me laugh.' She hesitated before saying, 'And they made me cry. I often thought of you, and wondered what you were doing. Did you receive my letter?'

'Yes – shortly after I got back to England. I was touched by it.' Leaning forward he kissed her cheek. 'Thank you for thinking of me. You've got no idea what that meant to me.'

Johnnie Ray scratched at the door. She let him in and he stretched out on the half oval rug in front of the fire and purred loudly.

'How are the twins?' Alec asked.

'Both are married. We don't see much of them. They went to live with their aunt and uncle shortly after our father came home from the war. Dr Fowler said my father wasn't fit to look after them. He was right, in a way, but it wasn't my father's fault.' Anger stabbed sharply at her. 'He was mentally ill, you see . . . that's how the cottage burnt down.' She shuddered. 'My father killed himself . . . and he was going to kill me. He changed his mind though.' She clapped a hand over her mouth. 'I'm sorry . . . I didn't mean . . . I don't usually talk about it.'

He looked horrified. 'Christ, Jilly! How bloody terrible for you. Thank goodness he didn't hurt you!'

'Tell me about the orphanage,' she said, abruptly changing the subject. What if her son hadn't been adopted into a good home, but brought up in an orphanage instead? She needed to know. 'Did you miss having a mother – your real mother?'

He looked surprised. 'I can't remember my real mother. What you can't recall, you tend not to miss.'

It wasn't the answer she'd wanted from him. She'd wanted him to say that the blood tie between mother and son had been too strong to be broken. Jilly had felt her son's heart beating strongly inside her own for the last five years. If they ever met on the street in the years to come, she wanted to be told that they'd know each other for what they were – mother and son.

'What is it, Jilly? Have I said something to upset you?'

It wasn't his fault. Alec was unexpected. She hadn't imagined he'd grow up to be so self-assured, or to find herself so in tune with him, as if they belonged together. Things had become too intimate between them on a mental level, too soon. He made her feel vulnerable again.

She poured his coffee in silence, and her eyes came up to his. 'Cream?' she said, all at once putting him back in his role of guest.

If she told him about her son now he'd be embarrassed, because he'd set the tone of the evening with his open friendliness, and had disarmed them all. She had to raise barriers, put some space between them.

She glanced at her watch. 'No, of course I'm not upset.

I must apologize. I shouldn't have asked you such an awful and personal question. I guess I'm a bit tired.'

Alec swallowed his coffee and stood up, a wry smile on his face. 'I should have realized I was keeping you up.'

Suddenly, she didn't want him to leave and regretted her manoeuvre. 'No, you're not. You don't have to leave yet.'

'I have work to go to tomorrow, too.' He picked up the tin. 'Thanks for this, Jilly.'

She followed him into the hall. 'Will I see you again?'

'Do you want to?' he said evenly.

'Don't be so exasperating, Alec. Didn't I just say so?'

'Reading between the lines is not one of my skills.'

'Coming up with the wrong answer is, though. Damn you then, Alec. Go . . . and forget all about me. But I warn you, if you do, I'm going to charge you storage for that tin.'

He laughed and kissed her on the end of the nose. 'Can you take Sunday off?'

'We close on Sundays, though we usually give the cafe a good scrub through in the morning. I'll be free in the afternoon.'

'Good. I'll pick you up and we'll go for a drive. I'll show you where I work and where I live, if you're interested. And I'll open the tin. I always felt brave when you were with me.'

It's me who will need to be brave this time, Jilly thought. She didn't want to lose Alec's friendship now they'd finally found each other again – but she wasn't going to deceive him, either.

'I like your Alec,' Will said, when he came in and they were drinking tea together in the kitchen. 'You should trust him.'

Jilly didn't pretend she didn't know what he was talking about. But it was none of Will's business and she wasn't going to discuss it with him. She rinsed her cup, dried it and hung it back on its hook. 'He's not my Alec. Goodnight, Will.'

'Ouch!' he said, as she walked off.

Jilly looked in on her mother, who lay on her back, gently snoring. A glass and the remains of a bottle of sherry stood on her table.

'You're a young woman still. You should stop drinking and take an interest in living.' Gently she kissed her cheek. 'I do love you, Mum, but sometimes I don't like you very much.'

'How long has my mother been drinking to excess?' Jilly asked Will the next morning.

'Since she lost the baby, I think.'

'You pander to her too much.'

'You know why. What happened to her was my fault and I feel responsible. If I hadn't put those marbles on the stairs she wouldn't have fallen and lost the baby. But whatever you thought, I didn't play with those marbles on the stairs to hurt her. I did it because the noise annoyed my father.'

Silence fell between them, then Jilly said quietly, 'I'm sorry I misjudged you. Let me put something to you, Will. Ask yourself why nobody else trod on those marbles. Could it be that they weren't there the night before?'

'Then how did they get there?'

'I think your grandmother put them there on the morning my mother fell. She hated my mother from the minute they met.'

The colour drained from Will's face. 'But Dad said it was my fault—'

She had a sudden horrifying memory of the beating Will had been subjected to. 'How would he know? She'd hardly have told him what she'd done.'

'You mean, it wasn't my fault?'

'I very much doubt it. The thing is, Will, my mother always wants to be the centre of attention. That's her nature. She's punishing you for what happened because she feels guilty. The more you do for her the more she'll demand of you. The worst thing your father could have done to her was to make her leave her job. She needs to be encouraged to find another, not to hang around here with a bottle in her hand and with only you and me for company.'

'Perhaps she could work in the cafe.'

'Definitely not,' Jilly said flatly. 'We've worked hard to get the cafe established, and we have our own lives to lead. I won't have her interfering. We'll be doing her a favour if we just stop waiting on her hand and foot, and encourage her to get an interest outside the home.'

'How can we do that?'

'I'll tell her to cook her own evening meal to start with . . . not wait for us to come home and do it for her, since we can eat at work.'

'What if she refuses?'

'Then she can go without. You're going to be busy in the evenings, soon. I'm going to send you to evening class to do a bookkeeping course. After that, you can do a business management course. There will be a pay raise with each qualification you earn.'

He smiled. 'What will I do with a business management course?'

'Manage the cafe when I'm not there, of course. We need regular time off, and will have to take holidays now and again. I'm tossing up between taking another girl on, or employing a cook. What do you think?'

'A girl will be cheaper. I'll be happy to take over the cooking. I enjoy it. I was thinking. If we bought a freezer I could cook the main dishes up in advance, and some of the puddings. We could also use frozen vegetables. It would save time.'

It was a good idea. 'Where would we put a freezer? We can hardly move in the cafe kitchen as it is.'

'Here, in the house. We'd simply take the trays of food in and heat them up. We could buy a small van.'

'Whoa!' she said. 'I can't afford all these things.'

'I can . . . you could make me a junior partner, you know.'

She gazed at him, wondering why she hadn't thought of something so simple. She laughed. 'You're as sly as a fox sometimes . . . partner.'

Fourteen

Sylvia didn't take kindly to Jilly's suggestion that she find a job.

'I'm not well.'

'You would be if you didn't drink so much. You're not being fair to Will. He's a young man who needs to make friends, and we both work hard. Soon, he'll have a share in the business. Besides that, he's going to night school to get some qualifications.'

'If it hadn't been for him—'

'Don't say it, Mum. Will didn't leave those marbles on the stairs, the old lady did. I'm surprised it didn't occur to you.'

Her mother didn't seem too surprised by what Jilly had said, but annoyed. 'You know, Jilly, you've become quite spiteful since you returned from London.'

Jilly had been expecting a showdown for some time. Now it had come she wasn't going to back down from it.

'And you've become selfish while I've been away. You have Will and myself waiting on you hand and foot. And you embarrassed Alec when he came to dinner, by flirting with him.'

'He enjoyed it. Men like to be made to feel they're attractive to women, you know, I'm still young enough to enjoy a man's attention. You've taken my stepson from me. Now you're jealous because Alec paid more attention to me than he did to you.'

So that was the problem between them, Jilly thought. Her mother looked upon her as a rival. She sighed. 'Don't be so ridiculous.'

'You couldn't hold on to the last man you had. Oh, yes, I remember now . . . he was a married man who preferred to go back to his wife rather than stay with you.'

The colour drained from Jilly's face and she felt sick. How that hurt. Even her mother seemed slightly taken aback by what she'd just said. Jilly ignored the jibe, though tears pricked her eyes. She was tempted to hurl Derek Fowler's name into the ring.

'Alec humoured you because you were drunk.' She attacked her mother's vanity. 'Have you taken a good look at yourself in the mirror lately? Will and I are worried about the amount of alcohol you drink; it shows in your face. Perhaps it's about time you did something about it.'

'And perhaps it's about time you learnt some respect for your mother.'

'Perhaps you should start earning it.' With that Jilly stomped off, leaving her mother with her mouth hanging open.

It was three days before Sylvia spoke to her again, and her mother looked as miserable about the situation as Jilly felt.

Alec prised the lid off the tin – wincing when it gave suddenly and he cut his finger. He sucked on the blood while he rummaged through the cutlery drawer to find a sticking plaster.

'Here . . . let me.' Jilly quivered as she wrapped the plaster carefully over the cut and his breath shivered through her hair.

From the top of the tin he took a piece of newspaper and unfolded it. A cheque for ten shillings fluttered out. 'The Brave Pilot,' he read out loud, 'by Alec Frampton. It was a cold day over the English Channel when brave Pilot Officer Oliver Richard set out to defend the coast of England in his deadly Spitfire . . .'

'Why did you change the pilot's name around?'

Alec had a job keeping his face straight. 'National security. I thought I might be captured and tortured by the secret service if I revealed the pilot's real name.'

When Jilly giggled, Alec laughed and picked up the cheque. 'It wouldn't be valid after all this time. I'll keep it as a memento of the past.'

'You could always ask them to replace it.'

'I could, but I don't need the money that badly.'

'You promised me thruppence if you won.'

'Did I?' His glance fell on the photo of his parents. Alec could see himself in his father's smile and his eyes were similar to his mother's. He gazed at the photo a long time, then laid it gently aside. 'I must buy a new frame for it.'

The clipping of them both came out next. Jilly was smiling without showing her teeth, her head cocked to one side like an inquisitive bird. Her eyes were screwed up against the light. As for himself, he looked solemn. He gazed at her and smiled. 'You had a tooth missing. It made you lisp.'

'Your memory is better than mine.'

When he went to set the pilot's flying helmet on her head she dragged it from his hands and threw it on the couch. 'Don't do that.'

Her vehemence surprised him. 'I thought the pilot was your hero.'

Why did she avoid his eyes like that? 'I was a child then. Now I'm not.'

He picked up the wings. 'These are yours, I believe.'

'They're part of the past. Leave them in the tin where they belong.'

Her vulnerability was all too obvious as she rose to her feet. There was sadness in her eyes, and a wary distrust. Her bottom lip trembled slightly, as though she were about to say something. Then her mouth tightened. 'I'll make some tea while you read your father's letter.'

It was obvious that the contents of the tin were having an unsettling effect on Jilly. He set it aside. 'I'll read it later. Let's go for that drive.'

'You shouldn't put it off, Alec. Your father had something to say to you. Something he wanted you to know.'

'I already know that he would have wanted the best for me.'

'Are you frightened that what you've done would disappoint him?'

'Hell, no. I've probably exceeded any expectations he'd have had regarding me.'

'Then why are you scared to open it?'

He hadn't thought she'd so easily put him on the defensive.

'Who said I was scared . . . all right, I'm scared. I don't know why. I'm a grown man, I might cry and then I'd be embarrassed. It's not manly to cry.'

'Nobody but us would ever need to know that you'd cried,' she said gently, bringing them close again. 'I'll cry with you if that will help.'

He threw the letter on to the arm of the chair, saying almost angrily, 'If it's so damned important to you to know what my father said, read it to me.'

He expected her to respect his privacy and throw it back at him, but she didn't.

'All right,' she said, her anger equalling his, and she slit the grubby envelope open with a fingernail varnished in white pearl.

She started reading in a strong, determined voice . . .

> '*My dear son, Alec,*
>
> *I'm on the eve of going to war, and I'm sad to be leaving behind the two people I love the most. If you are reading this, it's probable that I've become a casualty.*
>
> *Be the man of the house and take good care of your precious mother for me.*
>
> *My hope as I leave you is that you'll grow up to be a good man, always honest in your dealings with others.*'

Handing her his handkerchief, Alec said, when she gazed at him, her eyes awash with tears, 'Don't stop now.'

She scrubbed the tears away, sucked in a deep breath.

> '*Dearest son, not one of us knows what the future holds for us. I'll not demand that you make me proud of you. Instead, I ask that you just do your best, so you can always be proud of yourself.*
>
> *When you become a man, I hope you find love with a good woman, as I did with your mother. Be happy always, my son – and think of me sometimes.*
>
> *Your loving father,*
> *David Frampton.*'

Towards the end of the letter Jilly's voice had dropped to a wobbly whisper. Now her face was tragic as she gazed at him.

'Oh, Alec,' she said, and burst into sobs.

He was on his feet in an instant, gathering her into his arms, where she belonged, his own tears falling on the top of her head. He'd found his good woman. He was totally, irrevocably in love with Jilly Turner. He had been since he first set eyes on her in the cafe – and probably for all his life before that, and the one before that. All he had to do now was convince her of it.

There was something liberating about the tears trickling down his face, too. He couldn't remember the last time he'd cried.

He managed to manoeuvre her face round to his and gazed into her eyes. They were sodden and brown, and her dark eyelashes were clumped together into spikes. She gazed back, seemingly waiting for him to make the first move, a touch of curiosity coming to the surface.

He gave in to the irresistible urge to kiss her.

She didn't resist, but when he let her go she dried her eyes and gave him a little grin as she dabbed the tears from his cheeks. 'That wasn't fair.'

'Life has never been fair, as you've just proved. I never looked after my mother, as he requested – and you wanted me to kiss you, so stop complaining.'

She ignored his reference to the kiss. 'It's hard to argue with bombs when you're a small child – or mothers, come to that. It was her job to look after you, not the other way round. She did. She loved you, so she sent you away where you were less likely to suffer harm.'

He managed a weak grin in the face of her fierceness. 'She never met the Crutchly girls.'

'At least she didn't know she'd never see you again.'

Reaching for her cardigan, she said. 'Come on, let's go and see this school of yours. I hope it's not going to be as cluttered as your house.'

'This is all my great-uncle's stuff. I haven't had time to sort through it yet. The furniture is not to my taste. I don't quite know what to do with everything. I thought you might help me sort it out.'

Her eyes slid sideways. 'When did you think that?'

'Just this minute.'

'You think one kiss will turn me into Cinderella? It wasn't good enough.'

He grinned. 'I could manage a better one.'

'That wasn't an invitation. It would save effort if you called in a second-hand furniture dealer and gave the clothes to a jumble sale.'

'What about the china? Some of the things have value. That frilly china and glassware for instance. The cupboards are full of it.'

'Is there anything you particularly want?'

'No.'

'Then ask one of the auction houses to sell it for you.'

'I should go through it first.'

'You mean we, don't you?' She sighed. 'All right. If you get some boxes I'll come over in the evenings and help you sort it out – but only because I'm nosy. We'll do it gradually, and start with the clothes. Later, we'll make a list of anything that looks like it might be of value.'

Two weeks later the clothes cupboards were bare and the house smelled less musty. Alec had picked out a few pieces of china he'd taken a fancy to for display. Jilly carefully wrapped the other stuff and packed it in a cupboard in one of the smaller bedrooms.

'You know, Alec, this house doesn't feel like it's your home.'

'That's because it's filled with somebody else's lifetime. Mine only fits into a red tin and on to half a dozen coat hangers. I might sell it and move nearer to the school in a couple of years. I fancy living in a nice country cottage with a big garden. It was nice of Fry the spy to leave everything to me, though.'

Her reply was caustic. 'I expect it salved his conscience. Your life would have been different if he'd taken you into his home.'

'My uncle provided money so I could have a good education, otherwise I'd have probably been sent to work on a farm for a pittance when I was still quite young. I'm contented with what I had – parents who loved me, strangers who cared . . . like your mother. Like you. You still care; that means a lot to me.'

She gave him a sharp look. 'We knew each other for a short time.'

'But look what we had in common. Stop trying to fob me off, Jilly. Remember the pilot?'

A gaping wound opened up inside her. She was stricken with the thought that somebody might have told him about Rick Oliver before she'd had time to herself. Rick's betrayal still had the power to hurt. Yet she'd not been able to turn her youthful regard for him into hate. But like her lost son, she didn't want to think of him – or of the day after day she had waited for news, expecting him to come back and say he'd made a mistake by leaving her. Finally, her young and naive mind had accepted the conclusion that she'd been discarded. He'd had no intention of taking responsibility for the mess she'd been in, or the child he'd fathered. She'd grown up quickly then.

Her face flamed as her confidence sunk to an all time low. She was a shameful slut who'd borne a child while unwed. Her virginity had been squandered on some ne'er-do-well, so no decent man would ever want her. And Alec was a decent man. *Too decent for her.*

Had her mother told him out of revenge for the row they'd had? Surely not. She was too ashamed of the incident to mention it to anybody. She must know what Alec meant by mentioning Rick, though.

'What did you mean by saying, remember the pilot?'

'If we hadn't rescued him he'd probably have died. We shared that.'

If Rick had died, her son wouldn't have existed, and she wouldn't have lost him. She shrivelled with the agony of losing him every time he came into her mind. Yet to deny her son his life brought with it its own guilt. Without Rick her son wouldn't have existed. And because she couldn't bring herself to begrudge him that life, she also couldn't hate his father. A fleeting image of a baby's smile escaped from inside her, a feeling of intense love. She couldn't wish her infant away that easily, as if a genie had whooshed up out of a bottle and made everything painful disappear from her life.

She looked away from Alec's smile, feeling deflated – knowing how it would change if he knew about her affair. His eyes would evade hers, his voice become cool and distant with every contact, until he found some excuse to stop seeing her.

Jilly thought she was falling in love with Alec. She was comfortable with him, as if they belonged – had always belonged. He attracted her in all ways and she was becoming more aware of the physical tension pulling them towards each other. It would be agony all over again to lose him.

But how could she bring herself to trust him after what had happened with Rick? She must keep him at arm's length.

August was knocking at the window when things came to a head between them. Alec's garden was gleaming with red, yellow and white roses. Bees hummed about their work. Alec had just cut the grass and was raking the clippings into a pile. Jilly crept up on him and whispered in his ear, 'Boo!'

The next moment she was wrestled to the ground and was screaming for mercy as he tickled her ribs. 'Stop that!' Screaming with laughter she began to struggle and managed to grab hold of his collar and pull him down. He fell on top of her and she squirmed out from under, sprang to her feet and kicked lawn clippings all over him.

Grabbing her by the ankles he jerked her feet out from under her and she landed on his lap. Their smiles faded as they gazed at each other.

'Jilly, I—'

She scrambled to her feet. 'Don't say anything more, Alec. I must go.'

'You've just got here.' Desperation filled his voice. 'I *must* say it. I can't keep quiet any longer. I love you.'

'I know you do, Alec. I can't think about it now.'

'When can you think about it?'

Panic welled up in her. 'I don't know . . . I must go . . . my mother's expecting me.'

'I'll take you home.'

'No don't . . . I need to be alone. There's a bus in a few minutes. I'll ring you later in the week.'

She felt his eyes on her as she walked away, imagining the hurt in them. She could no longer avoid the issue. She'd have to summon up some courage and tell him.

All week she imagined Alec's bewilderment at her behaviour. She rang him, then lost her nerve and hung up before he could answer the phone.

'What are you being so twitchy about?' Will said on the Saturday, after lunch. 'That's the second time you've jumped down my throat this week.'

Miserably, she said, 'Alec's in love with me.'

Will smiled. 'And you're in love with him. Any fool can see that. What's the problem, then?'

'Nothing you can help me with.'

'Try me. You haven't told him about the baby, have you?'

'How did you know about it, Will? Did my mother tell you?'

'I'm not stupid, and neither am I deaf. The parents always treated me as part of the furniture. They had a big row about it and I overheard.'

'My mother wanted to bring my son up as her own.'

'No, she didn't. She wanted you to have him adopted out. She said it would ruin her life if people knew you'd had a baby. But my father wore her down. He said he'd treated you badly, and he wanted to make it up to you. She was furious, but she gave in to him.

'When you stayed in London rather than come home she was even more furious. She said you'd end up on the streets, and she was finished with you. For what it's worth, I think you made the right decisions and for the right reasons. I thought of you a lot when I was doing my National Service, and hoped you'd be all right.'

'Thank you, Will. But I don't know how Alec will take it.'

'There's only one way to find out, isn't there?' He handed her the receiver. 'Tell him the truth face to face.'

'But my mother—'

'Damn your mother, Jilly. This is your life, not hers.'

The phone rang for a long time. When she was about to hang up, Alec said, 'This is Alec Frampton.'

'Alec,' she said in a small voice, 'can you pick me up from work? I need to talk to you.'

'It's about time you did,' he said evenly, and hung up.

He didn't smile when she got into the car and there was a remoteness about him. 'Would you take me to where the Spitfire crashed?'

He looked surprised. 'Is there a good reason for going all the way to Blackbriar Caundle?'

'Yes, there is. You'll understand when I explain.'

'The explanation had better be good.'

'Oh, I promise you it will be,' she said bitterly. 'Don't be so damned scratchy. I hate it when you're cross with me.'

'I'm never cross with you, only at my own inability to understand what's going wrong between us.'

They parked the car up near where Rose Cottage used to be, and set off through the woods. The peaty smell rising from the bed of leaves stirred up memories of childhood.

Alec must have sensed it too, for he took her hand in his as they emerged into the clearing and said, 'You made my life here bearable, Jilly.'

'Don't say that, Alec. It just makes it harder for me to say what I'm about to.'

There was nothing left of the Spitfire, not even a screw or a rivet. No sign that Rick Oliver had ever been there.

He turned her to face him. 'Don't think I'll let you go that easily.'

'You will when you hear what I have to say.'

'Then, for pity's sake, let's hear it.'

'Rick Oliver came back into my life six years ago. I fell in love with him. I didn't know he was married until after he left. I . . . had his child, Alec. I gave him up for adoption.'

He gazed at her almost uncomprehendingly without saying anything. Above them the breeze soughed in the trees, and the sea sucked greedily at the bottom of the cliff.

Her mouth dried up. 'Say something, Alec.'

'You gave your baby up for adoption?'

Guilt tore through her, leaving her breathless with anguish. 'There was no real choice.'

'My poor Jilly.'

Angrily, she said, 'I don't want you to feel sorry for me. Now you know why I couldn't allow you to tell me you loved me . . . not without knowing. And I couldn't deceive you.'

'How badly you must be hurting from this.'

'It's my own fault. I allowed myself to be taken in by him.'

'Don't be so hard on yourself, my Jilly. Rick Oliver was always your hero. You couldn't have been more than seventeen at the time, and impressionable. As often happens with heroes, he turned out to have clay feet.'

'With a vengeance,' she said wryly. 'I was so stupid.'

'You wanted to be loved. We all do. Is that why you wanted to come here – to let me know that you're over him?' Tenderly, he caressed her cheek. 'Or was it because you needed to convince yourself?'

'It took a while, but I'm over him, though I can't bring myself to hate him. Don't make me cry, Alec.'

'Why not? You forced me to face my past and made me cry. Did you really think that what you've just told me would make me love you any less? We're only human, and I've been no angel.'

'It's different for men, though, isn't it?'

'It shouldn't be.'

Her heart leapt. 'I thought Rick loved me. Yet he left without giving me a second thought. My mother made me feel so ashamed. It was as though I was nothing, and my baby was something grubby, instead of the innocent, lovely child I gave birth to.' Tears were streaming down her cheeks now. 'All the time I was carrying him, I tried not to love him – but it didn't work. Giving him away nearly broke my heart, and I've been worried sick about what your reaction would be.'

He smiled at the thought. 'How can I not love you? The thing is, Jilly, our relationship seems to be a bit lopsided. I need to know something. How much do *you* care for me?'

'Oh, Alec . . . you know how much I care for you.'

'No, I don't. You've kept me at a distance. You can tell me now if you want. I'm all ears.'

'Are those ears? I thought they were wings.' She grinned

at him through her tears, elated beyond reason. 'I love you to pieces, Alec.'

He gave her the smile she loved so much. 'Say it again – louder.'

'I love you, louder.'

'Then will you marry me, your second best hero?'

Tears came into her eyes. 'You've never been second best in my life, you know. Yes, I'll marry you.'

He kissed her gently on the forehead. 'That son of yours will come looking for you one day, you know. We all need to know where we fit in. I had my past waiting for me in a rusty tin, and it contained all the love in the world. Your son will look for his past in you, and he'll find the same.'

'Oh, I do hope so . . . I miss him so much. But I can't allow myself to think of him too often. The pain of parting becomes unbearable.'

'You'll have to bear it, my love.' He drew her against his warmth. 'We'll have children of our own and you'll love them too. And come what may, you'll always have me to lean on.' He fished a jeweller's box from his pocket. 'I've been carrying this around for a couple of months now. D'you want to try it on?'

It consisted of a solitaire diamond surrounded by tiny rubies and set in gold.

'It's beautiful,' she said, as he slid it down her finger.

'You're beautiful.'

Love filled her like a shining light. 'Shall we get married in the registry office?'

He raised an eyebrow. 'No way. We can use the chapel at the school. I'd like to see you dressed like a proper bride, so I can show you off. That's why I showed the place to you in the first place. I'd planned to propose that day, but the students and a couple of the house masters kept coming in to leer at you under the pretence of praying, and there was no privacy.'

She chuckled. 'It's a pretty chapel, but I don't think I know enough people to fill it, though.'

'I don't know many people either. There's a challenge for us. I bet you ten shillings I can get more guests than you can to attend.'

'You're on, but I don't know anyone either,' she said, her eyes narrowing as an idea occurred to her.

'You're scheming, Jilly.'

'I am not—'

But her words were hardly discernible when he laughed, then stooped to claimed her mouth with his own.

Fifteen

Jilly's talk with her mother had brought about an improvement. Sylvia still drank, but with meals, and not as much. And she'd joined a group of people who went to the tea dances at the Pavilion in Bournemouth. Her mother had been fond of dancing, Jilly remembered, and she spoke enthusiastically about her new pursuit. It was nice to see her dress up and wear make-up again. But the atmosphere between them was still a little strained.

When she told her mother of the engagement, her mother said, 'Don't tell him about that other business else he'll run a mile.'

'I've already told him about my son.'

'You fool.' Her mother stared at her. 'Are you telling me he doesn't mind being second best?'

'Alec never has been, nor ever will be, second best. He understands that I was young and made a mistake. He loves me, and will support me in everything I do, through thick and through thin. And I really love him, Mum. I couldn't deceive him.'

'Love can soon turn sour.'

'I'll take my chances.' She held out her hand to show her mother the ring. 'Won't you at least be happy for me?'

'That must have cost him a pretty penny,' Sylvia said, then tears flooded her eyes. 'Oh, Jilly girl, despite the way you disappointed me, I do love you, you know. It's just that one thing crowded on top of another and I had Chris to contend with. When he died it was like being set free. Yet when I haven't got a man in my life I don't feel right. Why do I always make such a hash of things?'

Jilly sighed. It was typical of her mother to bring the conversation back to herself.

'Will you help me with the wedding? We're going to get married in the school chapel at Kingsmere Grammar School, where Alec works. And in four weeks' time.'

'You're getting married in a church . . . in four weeks?'

'That's what Alec wants. It's going to be a proper wedding.'

'Who's going to pay for this?'

'Alec and I will. I'll invite all my regular customers and I'm going to ask Peter to give me away and Audrey to be my matron of honour.'

'I hear that Audrey has a daughter now, though she never told us that. Someone else did. Sarah, her name is. She's getting on for four. Audrey nearly died having her and she can't have any more. Her husband has affairs, I believe.'

'Poor Audrey. I'm glad she had a child, though, since she wanted one. Perhaps she'd like to be a bridesmaid, too.'

Sylvia made an exasperated noise. 'Why include them, when they've hardly ever bothered with you?'

Jilly was beginning to suspect it was because her half-siblings had never felt welcomed by her mother. 'Because they're my sister and brother, and I'd like to get to know them a little better. And we'll send Dr Fowler an invitation, too.'

'I doubt if he'll come, especially if he knows about—'

'He does know, as a matter of fact. He'll get an invitation anyway. He examined me and provided the medical certificate, and wasn't in the least mean. Stop carping on about the past, I don't need your advice.'

'If you'd taken it in the first place and got rid—'

Anger flared up in Jilly. 'I refuse to discuss this with you.'

There was a martyred look on her mother's face now. 'Well, nobody can accuse me of not doing my duty. Don't say I never offered to take the brat off your hands.'

'Perhaps you should ask yourself why I didn't take you up on it,' she almost shouted.

As they stared at each other her mother's face flushed. 'Well, that's told me, hasn't it? I wasn't good enough for you, was I? You'd rather give your kid to strangers than to your own flesh and blood.'

Even knowing it was true, Jilly denied it to spare her mother's feelings. 'It wasn't like that. I couldn't bear the thought of my son being brought up with a lie. Did you consider how I'd feel, seeing my own child every day and trying to pretend I was his sister, when I needed so much to bring him up myself? What I wanted for him was a future free of the shame and tension attached to his birth.'

She might as well have not spoken. 'And after telling me I was a bad mother, you expect me to help you with your wedding.' Her mother heaved a sigh. 'Well, I suppose it will cause talk if your own mother isn't involved in the arrangements, especially when you've been living under my roof free of charge for all this time. All right, I'll help.'

'Thanks,' Jilly muttered ungraciously. She'd given up a good job to come back when her mother had needed her. It seemed as if her mother had forgotten that.

'The Kingsmere Grammar School chapel,' Sylvia mused. 'I'd forgotten Alec had become a teacher. And in a public school, at that. It will look good on the invitations. "Mrs Christopher Stainer requests the pleasure of your company at the wedding of her daughter—"'

'No, Mum. It will be worded more like this: "Alec Frampton and Jillian Turner request the pleasure of your company at their wedding in the Kingsmere Grammar School Chapel." Alec has invited you and Will over to dinner at the weekend, so we can fix a date.'

Her mother shrugged. 'If it's going to be that soon, people will think you're in the pudding club.'

'I don't care what people think. Oh, stop being difficult, do,' Jilly snapped, and walked off, seething. Why did her mother have to criticize everything?

Jilly had no qualms about taking her mother to Alec's house. It looked nice now they'd sorted it out. They'd changed the awful wallpaper in the lounge for something more to their taste, regency striped in cream and blue. The brown carpet had given way to grey shag pile. The coffee and side table were glass-topped, and they'd bought a comfortable dark blue lounge suite.

Jilly had wanted lava lamps, but Alec had laughed. 'We'll

go cross-eyed watching them when the oil heats up. What about those white lamps with the flower-painted bases from the local pottery? They'll match the lounge suite.'

Jilly had plans for the kitchen next. Nothing expensive, though; just a new cooker and counter tops. She'd redecorate and furnish the place gradually. After all, if Alec decided to sell the house it would pay them to make it look fresh.

Alec had bought a bed with a divan base and a thick mattress for the main bedroom.

He grinned widely at her when he showed it to her. Drawing her back against his body with his arms around her, he kissed her behind the ear. 'I bought it in a sale. The old one squeaked.'

They'd not made love yet, but it was getting harder to keep their hands off each other. She snuggled back into his warmth. 'It's a beautiful bed, Alec. Let's use it.'

He gazed down at her, his eyes like smoke, and said lazily, 'I thought you wanted to wait?'

'I thought I did, too. Now I know I don't.'

'Contrary woman.' He kissed her behind the ear. 'I'd allow you to lead me into temptation, but the bed's still wrapped in plastic.'

'So what?'

'May I remind you that your mother and Will are coming over for dinner?'

'Not for two hours.' She laughed when her suggestion brought him nudging against her. 'You respond well to stimulus, sir.'

'Let's see how well you respond, madam.' Grabbed up, she was tossed on to the bed. Alec plonked himself down beside her, his eyes alight with laughter. His lips claimed her mouth in a kiss so fiery she felt herself melt against him.

'Yes,' she whispered. 'I like it.'

'You can't throw out a challenge like that and expect to get away with it, you know.' He gazed down at her, his smile fading. 'Are you sure about this?'

'Don't you want me, then, Alec?' she teased.

'Want you? My God, woman, I feel like making a meal of you! I'd better make sure I have some protection first.'

'I'm protected. I went on the new contraceptive pill two weeks ago, just in case.'

He huffed with laughter. 'So, you planned to seduce me all along.'

'I guess I must have, since I adore you,' she whispered.

'Then let's get comfortable.' His fingers went to the fastenings on her blouse, then when he'd laid her breasts bare he gently kissed each raised nipple.

She shivered.

Stepping from the bed he pulled her up, then drew a flannel sheet from the cupboard and threw it on to the bed with a chuckle. 'I don't want your bare behind to stick to the plastic.'

They undressed each other with increasing urgency, and fell together on to the bed, the demands of the flesh uppermost in their minds.

Jilly hadn't imagined making love with Alec would be so exciting, or such fun. She spiralled upwards with each touch and kiss, making little noises of encouragement until her physicality slid into some sort of pleasure that was almost mindless. Alec was hard inside, her, and her pelvis arched to accommodate him as the blood pounded in her body with each exquisite thrust of him. The orgasm came quite suddenly, an erotic, prolonged and sensual pleasure that took her into the erotic heights, until she fell over the top and plunged, gasping, into a delightful void. It was something she'd never experienced before.

'Oh . . . Alec . . .' she gasped as he relaxed against her, his breath heavy against her ear. She drew the sheet around them, holding his warm and muscular body against hers and loving him.

When his breathing steadied he lifted his head and gazed into her eyes. He was laughing. 'That was something. You're a deliciously wicked bit of crumpet.'

'So are you.' She giggled, partly with relief that they'd broken through the physical barrier, and partly because she felt so good. She could feel him inside her still, and gently squeezed her muscles. 'Can we manage seconds, d'you think?'

'If you do that too often it's highly probable I will rise to the challenge.'

'How high did you say?' Giving a soft laugh, she squeezed again and he showed her exactly.

* * *

They were married four weeks later.

The morning was perfectly still, the trees a fiesta of bronze, ruby and gold. Downy thistle seed drifted in the air and horse chestnuts glowed with inner fire as they split their prickly husks in the need to be born. Under the trees, boys in maroon blazers and grey trousers scrabbled among the falling leaves to find the best and strongest of the nuts. These were threaded on string to serve a useful but short life as weapons in the game of conkers.

'You look wonderful, squirt,' Peter said, giving Jilly a swift smile as the car turned into the school grounds, its white ribbons fluttering in the breeze.

'I feel like the Queen of England in this Jaguar. It was nice of your uncle to offer to lend it to us for the day.'

'He's not a bad old boy, you know. He doesn't drive it any more and was pleased it was going to have a bit of a run, and a spit and polish.'

Boys turned to wave at the car as it passed. Jilly grinned and waved back.

The school and the chapel were built of mellowed stone. Ivy rambled over the walls in places and the high chapel window over the porch glowed like autumn jewels. A house-master strode towards the chapel, his long legs breaking into a lope as the car passed him. He slid through the church door while Peter was helping Jilly out of the car.

The wedding gown Jilly had bought off the peg was unfussy. Creamy white satin curved into the waist from a boat neckline, then flared out slightly, fuller at the back into a short train. Long sleeves came to a point on the back of her hand. Her drifting tulle veil was attached to three creamy roses. White and orange rosebuds formed a spray.

All in apricot, Audrey was waiting for her in the porch in a dress with cap sleeves that fell just below the knee. No longer blonde, her hair had been allowed to return to its natural light brown state, which she wore with a soft fringe. Audrey looked much happier than the last time Jilly had seen her. Sarah matched her mother, except her short dress had a square yoke, and she carried a flower basket rather than a spray.

'I know I said this before, but you look lovely, Jilly,'

Audrey said. 'I'm so pleased that life is working out for you. What do you think of my daughter?'

'She's so sweet, Audrey. I hope we can visit now and again.' She gazed from her sister to her brother. 'All of us. I missed you both after you'd gone.'

'Don't think we didn't miss you too. The adults seemed bent on keeping us apart. Still, that's water under the bridge, now. Things will be different now you're married. It's been difficult in the past . . . but now you'll have your own house. So yes, we'll keep in touch, you'll see.'

'I must say, I didn't imagine Alec Frampton would grow up into such a decent man,' Peter added. 'He's done well for himself despite his poor start in life. So have you, squirt. Audrey and I are immensely proud of you.

'That rather odd best man of Alec's is giving the signal. Go on Audrey, Sarah. Off you go, we'll be right behind you.'

Audrey kissed Jilly's cheek then arranged the veil over her face. 'All happiness, Jilly darling,' she said. 'You deserve it.'

The chapel was full of flowers. The sun shone through the windows in shafts of dusty colour as Jilly was walked down the aisle on the arm of her brother to the wedding march.

Jilly could see Alec at the front through the mist of her veil, Will by his side. Both tall, they wore black morning suits and were half turned towards her. Alec wore his special smile. Will was taking his role quite seriously, and she wondered how he'd handle the speech at the reception, which was being held in a marquee in the grounds of a nearby hotel.

Jilly had notched up a tidy number of guests from amongst her customers. She smiled at them all as Peter took her closer to Alec. Derek Fowler gave her a warm smile in return. He'd aged rapidly, and Audrey said he'd retired recently.

Her mother was sitting by herself in the front pew. She looked pretty in a blue crimplene dress with matching coat and hat. But she also looked overwhelmed by the company she was in. A wave of love rippled through Jilly. Bringing Peter to a halt she leaned down to kiss her. 'I love you, Mum.'

Her mother smiled and squeezed her hand. Jilly caught a faint whiff of sherry on her breath.

Alec took her hand in his and kissed it, whispering against her knuckles, 'I love you, my Jilly.'

The music stopped and there was a pause while the coughs and shuffles of the congregation quieted.

Then the school chaplain smiled at them and said in a voice that resonated to the rafters, 'Dearly beloved, we are gathered together here in the sight of God to join this man and this woman in holy matrimony . . .'

Jilly knew she'd always remember her wedding – remember the feeling of love and completeness it brought into her life.

The rest of the service took place quickly and they made their responses, their glances entwined and their hearts beating only for one another. Alec looked proud as the ring was slid on to her finger and he lifted the veil back from her face to tenderly kiss her – a little longer than was proper, which sent laughter rippling through the congregation. The school choir sang sweetly as the register was signed, witnessed by Jilly's mother, her half-brother and her step-brother.

Will was all alone in the world, like Alec had been. But Alec wouldn't be alone for long because she intended to give him a family to call his own. But then, there were her mother and Derek Fowler. How strange that so many lonely people had somehow connected, and had suddenly gathered together in one place, as though they'd attracted each other like metal filings to a magnet.

And the son she'd born and lost. Where was he at this moment of great happiness in her life? There was a moment when she pictured him running through a field of autumn leaves, giggling as he kicked them up in the air. A smile touched her lips and her heart sent a message of love to wherever he might be.

Then the church bells started to joyously ring, dispelling her faint feeling of melancholy. She walked with Alec back down the aisle together as man and wife, and out into the sunshine where a crowd of boys set up a huge cheer at the sight of them.

'Jolly good luck, sir,' they shouted out, and another suggested, 'Can we kiss the bride for you, sir . . . show you how it's done?'

'Certainly not,' Alec said, and grinned at Jilly. 'I'll show *you* how it's done,' and he did, making her blush.

Laughing and clapping, the boys threw confetti and rice over them.

Sixteen

25th August 1985

. . . I've enclosed a photograph of us all. Our eldest daughter, Susan, is on the left. She's twenty-two and is a teacher, like her father. She's engaged to be married.

Emma is four years younger. She intends to study towards a BA and become a librarian.

And Neil, I do hope we can continue to correspond and to get to know each other through our letters. You needn't feel reticent about asking me anything you wish to know.

Thank you again for your letter. I can't tell you how much it meant to me. As you didn't know how to start your letter to me, so I don't really know how to finish mine to you.

How odd, when you're my son, to find myself searching for words that won't embarrass you in any way. But I've decided to simply end as my feelings dictate, because these are the words I want to say.

Much love. I've missed you.

Jilly.

PS. It's a little late in the month to wish you a happy birthday, but I want you to know that it was never forgotten . . .

She stuck down the envelope, addressed it to Mr Neil James and propped it against the tea caddy, thinking, Not strictly true, Jilly.

'Do you remember when you stuck candles in a doughnut and we both sang happy birthday to him, Alec?'

'How could I forget? It was a hot day and you were down in the mouth. I thought it would cheer you up . . .'

'There was a reason I was down in the mouth.'

He grinned. 'A rather large one, I recall . . . and the doughnut—'

'Was a big mistake . . .'

September 1963

They'd just moved to the country, nearer to the school, and not far from the market town of Blandford.

The cottage wasn't as large as they'd liked, and needed some work doing on it, but both of them had fallen in love with the large back garden with its patio and orchard.

Feeling as fat as a hog, Jilly winced as the baby she carried tried to make a bit more space for itself. Rising to her feet, she waddled to the bathroom, the pressure on her bladder almost unbearable.

The bathroom was little more than a black hole, with a window that looked out over a tangle of grass and nettles and let in little light. Daddy-long-legs did a stealthy dance in the corners.

Sickly green walls matched the streaks in the bath. Patches of dirty cement yawned, where once they had hugged black and white tiles to the wall, and the bath was balanced on three Egyptian looking claw feet, and one red house brick.

When she pulled the chain dangling from a rusty cistern it released short spurts of brown water and hissed loudly at her.

'I hate the bathroom,' Jilly wailed, making her way round a heap of boxes to get back to her chair. 'I wish we hadn't moved. And I hate myself. I feel monstrously fat and ugly.'

'You look beautiful when you're fat and ugly,' Alec said. 'And the bathroom fitters and plumbers are coming to refit the bathroom next week. It will look like a palace afterwards.'

'You told me that last week.'

He kissed the top of her head. 'Never mind, my darling. It won't be long before Charlie is born.'

'There's two weeks to go yet,' she said. 'The last time . . . Oh God!' She felt stricken. '*He* was seven last month and I forgot!'

Alec didn't pretend not to know who she was referring to. He pulled the footstool over to her. 'Here, rest your feet on that. I'll bring you a cup of tea.'

He also brought in a doughnut ring, decorated with chocolate icing. It had seven yellow candles on it, flames fluttering. They'd been left over from the birthday cake she'd made for Alec.

'All together now. *Happy birthday to Richard . . .*'

Half-heartedly she joined in – and had just blown out the candles when she began to cry.

'Oh, Jilly, my love,' Alec said, taking her into his arms. 'I'm so sorry. I'm such a fool.'

'No you're not . . . you're a treasure. Only you could think of something like that to cheer me up.'

'It worked admirably, didn't it? We must do it every year, since you look *really* cheered up now, like a cat with its tail caught in the mangle.'

'I love it when you do unexpected things,' she protested, giving a hysterical sounding giggle. 'I'm tired, that's all. And my feet have swollen. Look, they're bulging over my sandals. I'm hot and my head aches today. I'm sick of the clutter, too. We haven't got enough cupboards to put everything in.'

'I'll put the boxes in the garage and we can sort it gradually. When the extension and the conservatory are built on we'll have much more room.'

'The nursery isn't finished yet. Where's Charlie going to sleep when he grows out of the crib?'

'He isn't even in the crib yet, so stop worrying about it. I'll put the cot up later. That will be one box less to walk around. And I'll paint the walls blue and hang the curtains tomorrow night. Everything will be ready for the little tyke's arrival, you'll see.'

When she had finished her tea, Alec led Jilly to the bedroom and tucked her under the bedspread. 'You have a nice rest while I start lugging those boxes out of your way.'

She slid her arms around his neck and kissed him. 'I'm sorry I'm such a misery. I'm mean to nag you.'

'Totally mean. You should be ashamed of yourself.' He held her close and whispered against her ear. 'It's my fault that you're mean. I deserve to be nagged. I should never have laid hands on you in the first place.'

She couldn't help but laugh at that. 'If I wasn't so pregnant I'd appreciate the laying on of hands now. As it is, stop making me laugh, Alec. This son of yours is already playing havoc with my bladder.'

'Go to sleep,' he whispered, kissing each of her eyelids. 'See, Johnnie Ray has come out from under the bed to keep you company.'

The cat landed lightly on the bed and snuggled up against her chest. He began to purr loudly.

As soon as Alec gently closed the door behind him, Jilly was awash with tears again. The late stages of her pregnancy had unexpectedly brought bittersweet memories of her son's birth and the trauma of their parting to the forefront of her mind. What if something awful happened to punish her? she thought. What if she lost the baby she was carrying? How could she bear it?

As it happened, she was woken by a rather strong, protracted contraction. When it abated she carefully got out of bed. As soon as she stood, her water broke and soaked through her clothing to puddle on the floor. She opened the door, yelling in panic, 'Alec, come quickly!'

Johnnie Ray skittered towards the door, nearly tripping Alec as he took the stairs three at a time.

He took one look at the mess she was in. 'Oh, my Lord, you've popped!' he said. 'You'd better get your nightie on. I'll bring up the bucket and mop, and get the bed ready for Charlie's birth.'

His presence calmed her. 'Don't worry too much. Babies usually take ages to arrive. Ring the midwife, would you? And my mother. She wanted to be here for the birth. If Will's not at the house try the cafe, since he'll have to drive Mum over. Let Audrey and Peter know, too. Thank goodness it's a Sunday.'

Alec ran around like a scalded cat, following her instructions, while she tried not to laugh.

But their baby didn't intend to do things so slowly. Alec hovered uselessly in the corner, giving her face the occasional swipe with a wet flannel, while she sweated, grunted and groaned for an hour. Then they heard a car. Relief washed over his face. 'The cavalry have arrived, thank God!'

Alec was banished to the lower floor, and the nurse had barely rolled her sleeves up when the baby's head pushed painfully through. Another ten minutes and a squalling bundle of red-faced fury was placed in Jilly's arms.

'It's a little girl,' the nurse said with a smile.

There was a moment when Jilly's initial surprise was suspended in time. She hadn't really considered that she might give birth to a girl.

Head to one side she gazed at her daughter, thinking that she looked like a creased-up and squashed version of Alec. Then the baby stretched. Her long skinny arms and legs quivered like the wings of an insect just released from its chrysalis. Her noise warbled to a whimper, her limbs folded back against her body, her eyes drifted shut and her little hand reached up to her mouth to bury her thumb there.

Jilly took a soft rug from the nurse and wrapped it around the child. 'Don't tell Alec it's a girl. I want to see his reaction myself.' She was filled with an incredible calm. 'I love you,' she whispered, and her eyes filled with tears as she kissed a sparse inch of downy darkness sprouting from her daughter's head.

It wasn't long before Jilly was cleaned up. Alec came in, a smile of expectation lighting his face, his eyes filled with curiosity. His arms came around her and he kissed the top of her head before gazing down at his baby. 'Hello, Charlie.'

The nurse strangled a laugh.

Jilly gazed up at him, her eyes alight with amusement despite her tiredness. 'I hope you don't mind, Alec, but I've decided to call him Susan Sylvia, after our respective mothers.'

'Whoops!' he said and chuckled. 'SS Frampton. She'll sound like a steamship. Mind you, she did sound like one earlier. Can I hold her?'

'Of course you can. She's your daughter.'

'So she is.' Taking his daughter gently in his hands Alec gazed tenderly down at her, then kissed the dainty foot that was sticking out of the blanket. 'Welcome to the world, my pretty Susie. I already adore you as much as I adore your mother.' His expression was full of pride, softness and love as he gazed at her. 'And how are you, my darling?'

'Empty, but full,' she told him. 'And you?'

'My cup runneth over,' he said simply.

Sylvia had become bored with playing the grieving widow. She was running out of money and only partly owned a home of her own.

Having a granddaughter had come as a shock. She was only forty-eight, after all.

She was fed up living in a large gloomy house, and thought she might sell her half to Will and buy herself a flat. At least she'd be able to take her friends home without the place smelling of cooking all the time.

The more she thought about it the more appealing it became. She cornered Will before he went to work one day.

'I want to buy myself a smaller place, Will.'

He hunched into his jumper and gazed at her through brooding eyes for a moment, then he smiled. 'Great, I've been thinking of getting rid of the house myself, since I've got plans of my own.'

'What plans?'

'I'm going to extend the cafe and move into the flat over the shop. I'll put this place on the market, then.'

'Where will I go in the meantime?'

'You can live here until it's sold.'

'By myself? Can't you just get it valued and give me my half in cash?'

'I'm in the middle of purchasing the cafe from Jilly, so I can't afford to buy you out at the moment. Besides, it's not worth the trouble and expense of transferring the deeds to my name when we're selling it anyway. It shouldn't take long to find a buyer, you know. Then you can buy your own flat. There're some new ones going up along Alum Chine Road.'

'I don't think I'll be able to afford one of those. Can't you let me have one of those that your grandmother left you?'

'No. I have good tenants in those.' He hesitated for a moment, then asked, 'What happened to the money Dad left to you?'

'There wasn't much when it was divided up. He left some of it to Jilly, don't forget, though I can't understand why. Mine's been spent on this and that. Bills for this place, mostly.'

'That's why it was invested, so you could pay your bills and have a small income from it.'

She shrugged. 'I decided to take it all at once. There isn't much left. I'll have to get a loan.'

'You won't get a loan if you haven't got a job.'

'Couldn't I move into the flat with you for a while, just until I find myself a place? I could always work in the cafe.'

Will shook his head. 'I'm fully staffed. Besides, I need some privacy. I'm sure you'll soon find somewhere to live. Go and stay with Jilly.'

'She's become too domestic. All she talks about is her husband and her baby. She doesn't approve when I have a drink and tells me I can't smoke in the house.'

'It's her house,' he said.

'The last time I went there, Audrey and Peter were visiting, and they looked down their noses at me.'

'I expect you imagined it.'

'I'm not stupid. I expect they tell lies about me, just like their uncle and aunt used to before they died. Derek Fowler always fancied me, you know.'

'I'm not interested in what he fancied, since I only met him once, and that was at Jilly's wedding,' Will said. 'Although you don't realize it, Sylvia, the world doesn't revolve around you. I have my own life to lead.'

'Well, there's gratitude for you. After I gave up my freedom to become a mother to you and this is what I get. You're as bad as Jilly. I wouldn't be surprised if you haven't ganged up on me.'

'I rather got the impression that you gave up your freedom for what my father could offer you. I didn't ask you to become my mother, and never, ever considered that you were.'

The stare they exchanged was broken by the thud of letters hitting the floor in the hall.

Sylvia backed away from an all-out row. Like most men, Will had become difficult to live with.

'Bills, most likely,' she grumbled. 'The electricity bill arrived yesterday. This damned place eats money. It's those big freezers you've got in the kitchen. I don't see why I should help pay the bills for running those.'

'You don't. You pay only a quarter of the bill,' he said. 'For God's sake, get a life, will you, Sylvia? I'm not responsible for you and I've got one of my own to live.'

'I've heard you sneaking girls in when you thought I was asleep.'

'I don't sneak, and it was one girl. I should be able to entertain my friends in my own home without you making comment, especially since I've lived here all my life. I tried to make sure we didn't disturb you.'

'You should have told me.'

'Give me a break, will you?' he said impatiently. 'I'm not fourteen any more, and I don't need to ask your permission. This is one of the reasons I want to live by myself.'

'You're just as nasty as your father was,' she said, as he slouched off.

He turned, his face sad. 'I've tried to get on with you, and helped you whenever I could. Do you have to nag on about my father?'

Guilt filled her. 'I'm sorry, Will. I didn't mean it.'

He nodded and moved off towards the kitchen.

She picked up the letters and threw them on to the hall table with some force. Bills and more bills! But no – there was an airmail letter! She picked it up, noting the American stamp. It had been addressed to her former name and posted to her old workplace. They'd readdressed it.

Turning it over she saw it was from Gary Carstairs. A smile relieved the sourness she'd been left with after her encounter with Will. 'I'll be damned!' she whispered, and ripped the envelope open with trembling hands. Her eyes scanned the letter. Gary was divorced, and was visiting England in March for some sort of reunion. He was touring England, staying for a month. He wanted to catch up with her and talk about old times.

She took a critical look at herself in the hallstand mirror, at the few streaks of grey in her hair. Those could be fixed, and she could go on a diet, get back to her old weight.

Gary Carstairs had been such fun to be with, she recalled, and she could do with some excitement.

Christmas took on a special sparkle now they had a baby to care for. Will drove Sylvia over to spend Christmas Day with Jilly and Alec. The house still hadn't been sold, and Sylvia grumbled, 'Will turned down the only offer we had.'

He shrugged. 'It was too low. The real estate agent said winter is a bad time of year to sell houses. We should wait until spring.'

Sylvia took a glass of sherry out into the conservatory and lit a cigarette, wrapping her coat around her against the cold as she stared out at the frosty garden.

The house smelled of roasting turkey and they'd decorated with holly, mistletoe and a tree covered in tinsel. There was a parcel for all of them under it. Sylvia and Will had placed their contributions there, too.

Jilly gave Will a kiss under the mistletoe. 'You know, Will, you're getting to be quite handsome.'

He looked embarrassed. 'Aw, shuddup, Jilly. You know I hate being teased.'

She laughed. 'I'm not teasing. I bet women fall at your feet. Tell me about your plans for the cafe.'

'I've just signed the lease for the premises next door, and I intend to live in the flat over it. We're going to sell cakes on the side. I've hired a cook to do the lunches, and I'll be putting on extra staff. I've also applied for a liquor licence.'

'Good luck with it, then. I've got a favour to ask you, Will.'

'What is it?'

'We would like you to be Susie's godfather.'

'Me?' A big smile slid across his face and stayed there as he picked Susie up and said, 'What d'you think of that, then, dimples?'

Susie chuckled and reached up to make a grab for his nose.

'You can't have that, I need it. But I've got something in my pocket you might like.' He pulled out a rattle, handed it to her and placed her back in her bouncer. 'There, that should keep you amused for five minutes.'

His glance wandered towards the conservatory. 'Jilly, your mother said she cashed in the investments my father left her. When the house sells, it's possible that she might not be able to afford accommodation for herself. I know it's none of my business, or even my problem, come to that, but I can't help worrying.'

'She'll have to get a job and rent a place if she can't afford to buy. Don't worry, Will. You're right. She isn't your responsibility. I know how manipulative she can be, so don't feel guilty about doing exactly what you want to do.'

'If the worst comes to the worst she can always move in with us for a time,' Alec suggested, but his expression told Jilly that he wasn't any keener on the idea than she was herself.

'That will be the last resort. She's lost weight, hasn't she?'

Will nodded. 'On purpose. She's put herself on a diet and has joined an exercise class.'

'At least she's taking a new interest in life.'

'She'll have to if she's going to fend for herself.'

'Oh, my mother can be quite enterprising when pushed to it. What's the betting she'll land squarely on her feet.'

Jilly's words came home to roost in April of the following year.

The house sold at the beginning of March. Will took a month off while the refurbishment of the cafe was being carried out – something Jilly was keeping an eye on for him.

Her mother paid her a visit one morning. 'Would you lend me a couple of hundred pounds until the sale is finalized?' she asked. 'I'm a bit short of cash. That's the trouble with losing weight, you have to replace all your clothes.'

Sylvia did look smart now, and her hair was arranged in a pretty style. Several years seemed to be shed from her, and she was wearing make-up again. She smiled a lot.

'Two hundred pounds is a lot of money, Mum.'

'Oh, I know you can afford it, since Will has settled up for the cafe.'

'But that's money Alec and I intend to invest.'

'A friend of mine asked me to go on holiday for a month. But if you won't lend it to me you won't, I suppose. It's my only chance before I start work. I've applied for a vacancy at the telephone exchange. The job isn't available until next month, though. I just felt like having a break first. It's not as if you won't get it back once the house sale goes through. These last few years have been hard on me, you know.'

And everyone else, but you don't seem to take that into account, Jilly thought.

'What about the money Chris left you in his will? Didn't you put that in your post office book? In fact, you could let me have the whole three hundred and fifty, to save me scrimping. You never know, I might find a place, and need a bit of a deposit in a hurry. That two hundred should have been mine, anyway. You know, he only left it to you to spite me.'

Jilly had forgotten about her stepfather's legacy. Initially, she'd used it to help her open the cafe. Then she'd replaced the amount once they'd gone into profit.

Feeling like Scrooge, Jilly thought of the money she'd saved in her post office book since she'd been a child. She'd meant to close the account, because Alec took care of the finances. But old habits died hard. If she closed it now, she could easily lend the money to her mother. She'd get it back before too long, after all.

'OK, I can manage the three-fifty. Look after Susie while I nip down to the post office. She has a bit of a cold and is asleep at the moment. Her nappies are on the change table, and her bottle is in the kitchen, made-up. It will need warming.'

Alec had taught Jilly to drive and had bought her a second-hand Mini to run around in a few months before.

It took her fifteen minutes to drive into Blandford, but then she had to find a place to park, and, as it was pension day, she had to join a long queue in the post office. She arrived home nearly an hour after she'd left.

She hurried up the path when she heard her daughter crying, and smelled the smoke of her mother's cigarette as soon as she opened the front door.

Glenn Miller was playing at full blast on the radio and her mother was dancing, wriggling her hips, a fag hanging from the side of her mouth. 'You were a long time,' she shouted over the music.

'For God's sake, Mum, can't you hear Susie screaming? And I've told you before, if you're going to smoke, do it in the conservatory.'

'I forgot.' Her mother threw the stub into the fire.

Jilly turned the radio down and went upstairs. Susie was standing up rattling the bars of her cot, tears running down her face and her nose streaming. Her nappy was soaked through, but her screams quieted to shuddering sobs when Jilly picked her up and soothed her. Jilly noticed a red welt on Susie's thigh when she made her comfortable, as if she'd been smacked. Her bottle dripped milk from the teat, and was stone cold. Jilly took her daughter downstairs and stood the bottle in hot water to warm through.

An empty glass stood on the table. The bottle of port in the glass cabinet had gone down considerably. Anger rippled through her. Her mother was so irresponsible at times.

'Hello, sweetie,' Sylvia said, coming close to kiss Susie.

Jilly smelt liquor on her breath and drew back. 'You've been drinking?'

'Only a port and lemon. That's what it's for, isn't it? It's the bottle I bought you for Christmas. Don't start making a fuss. Sometimes you're worse than your father was. I hope you don't go the same way. Sometimes, that type of mental disorder can be passed on.'

Susie's lower lip trembled and she buried her head in Jilly's shoulder.

'Did you smack Susie?'

'What makes you think that? She's in a bad temper, that's all. She's a right little vixen when she gets worked up, and you spoil her.'

'She has finger marks on her leg.'

'Oh, it was only a little tap. She threw her bottle at me and needed to be punished. Did you get the money?'

Her mother could wait! 'I'll give it to you after I've fed Susie.'

'Oh, it's going to be like that, is it? Look, Jilly, my friend has been waiting for me at the pub down the road for most of the morning.' Taking a cigarette from her packet, Sylvia ignored Jilly's warning look and lit it.

Susie started to cough.

Eager to get rid of her mother now, Jilly patted her
daughter's back then placed her in her high chair. Opening
her bag she handed over the cash to her mother. 'When will
you be leaving for your holiday?'

'In a day or two. Give me a lift to the pub, would you?'

'It's only a five-minute walk, Mum. I don't want to keep
Susie waiting for her lunch any longer.'

'That little madam has you running back and forth on the
slightest whim. Oh well, I suppose I can walk if I have to,
but my feet are killing me in these shoes.'

Serves you right, Jilly thought, eyeing the high heels. 'You
could always ring the pub and ask your friend to pick you up.'

Her mother's eyes slid away. 'No . . . I can walk.' She
hesitated before giving Jilly a more motherly hug than she
had for a long time.

Jilly felt herself stiffen in her mother's embrace. 'You'd
better not keep your friend waiting any longer.'

'No, I'd better not.' She gently patted her cheek. 'Goodbye,
Jilly girl.'

A thought came into Jilly's mind, one she decided to keep
to herself. Her mother must have snooped through her private
papers the last time she visited. How else would she have
known how much had been saved in her post office account?

'When will you be back?'

Her mother evaded her eyes. 'I'm not sure. I'll let you know.'

A month later Jilly received a letter from her mother saying
she'd married Gary Carstairs and had gone to live in America
with him.

She rang Will in panic. 'Did you know what she was
planning?'

'It's a surprise to me. I was about to ring and ask you if
you knew her new address. She asked me to settle her up
for the house in advance before I went away, said she didn't
want to lose the place she'd found.'

'Oh, Will. And did you?'

'I only gave her what she was entitled to. I didn't see the
harm when the offer and acceptance had already been signed.
I made sure that the settlement agency was signatory to the
deal, so the final settlement cheque would be made out to
me.'

Hearing a note of reserve in his voice, she said, 'Will, is that all you need to tell me? I don't want us to be less than honest with each other, especially now. I sense there's something else on your mind.'

She could almost hear him shrug. 'The person who bought the house bought the furniture, as well. But when I went to clear the cupboards out I found that everything of any value was gone. Mostly, it was my great-grandmother's china and silver. And the jewellery that used to belong to my mother and grandmother was gone from a little safe in my father's bedroom. That's why I wanted her address. I thought she might have taken it with her for safe keeping. Of course, someone might have come in after she'd left—'

Tears trickled down Jilly's cheeks. 'We both know that didn't happen. Will, I'm so ashamed, and so sorry. I'll reimburse you as best I can. I'll return the money you sent me for my half of the cafe to start with.'

'I won't hear of it, Jilly. You worked hard for that. It's my fault. I was discussing the jewellery with her before I left. She offered to get it valued and I gave her the combination to the safe.'

'She borrowed money from me, too. She lied, said she had a job to go to and wanted a holiday first. She used the house settlement as collateral, saying she'd pay it back as soon as it was through. And all the time she already had money. I fell for it. I can't believe my mother was so devious. How could she steal from us, her own kin, then go off without a word?'

'I don't know. I know she's your mother, Jilly, but I just hope she never comes back.'

Jilly couldn't find it in her heart to say the same, but nevertheless, over twenty years were to pass by before she saw her mother again.

Seventeen

1967

Alec had left Susie with Audrey.

Jilly had gone into labour early in that afternoon. Alec had called in the midwife, who had felt her abdomen, measured her blood pressure, then promptly called for an ambulance.

'What's wrong with her?'

'I'm taking precautions. Labour's begun prematurely. It's possible that it's false pains, but the baby also appears to be in the breech position.'

After he examined Jilly, the doctor confirmed it. 'We'll see how she goes,' he said. 'The nurse will ring me when she's nearer the time.'

Alec had stayed with Jilly, holding her hand and wishing he could do something useful.

She was trying hard not to show him her pain as he wiped the perspiration from her forehead, but she whimpered and groaned.

'My darling,' Alec murmured, 'I feel so inadequate.'

She mustered up a bit of a wry smile for him. 'Under the circumstances I'd expect you to be. In fact, I can hear your brain thrashing around in panic inside your skull. Do me a favour, Alec my love, go and do your worrying quietly in the waiting room. You're getting in the way of the nurse.'

Dismissed, he now prowled the hospital waiting room like a caged tiger and worried silently. It was worse than being with her, listening to her groans.

It was past midnight when the nurse popped her head in and smiled at him. 'The doctor has arrived. It won't be much longer. Try not to worry. I'll bring you a cup of tea.'

'How's my wife?'

'Bearing up . . . or should I say bearing down?' She cackled with laughter at her stale joke as she walked away.

Alec consumed the tea and arrowroot biscuits gratefully, since he hadn't had any dinner. It gave him the energy to pace some more.

His second daughter was born an hour later. On the other side of the barrier of a window, the nurse held up a tiny, fey-looking scrap with a wrinkled bum, bandy legs and hair like strands of gold. Her face greatly resembled Jilly's, right down to her snub little nose. Her translucent hands reminded him of frail seashells. Alec blew her a kiss and whispered, 'Hello, fairy,' as he fell in love for the third time.

'Can I see my wife?'

'They're still tidying her up but I'll make sure you can have a few words before they take her up to the ward. She'll be tired, though, a breech is always hard work, and she had a couple of other problems.'

'What sort of problems?'

'The placenta was torn, and she had some bleeding, nothing to worry about. She took a few stitches. Now, I must get your new daughter into the prem nursery. She's a bit on the small side so will need special care for a day or two.'

His anxiety knew no bounds. 'My wife's going to be all right though, isn't she?'

'Of course, Mr Frampton.'

'Isn't she sweet?' Jilly said a few moments later, smiling at him from a face drawn and pale from exhaustion. Her eyes drifted. 'I'm sorry I didn't give you a son this time.'

'Who needs a son when we've now got two beautiful daughters to love?' he said, then could have kicked himself when he remembered that Jilly probably might. But she didn't seem to have noticed his tactless remark.

'Do you like the name Emma Jane?'

He placed a kiss on her forehead. 'I think I prefer Gertrude Agatha.'

A grin twitched at the corner her mouth. 'Like hell you do.'

Smoothing the hair back from her pale forehead he gazed down at her. 'I love Emma Jane and I love you so much.'

'And look where that's got me!'

'You're the best thing that ever happened to me, Jilly. I think you must have been the first prize in some competition I won.'

Her eyes opened for a few seconds and she touched his cheek, a gesture of great tenderness. Her mouth trembled into a soft smile. 'You always needed someone to love, Alec. It was me who won the prize. I wish your parents could see you now, they'd be so proud of you, but then . . . perhaps they can.'

Even at times like this she made him feel loved. He wanted to cry like a baby as she was wheeled away.

But he wanted to strangle her mother, who'd gone off without thought to the damage her actions might inflict on her sensitive and vulnerable daughter. It had taken Jilly several months to recover from the woman's deceit. And she'd worried herself sick until Sylvia had finally written to them informing them of her address.

Alec didn't want to go home to a house full of empty rooms so he drove to where Audrey lived. She'd divorced her philandering husband the previous year, had moved and was soon to marry again. It was going to be a year of births and marriages. Will would be married next month, and Peter's wife was expecting her fourth child.

They were all friends now. Adulthood had brought with it certain insights, and had given them more perspective of their childhood, which was cemented by memories. Jilly had brought these people into his life, and they had now become part of his family.

Audrey's light was on. He could see her shadow moving beyond the curtain.

'I waited up,' she said, her face breaking into a smile. 'Well?'

'We have another daughter. She's lovely. She looks so much like Jilly. Everything went well, but it was a struggle for Jilly and it exhausted her.'

'Oh, Alec, congratulations! Jilly is stronger than she seems, and will soon recover.' She gave him a hug. 'You look tired out. I kept some dinner warm for you.'

'You're a lifesaver, I'm starving.'

'You'd better go and tell Susie that she's got a sister first.

She stayed awake as long as she could and I promised her you'd wake her up and let her know.'

Susie, a warm, sleepy bundle in a blue cotton nightdress, could hardly open her eyes.

'You have a baby sister,' he whispered against her ear. 'Her name's Emma Jane.'

'Is she pretty?'

'Of course. We only have pretty daughters.' He gently kissed her. 'Mummy sends her love. Go to sleep now, Susie, I don't want you to be tired tomorrow. I love you.'

But Susie was already asleep, with the addition of a small smile on her face.

The next day brought worry. Jilly's temperature soared, and she'd begun to bleed heavily.

'Don't worry,' she said unnecessarily before they wheeled her into theatre. When she returned, her face was nearly as pale as the sheet she was wrapped in. It was bad news. There would be no more children for them.

Alec sat by her bed until the anaesthetic wore off, holding her hand while her colour gradually returned.

He cried with her when the doctor told her. She gave him a wan smile when he mopped her tears away with a handkerchief soaked with his own tears. 'I so much wanted us to have a son one day,' she said.

Alec had never really craved a son. He loved his precious daughters too much. At the back of his mind was the thought that Jilly unconsciously needed to replace the boy she'd lost. But that could never be.

'A son would have been nice, but we have two lovely daughters to raise and must be thankful for them.'

'I am thankful for them. You just don't understand,' she said.

'Then help me to understand.'

'I really don't want to talk about it, Alec. It never really goes away and I can't share it, not even with you, because I don't know what it is.'

He knew what it was. Grief! He could only imagine what Jilly had gone through when she'd been parted from her baby. The finality of death was missing, though. Her son was alive somewhere, a twelve-year-old schoolboy, and she knew it. Jilly was coping with it as best she could. Now she had shut him out, and it hurt.

'Our daughters might provide us with a grandson one day.'

'I know,' was all she said, then looked at the daffodils he'd brought her and forced a smile to her face. 'They're pretty. Thanks, Alec. I'm tired now. Why don't you go and ask the nurse for a vase to put those in?'

When he came back with them she was asleep, her face wet with tears. He dropped in to gaze through the nursery window and admire his latest girl. There, tucked into a plastic crib, was Emma Jane Frampton, as dainty as a dragonfly. He wouldn't swap her for a son in a million years.

It was a week before Jilly came home. And as she'd done with Susie, Jilly said, 'I'm not very good at breastfeeding so I've put Emma straight on the bottle.' For a while there was an air of sadness and depression about her – then one day she seemed to shrug it off.

Shortly after that Alec was offered the job of deputy head. The position came with added responsibility and a rise in pay.

Over the next few years, several things happened. Will fathered a son and a daughter. Johnnie Ray died and was buried with pomp and ceremony at the bottom of the garden. He was replaced by a dog rescued from the pound, and two stray cats.

'Kingsmere has decided to allow day girls in,' Alec told her one day. 'I've put the girls' names down. They'll be educated free of charge, of course.'

They were well-educated. Susie went on to university, and Alec and Jilly were the proudest of parents when she graduated.

Alec's hair began to turn grey. Jilly placed a kiss on his forehead on his forty-eighth birthday. At least it was still thick. 'You're beginning to look very distinguished.'

At the end of term he was summoned before the school governors.

He returned home, a smile on his face. 'How would you like to be the headmaster's wife, next year?'

Her head cocked to one side and a smile glimmered. 'I'd have to help out with the school play and organize the school fête every year, wouldn't I?'

'You already help out. I promise not to make you wear a hat unless you want to. It would give you something useful to do, besides looking after me.'

'Yes, there's that, I suppose. It will keep both of us occupied until we're a couple of old crabs.'

'You'll never be an old crab. You're as beautiful as the day we first met – in Sunday School, wasn't it?'

'That was a long time ago, Alec.'

He hugged her against him. 'I don't think I've ever told you how happy I always feel when I'm around you.'

'You have, and you know I always cry when you say something like that.'

'We'll have some happy memories to share in our old age, then.'

She took in a deep breath. 'And some sad ones. It's been twenty-eight years since Richard was born. It's his birthday today. Alec, he's on my mind a lot lately, and I wonder why I can't forget him after all these years.'

He was glad she'd taken a small step towards the light. 'Because, my dearest love, Richard was lost to you when he was still alive. Because of that, your belief that you might see him again is alive, too. You could make your own enquiries, you know,' he suggested.

'I can't . . . twice I've made up my mind to. But then I get upset and think awful things. What if he doesn't know about me? What if he doesn't want to see me again, or hates me for what happened? What if he's been ill treated all his life, or . . . has died? Or perhaps he's a criminal serving time in prison. Or perhaps he doesn't want to know, and would reject me . . . *like I rejected him*?'

'Or perhaps he's just a normal bloke with a wife and family, just going to work and doing his best to keep the wolf from the door. Most of us are, you know.'

Relief filled her eyes. 'Yes, I suppose he could be.'

How fragile she was in her fears, how sensitive. Her wounds from her encounter with Rick Oliver were as raw as the day they were inflicted. He hated to see his Jilly hurting so much.

He didn't try to tell her that her fears were invalid: they weren't. But this was a problem that could be resolved by facing squarely up to it, herself. 'You didn't reject him.'

'It might seem so to him, though. My reasoning at the time now seems weak.'

'It would seem that way to you now. You were only seventeen and your thinking has matured.'

'But what about *his* thinking when he was that age? How could he help but resent a mother who had given him away?' Tears spilled from her eyes. Angrily, she scrubbed them away and retreated back into her shell. 'Let's stop talking about this, shall we? We're supposed to be celebrating your promotion. Would you like a glass of wine?'

'I would,' Emma said, looking and sounding so like her mother when she bounded in that Alec blinked and gazed from one to the other. But Emma had more confidence than Jilly would ever have.

'You're too young to drink.'

'And you're too old to cry, Mum. What's up?'

'It's nothing.'

'On the contrary,' Alec said. 'It's your big brother's birthday, and we're celebrating.'

'Some celebration. Where's the doughnut?'

'I forgot it.'

'You don't have to make a big thing of it, you know.' Emma gave her a bit of a hug. 'He must be ancient, by now.'

'Twenty-eight.'

'Like I said, ancient. Is there anything to eat? I'm starving.'

'You can have a piece of cake. But not too big, because we're going over to your uncle Will's restaurant for dinner tonight.'

Emma gave her mother a grin. 'Oh yes, so we are. Isn't it to celebrate his award for excellence or something?'

She nodded. 'Don't be too long getting ready. I don't want to be late, so we need to leave in two hours.'

'I won't be long. I'm going to wear jeans and –' she rustled the paper bag she was carrying – 'my new slogan tee shirt.'

'What's the slogan?' Alec asked.

'Very establishment, so you don't have to make a fatherly fuss.'

'I never make a fuss. It's a waste of time with females, since they're low on logic. I'm going to be head of school next year, Emma.'

'Oh, are you? Well, I expect they had to choose someone who knew the place and could conform to their fusty old teaching practices. I must say I'm looking forward to Will's party. How clever of him to win an award. I'll take the dog for a walk after I've changed, shall I?'

'Yes, do,' Alec said. He felt miffed. Such a fuss over Will's award, when his headmastership had hardly got a mention. 'I'm going to ring Susie and tell her about my new job,' he said.

'She phoned earlier and said she'd be home for the weekend, so I wouldn't bother. You can tell her then.'

'Have I got to go tonight?'

Consternation filled Jilly's eyes. 'This is Will's big day, Alec. Besides, I need you to drive us. My car is making a funny noise. I can't trust it, and you know I don't like driving that big one of yours. I can hardly see over the steering wheel.'

They both cringed when the bathroom door thumped shut behind Emma.

'Can't that girl do anything quietly?' he said, and they grinned at each other.

Later, Alec lounged on the bed and watched Jilly dress after bathing. As she slithered into a fiery red shift, her head got stuck. He heard her swear and watched her hands emerge to fiddle with the fastening. He could have undone it for her, but her neat body was clad in a pair of stockings with suspenders over a pair of black lace panties.

Crawling to the end of the bed he kissed the space between stocking top and lace.

'Stop it, at once,' she said, her voice muffled by the material. He grinned when she took the dress off to attack the fastening properly. 'Come here, Mrs Frampton. I fancy you like crazy.'

Her laugh teased him. 'Not now, you don't.'

'I'm taking the dog out,' Emma shouted up the stairs and the door slammed behind them.

He made a dive for Jilly and flipped her over on her back, holding her hands above her head. 'Damn it, Jilly. You know exactly how to turn me on.'

'It doesn't take much, and you've always liked me in black knickers.' She batted her delicious brown eyelashes at him. 'We've got about twenty minutes before Emma comes back.'

It was sufficient time for them to indulge in a highly erotic exercise that satisfied them both. By the time Emma returned they were dressed and seated demurely on the couch, the picture of model parents.

'It's a warm evening, aren't you going to be hot in that sweater?' Alec said to Emma.

She giggled. 'Oh, don't be so old-fashioned, Dad. It's the latest fashion. It doesn't matter what you feel like, only what you look like.'

He threw up his hands in mock horror. 'Who am I to argue with the latest fashion?'

'You have a ladder in your stocking,' Emma pointed out to her mother.

'Damn it!' Jilly said, and blushed when Alec chuckled.

They made the restaurant with time to spare. The place was in darkness.

'We must be first here. Good job I've still got a key.' Thrusting the door open Jilly said, 'Is anybody there?'

In an instant the lights were flicked on, and the silence of collective bated breath became a cheer. They were all there, Alec's friends from school, Will, Audrey, Peter and families. And there was Susie, who flew across the room to give them all a big hug.

Alec grinned when he saw the banner: 'Congratulations to Alec Frampton, Kingsmere Grammar School's next headmaster.'

Emma threw her sweater aside and giggled. Her tee shirt read 'My dad is a headmaster. ~~Dispite~~ Despite that ~~floor~~ flaw, I love him heaps.'

A warm glow filled Alec. He could feel his grin spreading from ear to ear. Drawing Jilly against his side he kissed her cheek and whispered, 'You knew all the time.'

'The headmaster told me yesterday. Congratulations, my love. You deserve it.'

It was winter when Sylvia Carstairs reached Dorset.

Widowed for the third time, she was looking forward to

seeing her daughter, and the two granddaughters Jilly had written to her about. They'd be grown-up by now.

She'd lost the love of her life in Gary. They'd had fun together over the past twenty years, throwing lavish parties and doing all the things they'd wanted to do, like travelling around the countryside in a luxury trailer.

Money had been no object with Gary, though his grown-up children had disapproved of his lifestyle. Gary had headed a thriving business, which had been passed down by his father, and was now managed by his two sons.

Gary had suffered a heart attack just outside Las Vegas. He'd dropped dead behind the wheel and they'd run off the road. Sylvia had spent several weeks recuperating, first in the hospital while her broken bones healed – then in the home they'd shared, with a private nurse looking after her.

Unexpectedly, there had been more bad news, though. It had knocked the stuffing out of Sylvia.

The house they'd been living in between trips was registered in the name of the business, which in its turn had been signed over to Gary's sons, years before.

When Sylvia had recovered, they offered her a business-class ticket home and a small amount of money.

'I was married to your father for twenty years,' she told them. 'We loved one another. That will count for a lot in a court of law. I deserve more of the estate than that.'

His sons told her, 'Father has no estate. You've been company liabilities for several years now. You have our offer. Take it, or leave it.'

She'd taken it. She'd go home to Jilly. She wouldn't turn her away.

Boarding the train at Waterloo Station, she travelled through familiar countryside. Brown crumpled earth ploughed into ridges, bare hedges, tree shapes stark against a pewter sky. The rooks rose into a cold and misty horizon. Home, she thought, and was glad of it. She felt like winter herself, as if Gary's death had sucked the marrow from her bones.

She had taken time to reflect on the journey home, and knew her faults. It was too late for her to change, even if she had an alternative.

A taxi took her from the station to a large thatched cottage with the bare bones of a wisteria growing around the door and gnarled, pruned rose bushes. Smoke drifted from a chimney to scribble lazily against the sky. It had been raining. Water dripped from everywhere.

There was no answer to Sylvia's knock. She gazed at the hanging basket and smiled as her fingers easily found the small chunk of metal. Jilly had always been predictable.

'Anyone home?'

From the back of the house came the sound of frantic barking.

'Shuddup, Fido!' she growled, and leaving her cases in the hall, went though to the lounge. The place was warm, and had a homely feel to it, in a predictable, chintzy sort of way. Not Sylvia's style, but beggars couldn't be choosers.

Jilly might turn her away, she thought.

'No, not my Jilly,' she whispered out loud. She smiled at the photograph of the two grown-up girls on the mantel-piece. Her granddaughters, and she couldn't remember what their names were. Jilly had always wanted to be part of a family, now she had one of her own.

Helping herself to a glass of sherry, Sylvia lit a cigarette, remembering too late that Jilly didn't like her smoking in the house. One wouldn't hurt. She sucked the last shred of smoke through the stub, then threw it into the fireplace.

The dog settled down. Sylvia seated herself in an over-stuffed armchair and swallowed the sherry. Her eyes drifted shut. She was tired. The silence of the house was wonderful, except her head was filled with the tick, tick of the clock.

A cat came to sit on her lap. Its purring filled the void between ticks and was comforting.

She thought she heard voices in the distance . . .

Eighteen

'Who is it?' Emma whispered.

Jilly gazed at the woman sitting on her couch. She hadn't heard from her in months, not since getting a post-card saying they were heading for Las Vegas. Despite the blonded hair and make-up, how old and wrinkled her mother looked after all this time. And unhealthy. Her face was gaunt and lined, and she had bags under her eyes.

'It's my mother. Your grandmother, Sylvia Carstairs, from America.' Her mother's presence raised a faint feeling of dismay in Jilly, as if she posed a threat to the well-being of her family. A tiny fist of fear struck her in the midriff. 'I wonder what she's doing here after all these years . . .'

'Her cases are in the hall. Will she be staying with us? Should I make the guest room ready?'

Torn between duty, her instinctive need to punish and a niggling unease, Jilly dithered. 'I don't know, darling.'

But there was an inevitability about it when her mother woke and confirmed what Jilly's intuition had already supplied her with.

'He's gone . . . Gary's dead. God, and I miss him so much. Don't turn me away, Jilly girl. Let me spend some time with you and my granddaughters. I'm ill. I need you.'

'Oh, Mum.' Jilly burst into tears.

Sylvia passed away the following June, her skin gradually taking on the hue and texture of yellow parchment as the disease insidiously destroyed her organs and sapped her of her strength.

Jilly looked after her mother with as much love and care as she had in her. From time to time she couldn't help but resent this intrusion into her life and the lives of those she loved.

'The girls are pleased they've got to meet their grandmother,' Alec told her. 'Poor Sylvia. She's only got a few weeks left, then it will be over for her.'

Illness didn't change the leopard's spots, though. While she drew breath, Sylvia still indulged her habits. 'It won't make any difference now, so why should I bother?' she said.

When she was forced to take to her bed, she had them all running back and forth to do her bidding.

Increasing pain put her mother in a hospital bed where she lingered on in a narcotic-induced stupor for a week. Towards the end she clutched Jilly's wrist. 'You're the sunshine in my heart, Jilly girl.'

'Your only sunshine?' Jilly whispered, choking on the words.

'That's right . . . you make me happy when skies . . . are grey. I've got to tell you something . . . the letter . . . him . . .' She gave a sigh and lapsed into unconsciousness.

Jilly was at her bedside when her mother exhaled her last rattling breath, called to the hospital in the middle of the night by the nurse.

She kissed her mother's face, made peaceful by death. 'Goodbye, Mum, I love you,' she whispered.

Alec was waiting for her outside. He folded her in his arms and held her gently, so she felt comforted. 'I'm so sorry, Jilly.'

She looked up at him and smiled, feeling an odd sense of relief. 'My mother was happy with Gary Carstairs, you know. She always loved him. They were lovers during the war when I was little.'

'Sylvia was good to me when I was a child. I liked her a lot and thought she was very glamorous. I used to wish you were my sister, so she would be my mother.'

'I'm glad she wasn't. Were you very lonely, Alec?'

'Not when I was with you. I've always loved you, Jilly. I could never understand what it was about me that attracted you, though.'

'Your funny accent,' she said. 'You've lost it over the years, though.'

'Fair dinkum?' he said, raising an eyebrow and sounding so convincingly amazed that she grinned at him despite the sadness of her mother's death.

'Fair dinkum! Now, stop fishing for compliments. You should be ashamed of yourself. Take me home, Alec. I've got a busy day ahead of me making arrangements for her funeral.'

The church was crowded with people on the day of Sylvia's funeral. They were there to pay their respects – to Jilly first, and then to Alec – rather than to mourn Sylvia, who they'd hardly known. People approached Alec – the men with their hands extended and the women with a smile. Alec handled them all with ease and confidence as befitted his position in life. He had an easy-going, pleasant manner that endeared him to people.

Back at the cottage, Jilly watched him. Loving him.

The day was painted with sunshine. The air smelled of roses and the lawn was stippled with shade. A blackbird in the hedge was stalked by the cats, who narrowed their eyes and looked fierce. It sang mockingly and flitted from branch to tree to hedge and back again, teasing them. Bees droned through the flowers.

The day was alive. Her mother was dead. Dressed in a slim black shift, Jilly served tea on the terrace, sandwiches and fruit cake. At least she'd known her mother. *Richard hadn't known his. Might never know.*

Where had that thought come from? Now was not the time to think of him. She moved on, but another thought popped up. Alec hadn't known his mother, either. She wondered; perhaps Alec's mind retained a perfect picture of her, a memory picture of him being in her arms and her breath warm against his cheek.

A wave of love for him almost swamped her. As if Alec had felt the surge of it, he turned, searching for her amongst the crowd. Their eyes met, and she felt a familiar lift of her heart as they exchanged a smile.

He excused himself, made his way to where she stood, turned his back against the guests and brought her into his arms and against his shoulder. No one approached as he claimed a moment of tenderness with her. 'You're looking a bit fraught, my love. How are you holding up?'

'I'm managing. People are beginning to gradually drift off now.'

He kissed the end of her nose. 'It will soon be over.'

The drift became a general exodus. Audrey, Peter and Will helped clear the dishes away, then left. Emma and Susie washed and dried them and the house was back to normal.

Only it wasn't back to normal. Her mother had gone. Dying was a different kind of departure. So final. 'You know where you stand with death,' she said to Alec. 'She hurt me when she went off without a word. I was angry for a long time. I'm glad she came home when she needed someone, to us. It makes you feel . . . wanted.'

He knew where she was coming from better than she did herself. 'You should find him,' he said.

Yes, she thought, one day I'll find the courage. Perhaps my son has unconsciously retained an image of me. Perhaps we'll recognize each other in a soul sort of way.

And perhaps you won't, the more sensible part of her told her.

Susie lived in a flat with other teachers, near the secondary school where she worked. Engaged to a builder, she intended to marry in the spring. Emma was looking forward to going to university the following year.

Jilly suddenly felt at a loose end. The house was empty without her mother to keep her occupied. Three months had passed since her mother had died. Jilly still couldn't bring herself to clear out Sylvia's room. She'd refused the offer of Alec and Emma's help.

She hadn't been able to shake off the slight depression she'd lived under since her mother's death. It had been raining for a week, the windows had been closed. On the first fine day she went out into the garden to pull the weeds from the rose bed.

When she went back indoors she inhaled the acrid yellow smell of stale cigarettes. Grief hit her with a short, sharp poignancy and she rushed up the stairs.

Throwing open the door to her mother's room, she gazed

at the unmade bed, the dirty ashtray and sticky glass still standing on the bedside table. Through a blur of tears she threw open the windows, rolled up her sleeves and started work.

She dragged the cardboard box of her mother's clothes down the stairs and into the garden – went back up and emptied the bedside drawers. There was a picture of herself in a frame, and one of her mother with Gary Carstairs, taken during the war. Her mother had been beautiful. She picked it up, ran her thumb over it. No wonder she'd attracted men. Jilly felt glad she had found happiness with Gary in the end.

Jilly found something else too – something quite unexpected.

When Alec came home from work she was up a ladder, slapping white paint on every surface she could reach.

'You should have let me do that,' he said.

'I needed to do it.'

'You're angry about something.'

'Life is so short. This room was the nursery. Do you remember when Susie arrived unexpectedly, and you had to rush to get it ready for her? You painted it pink. Then you painted it blue for Emma. But she turned out to be a girl, too, so you painted it pink again. Then I couldn't have any more children, when I really did want us to have another child, Alec.'

'I know,' he said. 'You wanted a boy.'

'We painted it lilac for Mum. There are several lives layered inside the paint.' What he'd said suddenly registered. 'What do you mean, I wanted a son? We both did.'

'You forget I already had a school full of boys,' he said. 'I was quite content with our daughters. I thought you wanted a son to replace Richard.'

'You got that wrong, you fool. Nobody could replace Richard.' She huffed out an incredulous laugh. 'How odd that you've been thinking that all these years.'

'It was logical.'

'Phooey to logic! What I really wanted was a son who took after his father.'

He came to stand beneath the ladder and gazed up at her. He'd never picked that up. After all this time, how little he knew her. 'And now you're painting it white. Why?'

'Because everything seems to have come to a standstill. The girls have grown up, Mum has died and I have nothing to make me feel useful, except being your wife. Besides, there was only white paint in the shed.'

'Then let's prepare for the future. One day we'll have grandchildren. Let's paint the walls sunshine yellow and give the room a blue ceiling with clouds, rainbows and ducks in a pond. Paint a circus tent around the widow and cover that wall in elephants, clowns and stripy tigers. Emma likes drawing. She'll probably help you.'

You're my sunshine, Jilly girl, her mother had often told her, and she remembered a feeling of love between them. 'Remember the jewellery Mother stole from Will?' she said abruptly.

He nodded.

'I found it in a shoebox in the wardrobe.'

'Ah . . . I see . . . so that's the real problem. You'd rather have believed the lie Will told you about somebody robbing the house. It made you feel better.'

'I didn't believe it. I just don't like knowing she was a thief.'

'Think how good you'll feel when you're able to return it to Will.'

The ladder wobbled as she descended it, as if one leg was slightly shorter than the other. The paint tray slid from the top, splattering the carpet and Alec's trousers with white dots of varying sizes.

'I was going to change the carpet anyway,' she said. 'It's worn, and it smells of cigarette smoke.'

'Why don't you simply pull it up? If the floorboards are OK I'll give them a scrub at the weekend, and we'll get a couple of bright rugs.'

She took his face between her hands and kissed him. 'I'll do the scrubbing. You have the garden to catch up with, remember? Mum's stuff is in that box downstairs. Would you run it over to the charity shop for me, tomorrow? I kept her jewellery. There are a couple of good pieces. I thought the girls might like to have them. And there's some money that can be shared between them. Not much, just a few hundred.'

'I'll take the stuff to the charity shop now, get rid of it. And I'll buy some paint.'

'Thanks Alec. A circus sounds like a lovely idea. I hope the girls don't feel pressured into providing us with grand-children because of it.'

'They won't,' he said. 'Haven't you noticed how inde-pendent they are?'

Picking up the brush, she painted, 'I love you, Alec' in large letters, then turned and smiled at him. 'Just remember that this is written under the circus.'

That had been yesterday . . . and now this. A letter from her son, found hidden under the carpet.

Just as she thought she'd sorted out her feelings about her mother – the ultimate betrayal. How could she have kept this from her?

The clock struck three, the dog gave a bark and both of the cats came up to remind her it was nearing teatime.

She went down to the kitchen, her feet automatically dodging the attentive creatures, her mind a stew of churning emotion that now bubbled between annoyance and elation. It also touched on a deeply buried hurt that scared her with its intensity and the intent to claw the seal from the door to her dungeon.

'Oh my God!' she whispered, feeling a momentous thun-dering in her heart. 'I expected to have to face this one day, but not so soon after my mother's death.'

But without that she'd never have known that her son had wanted to meet her. Then she remembered that her mother had tried to tell her about it as she'd lain dying.

The thought of meeting her son at long last made Jilly feel frighteningly alive, so all her senses seemed to function at once. She had to yell out loud with the joy of feeling so alive.

The air coming through the window smelt of nuts, mush-rooms and newly mown grass. The rake made a scraping sound as its teeth gathered the autumn leaves. Her tongue tasted the salt of the tears running down her cheeks, but the tears tasted like joy. She could feel her son's head pressing warmly against her body, dark-capped and sweet, her tears washing over him. She'd never been able to feed her daughters, had never wanted to get as close to them as she had to the son she'd lost – lest she lost them too.

There was an image of the door. Two inches of solid wood. She could see herself reflected in the shining surface of the polished brass doornob, a young, scared girl about to give her heart away.

Trembling, she reached out to open the door. There was no resistance. On the other side was an empty room flooded in sunshine, and the shadow of a man.

She blinked and it was gone.

Jilly didn't quite know what to do, so she did something sensible. She put the kettle on and decided to tell Alec about the letter over tea . . .

Nineteen

Dear Jilly,

My company is sending me to London in April to attend a couple of business meetings and to observe the London Stock Market in action.

This will provide an opportunity for us to finally meet (again!). I'm looking forward to it with pleasure, plus a small dose of trepidation, even though I feel I know you quite well through your letters . . .

Butterflies fluttered in Jilly's stomach. No, they were flapping like demented bats.

'Alec!' she yelled, and he came running through to the sitting room, alarm on his face.

'Are you all right?'

'Neil's coming over to England next month. He wants to meet me!'

'Of course he wants to meet you.'

'What shall I do?'

'Make an appointment to get your hair done, I suppose.'

Picking up a cushion she beat him with it. His arms folded around her and the weapon, rendering them both harmless.

He laughed and kissed the end of her nose. 'You're going to be impossible to live with between here and next month.'

'Come with me?'

'No, Jilly. This is something you have to do by yourself.'

A week later and it was Mothering Sunday. There was a tissue-wrapped package tied in red ribbon on Jilly's breakfast tray.

Her family were seated on the end of the bed watching her with expectant expressions on their faces. She drank the mug of tea then picked up the spoon to eat her cereal.

The three gazed at each other. 'Aren't you going to open your Mother's Day present?' Alec asked her.

She gave a little grin. 'I was going to eat my breakfast first.'

'And keep us waiting? No way!' He lifted the tray from her lap, set it aside and placed the package in its stead. 'Open it.'

Their daughters exchanged a glance and grinned.

'Wait,' Emma said as Jilly untied the red bow. She handed over a handkerchief.

'What's this for?'

'You always cry when you're happy.'

Unwrapping the package Jilly stared down at the hotel brochure and reservation, her eyes widening. 'I used to work here.'

'That's why we booked it. We thought you'd feel more comfortable there. It has a good reputation and is only a stone's throw from where Neil will be staying. And there are two tickets to the Adelphi theatre, so you can take him to see *Me and My Girl*.'

'Perhaps they should rename it *You and Your Boy*.'

Jilly managed a wry smile for Alec's joke.

Susie said, 'When you see him you could suggest that he comes down to attend my wedding if he's still here. I mean . . . we'd love to meet our brother, wouldn't we Em?'

Emma nodded. 'I'm absolutely agogified!'

'Whoops, we have an arts student in the house,' Alec said, and they exchanged a grin.

'You know, if this gets out it will cause talk.'

Susie's voice was fiercely loyal. 'We've discussed this, haven't we Dad? We don't care if you don't. Besides, times have changed, Mum, and people are much more accepting now.'

Alec's voice was suddenly uncertain. 'You do like it, don't you?'

Jilly gazed at his anxious expression and at the encouraging smiles of her daughters. How hard they'd tried to please her. Whatever she'd lost of worth in the past, and whatever happened in the future, she was still in possession of an abundance of happiness and the joy of having a wonderful, nurturing family.

'I love it. The three of you are worth your weight in gold, you know. This is the best Mother's Day I've ever had. Thank you so much.'

When she began to weep the girls began to cry too and they all hugged each other tight.

Alec blew his nose, said, 'There . . . now I've managed to make you all cry. I think I'll go off to take the dog for a walk.'

The day before Jilly left for London, Alec dug the red tin out of the attic. 'I remembered that old article had a photograph of Rick Oliver attached. It's discoloured, but you might like to give it to him in case he wants to follow it up.'

She smiled as she thought of the shock Rick Oliver would get if Neil knocked on his door.

'There's also Rick's wings and the flying helmet,' she said. 'Would he want those, d'you think?'

'The helmet went mouldy, I threw it out years ago. Besides, those were our memories.' Alec picked up the wings and placed the emblem on her outstretched palm. The threads had tarnished. Her hand folded round it and for a moment she remembered a golden youth who'd risked his own life to help defend his country. A true hero who she'd worshipped.

Then she remembered a man who'd walked away, leaving her to face the trauma of birth and loss of her child without support.

Opening her hand, she tossed the wings into the fire. It was a moment of catharsis and she grinned at Alec when Rick Oliver crashed for a second time. 'I feel suddenly light.'

'Ahah! The Incredible Lightness of Being,' he said.

'Trust you to come up with something I've never heard of. What's that supposed to mean?'

'The Tibetans have a theory that the mind consists of layers of compressed memories. As they're discarded, so the spirit grows lighter.'

'I'll remember that the next time I feel compelled to contemplate my navel.' Carefully folding the newspaper clipping back into its creases, she grinned at him. 'You never know, Neil might be in need of this particular layer.'

'You do feel comfortable about this now, don't you?'

'I didn't expect it to come so soon . . . but yes, I'm comfortable with it. I've been waiting for this day for the past twenty-nine years.'

He grinned. 'A contradiction if ever I heard one.'

She snorted in exasperation. 'You know very well what I mean, Alec Frampton. I owe Neil his past, and whether he likes me or not I can only be myself. I'll rely on my instincts to carry me through.'

'They've always stood you in good stead, my Jilly.'

'Neil has to be nervous, too, probably more than I am. I think I'd rather be in my shoes than his. I have trouble believing that the infant I parted with is a grown man. There's such a big void there. He was so little when I handed him over – so helpless. He'd just started to smile.'

'You'll have to get used to him being an adult.'

'But I've completely missed out on his childhood. I feel sad about that, because there's such a gap. Knowing he didn't give me a thought, because he was unaware of me when he was growing up, is difficult to grasp. It makes me feel sort of . . . immaterial . . . like a shadow hanging about in his background that he never noticed.'

'You know he was happy. He had a good childhood with people who loved him. And wasn't that the reason you parted with him in the first place? I'm sure he appreciates that . . . so just keep it in mind. Come on, let's go to bed. We have to be up early for you to catch the train.'

And later, she remembered something that had been on her mind. 'It's our silver wedding anniversary next year. Could we do something special? A trip to Australia, perhaps?'

'Exactly what I was thinking, since I wouldn't mind taking a memory lane trip of my own.' His voiced dropped to a murmur as he whispered in her ear. 'And because I love you and you're wearing that little black lace number, my thoughts, as well as other parts of me, have turned towards the carnal. So I'm also thinking we might have a little celebration beforehand . . . like now?'

Jilly grinned. 'D'you know what, Smart Alec? Because I love you too, and you're wearing nothing but your birthday suit, which is a rather obvious hint in anyone's language, I think that's a damned good idea.'

It was the first time Jilly had revisited London. She'd forgotten how busy, and how beautiful the city was.

Her hotel room was one of the better ones. It overlooked a pretty little park and the Thames Embankment beyond. The place brought back memories she thought she'd left behind.

Her loneliness for one. She'd found it hard to make friends, except for the Irish girl she'd shared a room with. That had only lasted a few months before she'd moved on. And although Jilly had worked with young men, she'd never been able to form an attachment.

She'd worked hard to fill in the time, she remembered, and saved as much of her meagre wage as she could. On her days off she'd walked for miles, visiting art galleries and wishing she could afford to go to the theatre, the opera, the ballet, or any other attraction London offered.

The rest of her wage was spent on essentials. She'd never been smart or trendy, her most adventurous fashion being a comfortable caftan, which although years out of date and faded almost into extinction, she sometimes still wore.

Today, she was dressed in a grey suit with a pale-blue flowered shirt. Her sensible headmaster's wife uniform, Alec called it, and urged her to buy something new while she was in London.

'You'll want something nice to go to the theatre in.'

Not far from the hotel she found a small boutique. She thought, Little black dress, as she went in, but came out with a soft and expensive cream-coloured shift with a caramel belt and a checked wrap.

She treated herself to a small shoulder bag and strappy sandals with frivolous heels, then painted her finger and toenails in cinnamon pearl.

Changing into a russet blouse over beige pleated slacks, she eyed herself critically in the mirror. Was that a grey hair? Plucking it from her head she picked up her hair brush.

'Damn it, stop prevaricating,' she told herself.

The room was decorated in restful shades of grey and

blue. When she'd worked here the rooms had been brown and cream. 'Damn it, stop admiring the furnishings,' she told herself. But then, she recalled the nights she'd fallen asleep, grieving for her lost son, her face wet with tears, the memory of his face soft against her cheek, and his nuzzling mouth and his tentative, beginner's smile. That memory had never been far from the surface, she thought.

He was ten minutes away.

She must stop putting things off.

He was not her baby son any more.

Jilly wished Alec was with her as she crossed to the telephone and dialled the number of Neil's hotel. She was put through without fuss.

Too fast, before she could prepare herself.

'Neil James,' a deep voice said, and she smiled at the warmth it contained. But her throat dried up when she tried to speak and her voice came out as a timorous, mouse-like squeak.

'Hello,' he said cautiously into the silence. 'Is that you . . . Jilly?'

'Yes, it is,' she managed to get out. 'I have tickets for the theatre tonight and I wondered if you'd like to go. They were a present from my family . . . for us.'

She could have kicked herself for differentiating between them, but couldn't take it back now.

'I'd love to go to the theatre. How about I take you out to dinner first?'

'That would be lovely.' His friendly Australian accent reminded her of Alec's when they'd first met. Suddenly, she couldn't wait to meet him. 'Are you doing anything now? My hotel is just around the corner. I could be there in ten minutes . . . that's if you haven't got anything more important on – meetings or something.'

He chuckled. 'I was just about to suggest the same thing, since I'm dying to meet you. I'll go down to the lobby. There's a coffee shop we can use.'

'Neil,' she said, slowly, because her hands had begun to tremble, 'I have to tell you this . . . I'm totally terrified.'

'So am I. My knees are knocking together. I'm surprised you can't hear them.'

Jilly hadn't expected that. She laughed when she realized he was teasing her, said drily before hanging up, 'I'm glad we've sorted that out. I'll see you in ten minutes, then.'

She avoided treading on the cracks in the pavement as she walked along the Strand. She didn't want to invite bad luck. Her mind was in a ferment, filled with excitement, so she felt as though she could fly. She certainly didn't feel like a forty-seven-year-old mother off to meet her grown-up son for coffee.

A man in uniform tipped his top hat at her. She stepped into a revolving door with a small group of people and was deposited on to a deep carpet of royal blue on the other side.

To her right were the lifts. One made a pinging sound and the doors slid open.

The coffee shop was on her left, on the other side of a pillar. Partially concealed by it she peered into the interior. There were two couples at the tables and a couple of businessmen sitting by themselves in lounge chairs.

Neither of them looked like Neil should look.

When somebody behind her cleared his throat and said, 'Are you looking for me?' she spun around.

'I've just come down in the lift,' he said.

Recognition thrust through her. Not a surface recognition, but something that went much deeper, the certainty that she knew him – would have known him even if she hadn't seen his photograph. He resembled Rick Oliver. Yet she saw herself strongly in the brown depth of his eyes and in the unruly hair, which curled this way and that.

Tanned and well-built, he drew the eye of passing women.

They smiled at the same time. Neil's smile was full of natural charm and crinkled the corners of his eyes.

'It's been a long time, such a *long time*,' she said, her glance devouring his face. She wanted to hug him tight, but felt the uncertainty and reserve in him.

Take it slowly, she told herself.

He nodded, leaned forward to kiss her cheek, then, taking her by the elbow, he guided her into the coffee shop.

She gave him the cutting while they waited for service, pointed to Rick Oliver. 'That's your father. I named you after him . . . Richard. It's the only photo I have, I'm afraid. He was eighteen there. My husband kept it all these years. You can have it if you'd like.'

'My mother kept Richard as my second name.'

A tiny flicker of anguish appeared. Alec's advice came to her. *He had a happy childhood, that's what you wanted for him.*

Of course . . . of course. Stop being so sensitive. Her hurt fled as she blessed the woman for giving him that.

He examined the cutting, his lips pursing, but grinned when he saw the photo of Jilly and Alec. He gazed up at her, a smile spreading across his face. 'You haven't changed much. Is that your husband?'

She smiled at the thought of Alec; he'd be waiting for the phone to ring later, worrying about her. 'Yes, it is.'

'You told me he was educated in WA?'

'Alec was orphaned during the war. He was placed in an orphanage and sent to Australia to live when it ended. He was my best friend and I missed him a lot.'

'Did you keep in touch?'

'Not in a conventional way. He wrote me letters and didn't post them, but gave them to me when we met again. He'd left all his wordly goods with me, too, in a battered red tin that he stored all his private things in. That's where the cutting has been kept. Your father was our hero when we were small.'

'I can see why. Did you love him very much . . . my father?'

She hadn't expected him to ask her that. 'I . . . I thought I did. He came back into my life when I was seventeen, and he dazzled me.'

'And now?'

'He was my first love, Neil. I was crushed when he left. It took me a long time to recover from that . . . and from what followed. Yet I can't bring myself to completely despise him. I've never regretted your existence, you know, only losing you. It was such a relief when I discovered your letter amongst my mother's things. Just knowing you were alive and well was wonderful.' She felt a lump growing in her throat. 'I'm sorry you had to wait such a long time before I was able to reply. It must have made you feel sort of . . . redundant.'

He placed his hand over hers and smiled. 'What's a year when you waited for twenty-nine?'

They drew back when the tea was served. Afterwards they strolled along the Embankment. The day was full of sighing winds, the ground wet-slicked and shiny from the sudden showers, and the sky full of coloured rainbows and singing birds.

Jilly drew in a deep breath. Everything about her was heightened, shining with newness, as if she'd been reborn and was seeing it for the first time. Her elation knew no bounds, her body fizzed with it, as if an electric current had been run through her nerves.

This is the happiest day of my life. I want to say something from my heart. That is, I love you, my beautiful son.

When she'd handed him over on that awful day, he'd been wrapped in a parcel of her love, her despair, and her hopes for his future.

He'd had more love than he'd ever known about. Her despair had been resolved, and now was his future.

All of her hopes had materialized in the shape of this man, who was still her beloved son. And if this precious time was all she could have of him, then she'd be happy and make it last for the rest of her life.

Neil took her hand in his. Once she'd curled her hand around his tiny fist. Now he curled his around hers, and it was warm and solid when he said, 'Tell me about my sisters . . .'